D0012457

Hair Brained

A Bad Hair Day Mystery

NANCY J. COHEN

Regina Public Library
BOOK SALE ITEM
Non-returnable

Hair Brained, Copyright © 2017 by Nancy J. Cohen
First Edition: September 2017
Published by Orange Grove Press

Digital ISBN: 978-0-9970038-7-1
Print ISBN: 978-0-9970038-8-8
Edited by Denise Dietz from Stray Cat Productions
Cover Design by Boulevard Photografica
Digital Layout by www.formatting4U.com

This is a work of fiction. Names, characters, places, and incidents either are the product of the author's imagination or are used fictitiously, and any resemblance to actual persons, business establishments, events or locales is entirely coincidental.

All rights reserved. This book is licensed for your personal use only. No part of this work may be used, reproduced, stored in an information retrieval system, or transmitted in any form or by any means (electronic, mechanical, photocopying, recording, or otherwise) without prior written consent by the author. Any usage of the text, except for brief quotations embodied in critical articles or reviews, without the author's permission is a violation of copyright.

Chapter One

"What's keeping Dalton so long?" Marla said, casting an anxious glance at the doorway. She stood by the kitchen sink with a dishtowel in hand, wondering about the phone call that had torn her husband away from their guests on New Year's Day. He should have returned the call later instead of disappearing into another room, especially with company over.

"Maybe your friends Tally and Ken are coming after all," Marla's mother, Anita, suggested. Her warm brown eyes regarded Marla from under a crown of short, white hair.

"If that's the case, why would Tally notify Dalton instead of me?" Marla had invited the couple to their party, but Tally had declined. Her best friend hadn't mentioned plans for their traditional New Year's Eve date, either. If she didn't feel like going out with a new baby at home, wouldn't Tally have said so?

"Maybe it's a work call." Anita stacked a trio of dirty serving platters in the sink to free up more counter space.

"Dalton's partner is supposed to be covering for him today." As a homicide detective on the Palm Haven police force, Dalton was often on call. Marla had hoped that wouldn't be the case during their party today. But when he reappeared in the kitchen doorway with a somber expression, her heart lurched. His news couldn't be good.

"Can we talk in private?" he said, his voice gruff.

1

"Sure." Marla tossed her dishtowel onto the kitchen counter and followed him toward the study. Laughter and chatter from their guests reached her ears as they passed the living room of their single-story house.

She faced Dalton inside their home office, where his tall frame and broad shoulders dominated the space. A lock of peppery hair fell across his brow, creased with concern.

"Tally and Ken are missing," he began without preamble.

"What do you mean?"

"They went out last night and haven't come home."

"Who told you this?"

"Mrs. Phelps, their babysitter, phoned me. We're on her emergency call list."

"Luke is safe at home, then?" Marla couldn't conceive of Tally leaving her four-month-old for any length of time.

"Yes, he's okay. According to the sitter, Tally said they might be out late and would get a hotel room if that were the case. Mrs. Phelps fell asleep waiting for them. When they failed to show up this morning, she figured they were sleeping in. But as the day wore on, she got worried. She tried to call, but their phones went straight to voice mail."

"Tally would never leave Luke for so long without contacting the sitter." Marla didn't voice her fear that something serious must have happened. Tally, in her mid-thirties, had tried to get pregnant for years. Their child meant everything to her. It was unimaginable for Tally to be apart from Luke for an entire day without notifying anyone.

"I called Kat and asked her to look into car accidents and hospital admissions," Dalton added, compressing his mouth into a thin line.

Marla hoped his partner's research wouldn't bring bad news. She gaped at Dalton as the repercussions hit. "We have to get Luke. I'm listed as his guardian in the event—"

"I know. The sitter is packing the essentials for us."

Tally and Ken had appointed Marla as the child's

guardian in their estate documents. Tally had no close relatives and didn't trust her brother-in-law in that role. Phil, a confirmed bachelor, lived out west and preferred his single lifestyle.

"Let me try to call Tally," Marla said, her throat dry. "Maybe she'll answer if she sees me on the caller ID."

"Don't bother. I've already tried. This isn't good, Marla."

"I agree." Icy fingers of dread made her stomach clench and her pulse race. "What will we tell people?"

"Tally has a family emergency and needs us to take her child for a few days."

"Our mothers will want to know more." Dalton's parents were at the party along with Marla's widowed mom and her latest boyfriend.

"We don't have enough information at this point. We'll have to break up the party, and then we're outta here."

So much for a peaceful start to the new year, Marla thought. Today should have been a time for celebration. She prayed it wouldn't be a holiday that marked a tragedy hereafter.

Forty minutes later, they entered the development where Tally and Ken lived. The upscale community in the western suburbs of Fort Lauderdale boasted high-ceilinged homes with barrel-tile roofs and manicured lawns.

A sixtyish woman with bleached-blond hair answered the door at Tally's house. After they identified themselves, Mrs. Phelps gestured for them to come inside.

"Thank God you're here. I've been worried sick. Have you heard anything from Mrs. Riggs? She adores her son and would never neglect him like this."

"Tally hasn't called us either." Marla entered the foyer. The smell of furniture polish mingled with the faint scent of vinegar used to clean tile floors.

"My partner, Lieutenant Katherine Minnetti, is investigating." Dalton peered around the place as though

3

searching for clues. "If you give me your contact information, ma'am, I'll be in touch when we learn more."

"Oh, please. I couldn't bear it if something terrible has happened to them." The sitter's round face paled, reminding Marla of pastry dough, especially with the woman's rotund figure.

The living room stretched to a set of French glass doors that opened onto a screened patio. The aqua water in the fenced pool looked pristine, as though the pool service guy had just been there. Every surface indoors, too, appeared freshly wiped down. Marla wondered if Tally had been upset recently. She tended to clean when stressed.

A baby's gurgle turned her toward the sound. Luke sat in his stroller in the formal dining room that opened into the kitchen. She padded over to greet him while Dalton questioned the sitter regarding Tally's whereabouts. The baby wiggled his arms and legs in constant motion, cooing when he spotted Marla. She smiled in response, stooping to take hold of his tiny hand. Poor little thing. Her chest tightened. Tally would never abandon her child.

The sitter wrung her hands as she related her story. "Mrs. Riggs … Tally … said they hadn't meant to go out on New Year's Eve. She was sorry for calling me last-minute, but her husband had an urgent work-related appointment. Tally decided to accompany him, saying they'd go out for dinner afterwards. They were lucky I was free. I'd been booked for the night, but the wife got sick and the couple cancelled."

"I gather you've worked for Tally before?" Dalton inquired.

"Oh, yes. I live in the neighborhood. I'm widowed, you see, and I like to help the young mothers who want an evening out. Plus, the extra cash comes in handy." She collected her handbag from a nearby chair.

"What time did Tally say they'd be home?"

"She didn't. As I told you on the phone, she said they

might be late, in which case they'd get a hotel room. I expected to hear from her this morning, even if they'd slept in. I got worried when Tally didn't contact me and I couldn't reach either one of them. Look, I wrote down Luke's feeding schedule. It's in the kitchen, along with his diaper bag."

"Thanks, I'll get them," Marla replied. At least Tally hadn't been breast-feeding. That would have been awkward. Her friend wanted to regain her figure fast and go back to work at her dress boutique. Had the employees there heard from her? No, the shop was closed for the holiday. And why would Tally contact them and not the babysitter?

"How did Tally seem when she spoke to you?" Dalton persisted.

Marla recognized his hunched shoulders as a sign of tension. His anxiety increased her own concern. She gnawed at her lower lip, letting go of the baby's fingers and straightening her spine. She'd better see what was packed in that bag before the sitter left.

"She appeared rattled, if you ask me," Mrs. Phelps said with a shrug. "Her words came in a rush, and her face looked drawn. Her husband, Ken, was already in the car when I arrived."

Had Tally suspected his call wasn't work-related at all, but instead was an assignation with another woman? Marla had spied him coming out of a restaurant with a brunette one day while driving through Wilton Manors. So when Tally complained that he was acting distant, Marla wondered if he was having an affair. Castaway Café seemed an odd choice for him to meet somebody without being noticed. A heterosexual couple would stand out in that place where gays congregated. Then again, no one would think to look for Ken there.

Anyway, was this why Tally had joined him last night? To see if he was lying to her? Or did she already know the truth? Tally had been evasive in her conversations with Marla lately, so maybe she'd discovered what Ken had been hiding.

Marla wandered into the kitchen and spotted the bulging bag on the counter. A quick glance confirmed its contents. She found the feeding schedule and stuffed it inside. Then she scanned the countertops, searching for messages or any other indication of where Tally and Ken might have gone. *Nada.* The dish drainer was empty, the counters clean. No stray papers cluttered the granite. Things were almost obsessively neat.

With a sigh, Marla slung the bag's strap over her shoulder. Holy highlights, that thing weighed a ton! How did mothers do it? Back in the living room, she shot a panicked glance at Dalton as he shut the door on the babysitter's retreating back.

"Wait, how will I know what to do?"

Dalton rounded on her, his eyebrows arched and his gray eyes like polished pewter. "What's there to know? You change the kid's diapers, feed him, and put him to sleep."

Oh, yeah. Easy for you to say. You've been through it once with your daughter.

"Put him to sleep in what? We don't have a crib in our house."

"That's okay; we'll rig something up that will work for tonight. This shouldn't last too long. Tally and Ken will reappear at some point."

"Yes, but what if they don't? I mean, we're not equipped to handle an infant. Our house isn't child-proofed. We don't have a crib or a changing table or any of the other stuff."

"Including a car seat, now that you mention it. I'll look in the garage. Maybe Tally's BMW is still inside." He loped off in that direction, hollering a few minutes later that Tally's car was parked there, and he'd retrieve her equipment.

Meanwhile, Marla wondered what she would do if Tally failed to show up in a timely manner. She had clients scheduled at the salon, as well as other commitments.

Dear Lord. Her throat closed until she reminded herself this wasn't about her. It was about caring for Luke.

Moisture tipped her lashes. Nothing terrible had better have happened to his parents. Whatever the reason for their absence, she'd give Luke her loving care. Ensuring his safety was all that mattered. And Brianna could help. Dalton's fifteen-year-old daughter might get a kick out of having a baby in the family, if only temporarily. They'd figure out the rest as they went along.

She followed Dalton outside as he went to fasten Tally's rear-facing car seat inside his sedan. A cool January breeze stirred her hair, the afternoon sun bright against a clear blue sky. Normally, she liked the change of weather in South Florida, but now it made a shiver grip her spine. She hoped the wind wasn't a harbinger of ill tidings. New Year's Day should be filled with hope and renewal, not uncertainty.

After Dalton settled Luke into his safety harness, Marla hurried back to the house to lock the front door with the spare key Tally had given her for emergencies. At least she'd had the foresight to bring it.

"Wait," Dalton called. "We should take the stroller. It'll fold up and fit in the trunk."

"Okay." Marla stood by while he went to retrieve the device. She needed instructions on operating these things. Baby care was a strange new world to her.

Soon she'd secured the house, slid into the car, and eyed Luke in the rear. Satisfied he was safe, she faced forward and pursed her lips. "Now what?" she asked Dalton as he pulled out of the circular driveway.

"We'll take care of Luke until Tally contacts us. Maybe they went somewhere without cell service, or they turned off their phones for some reason. I'll check in with Kat as soon as we get home."

Marla folded her hands in her lap, imagining all sorts of awful possibilities. They should have done a more thorough search at Tally's house for clues as to where she and Ken might have gone. While part of her hoped this was all just a

7

mishap and her friend would turn up at any minute, the other part made her stomach roil in anticipation of bad tidings.

Focus on the baby. Luke was the one who needed care. That meant she had to keep a clear head, but it wasn't easy with anxiety clouding her mind.

"I'm worried," she blurted, unable to contain her heart-pounding fear.

Dalton's brow furrowed. "So am I, but we'll find them. If all else fails, I can put out a bulletin on Ken's car."

They lapsed into silence except for the child's squeals and coos from the back seat. Thank goodness he wasn't a screamer, Marla thought, unsure what she'd do if he started howling. The poor kid was bound to miss his mother, but at least she and Dalton were familiar faces.

They made it home in record time. Dalton helped unfold the stroller and place Luke inside. Marla wheeled him into the house while her husband hefted the baby bag.

She'd barely made it into the foyer before the dogs came bounding at them. Oh, no. She'd forgotten about their pets. The crowd had left, but Ma must have let the animals into the house before leaving.

"Down, Lucky," she ordered their golden retriever, whose paws landed on the stroller. Spooks, their poodle, leapt at the strange contraption and barked.

That set Luke off. He uttered a cry that cascaded into a series of wails.

"Get them away from us," she called to Dalton, picking Luke up and swaddling him in her arms.

Dalton's sharp commands brought the dogs under control. Freed from their blockade, Marla headed into the kitchen and regarded the dishes strewn across the countertops. Someone had washed and dried everything, but it all had to be put away, along with the folding chairs and other remnants of the party.

Her shoulders sagged, and she sank into a seat at the

kitchen table. Luke continued to howl, his ear-piercing cries grating on her raw nerves. She rubbed his back to soothe him. "Don't worry, Luke. We're here to take care of you." But in truth, Marla had no idea what to do. It had been years since she'd cared for an infant as a nineteen-year-old babysitter. Should she have picked him up, or would that spoil him into crying for attention all the time?

"He probably needs his diaper changed," Dalton said, trailing after her. "All this excitement would have made him wet himself."

"Oh, joy. Or maybe it's time for a bottle. Get his feeding schedule for me, would you? It's in the diaper bag." She reviewed Mrs. Phelps' instructions. "Yes, he could use a feeding. I'll change him first, but where should I do it? We don't have a changing table."

"Put a towel down on the guest bed and use that for now. You'd better bring a supply of plastic bags in there for garbage. I'll get a bottle ready while you're occupied."

Brianna appeared in the archway. The slim teenager still wore the makeup she'd applied for the party, but she'd tied her toffee hair into a ponytail and changed into jeans. "What is that racket I'm hearing? Oh, cool. You brought Luke home." Her brown eyes rounded. "Wait, what's the matter with Tally?"

"We don't know where she's gone." Dalton related what the babysitter had told them.

"That's weird. You'd think she would tell somebody what's happening."

"Would you like to help?" Marla said, gesturing to her. "If so, please carry that bag into the guest room. Luke needs a diaper change. The dogs have upset him, and so has all the commotion."

His cries eased as Marla held him. She picked up a towel from the linen closet along the way, then realized she'd forgotten the trash bags Dalton had mentioned. Leaving Luke with Brianna, she hastened toward the laundry room off the kitchen where they kept their supplies. Her trembling fingers plucked a box of small-sized plastic bags from a shelf.

It wasn't only her hand that shook. Her entire body trembled. *You can do this*, she told herself on the way back to the bedroom side of their house. It wasn't as though she shouldered the responsibility alone. Brianna and Dalton were there to help, and her husband had already raised a child. He could guide her.

Nonetheless, she felt awkward as she went to change the baby, even though she'd helped Tally with Luke before. Maybe it was because doubts assailed her. Was she up to the task of mothering an infant? When she'd agreed to be his guardian, had she truly believed the role might be hers someday?

Brianna had already unfastened the soiled diaper. Marla made quick work of disposing of the wet item and wiping Luke's bottom.

"Don't lean over him too close," Brianna warned. "He might pee again. You have to watch out for boys."

"You're right." After patting him dry, Marla sprinkled Luke's bottom liberally with powder before putting on a dry diaper. His blue eyes, so like his mother's, gazed up at her, and her heart melted. "You'll be fine," she said in a soothing tone. "We'll take good care of you until your mommy comes home."

She put the baby's outfit back on, planning to change him into pajamas after his last bottle for the evening. Lifting him into her embrace, she cuddled his warm body to her chest. He was so small and totally reliant on her.

"Don't worry," Brianna told her with a perceptive grin. "I'm here, and Dad will help."

"I know. But what happens when I go to work? I have clients scheduled for tomorrow. They're depending on me, too. I don't like to disappoint my customers."

"It's your salon. Can't you bring Luke along and sit him in his stroller?"

Marla cast her a wry glance. "I barely have time to eat when it's busy, so how could I give Luke the attention he deserves? I'll call Ma and see if she can come by."

"I'm off from school until next week. I can babysit. What's the going rate these days?" Brianna asked with a teasing poke at Marla's elbow.

"I'll speak to your dad about it, but it'll be a long day. Maybe my mother can come over for a few hours. You can have the morning, and Ma can take the afternoon shift if she's free."

"Or maybe Tally will show up at our door. It's unlike her to leave you in the dark."

Lately, it's been rather common, Marla thought. "I wonder if your father has spoken to Kat yet." She led the way back into the kitchen, toting Luke under one arm and lugging the tied garbage bag with her free hand.

Dalton was speaking on his cell phone. He stood by the kitchen sink, near where a capped bottle stood on the adjacent counter. Noting Marla's entrance, he wagged his finger at it. He must have prepared the bottle before calling Kat.

"Ken drives a gold-colored Acura RLX," he said on the line. "You should be able to get his tag number. I have no idea which direction he might have taken. I'd say to concentrate on the tri-county area first, then we can expand our search later if necessary."

"Dalton, I just thought of something," Marla said as soon as he'd hung up. Grateful to Brianna who took the trash bag and dumped it into the larger one in the garage, she shifted Luke to her other arm. "If Ken got a call before he left the house, is it possible to trace its origin?"

He stared at her. "That's an idea, although they have a land line too, don't they? The call might have come in on either phone. I'd wait to see what develops before contacting their service providers. If they don't show up, maybe their GPS is active, and we can find them that way."

"So nobody who meets their description has been admitted to any hospitals?"

"Kat said there were some John Does. She's investigating further."

"What's a John Doe?" Brianna asked with a perplexed frown.

"Patients whose identities have yet to be established. Watch the news. All sorts of scum end up in the ER along with accident victims."

Marla gawked at him. "You don't think Ken got off I-95 at the wrong exit, and they were attacked, do you?" It had been known to happen, especially in Miami.

He spread his hands. "Who knows? It's damn peculiar that they haven't tried to contact us."

"Maybe they had car trouble and have been out of range for cell service."

"I suppose we could check with Road Rangers and the towing services."

"And hotels in the area, since the sitter said they might have gotten a room somewhere. But why would they have gone out on New Year's Eve so suddenly? It doesn't make sense."

"Mrs. Phelps said Ken's call had been work-related," Dalton reminded her. "I'll visit his office when it reopens to see if his colleagues know anything. Meanwhile, Luke needs to be fed. Mrs. Phelps wrote down which formula he drinks, in case we have to buy more supplies."

Marla sat at the kitchen table with the baby in her lap. Dalton brought over the bottle, and she tickled Luke's lips with the nipple until he grasped onto it. He made loud sucking noises as he drank, his gaze fixed on hers. Oh, gosh. Her heart softened at the trust in his eyes and at the scent of his formula mixed with his powdery baby smell.

What if he was her own? *No, don't go there, Marla. You have enough to do right now taking care of Tally's child.*

"You said Ken drives a gold-colored car," she remarked. "Isn't that unusual in Florida?"

"You mean, compared to all the white and silver models?" Dalton replied. "The technical term for his color is gilded pewter metallic. The RLX retails for around sixty thousand dollars with add-ons."

"His business must be doing well." She glanced at Brianna, who'd taken a seat opposite and wore a broad grin on her face. "What are you smiling about?"

"You and Luke. You look so natural with him. It would be nice to have a baby brother."

Marla's cheeks heated, but she didn't comment. It was one thing to care for a teenager and quite another to satisfy an infant's needs. Luke required a level of care she didn't know she could provide.

She finished the feeding session, aware of Brianna and Dalton's keen observation. Did she pass muster? Her doubts got cast aside as she burped Luke and changed his soiled diaper. Dalton rigged the guest bed to serve as a crib, and she put the baby down for his afternoon nap. If his parents remained absent, she'd have to look into the possibility of buying basic nursery items.

Luke cried as she stepped from the room. She remembered Tally saying he often fussed before going to sleep, but the temptation to pick him up almost made her return. Logic told her he'd been fed and changed, so he should be comfortable. She steeled herself against his wails while lingering in the hallway.

Shortly thereafter, his cries segued into whimpers, until finally silence reigned.

She dragged a hand across her face. This day had been exhausting, but she wouldn't be able to sleep tonight until she'd reviewed things with Dalton.

"What else can we do?" she asked him at the dinner table. They ate leftovers from the party. She was so tired that her appetite had fled. It took too much effort to chew and swallow, but she forced herself to eat for the energy.

Dalton looked as fatigued as she felt. Lines creased his brow, and his mouth curved downward as he regarded her. "I can broaden the search tomorrow. They can't have just disappeared."

Tally, where are you? Marla hoped for a simple explanation that they'd laugh off together someday. But dread wove its insidious fingers into her psyche. She'd never be able to get any rest at this rate. Her heart pounded, its pace accelerating when the phone rang. She glanced at the wall clock as she snatched the receiver. Six-thirty. Maybe Dalton's partner had news.

"Hello?" Her voice came out as a squeaky croak.

"Hi, may I speak to Marla Vail, please?"

"That's me."

"I'm a nurse at Southwest Regional Hospital. Now don't get too alarmed, but we have a patient here in ICU who has you listed as an emergency contact. She was in a car accident last night. Her name is Tally Riggs. How soon do you think you can get here?"

Chapter Two

Marla's knees quaked as she and Dalton rode the hospital elevator to the floor that held the Intensive Care Unit. What would they find there? Her friend surrounded by tubing and wires? Was Tally even awake? The nurse hadn't given much information over the phone, just that Tally had sustained serious injuries. She'd been stabilized for now but wasn't out of the danger zone.

"The nurse didn't say anything about Ken. Do you suppose he's been hurt, too?" Marla said in a hushed tone to Dalton, even though they were alone in the lift.

"We'll find out soon enough." His stony eyes didn't betray his emotion, but she knew he was worried from his tense posture.

She gripped her stomach as a wave of sickness hit her. What would they find when the doors opened?

Her nose wrinkled as they stepped into a corridor beside a bustling nurses' station. The antiseptic smell reminded her of her father's last days. Her body trembled, and her pulse raced. Beyond the nurses' station were cubicles walled off by glass partitions. Patients lay against white sheets, looking as pale as their bed linens. Their faces were barely visible behind the apparatus that supported them. Marla scanned the group but couldn't identify Tally among them.

One of the nurses, a short woman with auburn hair, glanced up and smiled at their approach. Marla's throat tightened. She couldn't find her voice to speak, so she let Dalton take the lead. As they neared, she clutched his arm, needing the reassurance of his firm presence.

"Hi, we're Marla and Dalton Vail. Somebody called us about our friends, Tally and Ken Riggs." Dalton's deep voice flowed over her like warm honey, soothing her nerves.

Thank God she had him to lean on. She couldn't have done this alone.

"Oh, yes. The doctor wants to speak to you. Come this way, please." The woman wearing blue scrubs guided them briskly down the corridor and into a lounge. The waiting area had a TV, vinyl-upholstered chairs, a coffee table, and a magazine rack. A potted plant stood in one corner. A counter held a coffeemaker that looked half-empty. Marla wondered why the room wasn't filled. She'd be here all the time if a loved one was in jeopardy, but perhaps visiting hours were over for the evening.

"Have a seat, and I'll page Dr. Gillis."

The nurse scurried out before Marla could mobilize her tongue to ask questions. Was the woman avoiding their inquiries on purpose? It wasn't a good thing when the doctor had to relate the news.

Unable to sit still, she joined Dalton in pacing the linoleum floor until heavy footsteps sounded from the corridor. She stared at the open doorway, relieved to see a gray-haired man in a white coat approach them. He had warm brown eyes and a welcoming smile.

"Mr. and Mrs. Vail? I'm Dr. Gillis. Please, have a seat." He shook their hands and then waited until they'd complied. "The police informed us you were on Mrs. Riggs' ICE list. In Case of Emergency," he clarified.

"Yes, we're close friends," Dalton acknowledged.

"It took the rescue team a while to retrieve the couple. When we got them in the ER, our priority was to stabilize the injured woman. That's why you didn't hear from us until today."

"Do you know what happened?"

"Their vehicle went off the road last night. I'm sorry to have to tell you this, but Mr. Riggs did not survive the crash."

"Oh, my God. No, it can't be true." Marla clamped a hand to her mouth. This wasn't possible. Ken ... dead?

Dalton leaned forward. "Ken has a brother, Phil. Do you know if he's been notified?"

"We're doing that now."

"Tell us more," Dalton said in a flat tone.

How easily he could turn on detective mode and shut out his feelings, Marla thought. These were his friends. How could he act so unruffled?

"Mrs. Riggs sustained serious damage in the accident. Keeping her alive is our main concern." The doctor rattled off a bunch of medical terms, but Marla only heard words like "lung puncture" and "brain swelling" and something about the danger of her spleen rupturing.

With each pronouncement, her gut clenched. Fear churned her belly at the thought that Tally might not make it. If only this were a nightmare and not reality.

"So Tally is unconscious?" she asked, once she could speak beyond her constricted throat. At least her friend wouldn't suffer any pain that way. Her body must be bruised all over.

"Yes, ma'am. It might be weeks before she wakes up. We'll have no idea of the residual damage until then," Dr. Gillis said, enunciating each word. Marla surmised he was used to dealing with frantic family members whose anxiety caused selective hearing.

"You mean, she might be permanently disabled?" Marla's pitch rose. Tally had to be all right if she made it through this crisis. Luke needed his mother.

"I don't care to sugar-coat things for you, ma'am. Your friend is lucky to have survived. Our ER is filled with patients injured on New Year's Eve. The holiday is another reason why it took so long to identify her."

17

Dalton gave Marla's hand a squeeze. For a brief instant, pain flickered across his expression. But then he suppressed it into his detective's mask and retrieved his cell phone.

"I should check with Kat. It's odd she hasn't heard about the accident. She's been checking the reports."

"Dalton is a police detective, and Kat is his partner," Marla explained to the doctor. "We feared something bad might have happened when Tally's babysitter called us to come over."

"Would either of you know if Mrs. Riggs has a living will?" the physician inquired.

Marla exchanged a startled glance with Dalton. "Um, I think so. I have a bunch of her papers at home, including power of attorney. I'm listed as Tally's successor trustee after her husband."

"We'd appreciate having a copy of those documents when you get the chance. I assume the brother will take charge of Mr. Riggs' body when it's released?"

Marla's mouth opened and closed like a beached fish, but she couldn't edge any words past her thick tongue.

"That's right," Dalton agreed. "Phil would be the one to make funeral arrangements. If you'll excuse me, I'm going to call my partner with this news." He rose and strode away into the corridor.

Marla stood, anxious to learn more about Tally. "So what are my friend's chances?" she asked, avoiding any thoughts of Ken. She couldn't believe he was gone, but she'd deal with it later. Tally needed her strength through this ordeal.

"The next forty-eight hours are crucial. If she makes it to the weekend, I'd say we have a fighting chance she'll come out of this alive. But that's all I can predict at this point."

"How often can we visit?"

"Two visitors are allowed at a time from eleven in the morning to eight in the evening. So to clarify, you're the person to call if we need to make a decision on her care, and not the husband's brother?"

"Yes, that's correct. Unfortunately, Tally doesn't have any close relatives. We're like family to her."

"I'll make a note in her chart. You can come see her now. Don't be frightened by the equipment. It's helping to save her life."

"Thank you so much, doctor." Tears tipped her lashes at his kindness. She was grateful he showed compassion, especially when he must relate bad news on a regular basis. Tally was fortunate to be under his care. Actually, what type of specialist was he? Did the hospital have Tally's insurance info so she could get whatever interventions were needed?

Marla asked at the front desk. The nurse reassured her that the police had called in that information once they'd retrieved Tally's wallet. Marla said goodbye to the physician and followed Karyn, the nurse, to the proper cubicle.

Tally's wan face was barely visible beneath the ventilator tube and tape keeping it in place. Her chest rose and fell beneath the flimsy hospital gown, and her eyelids remained closed. An IV machine dripped fluid into her arm, while other wires and tubes snaked to various devices. Karyn explained the purpose of each one, but Marla's ears closed. She could only take so much.

"Her lips look dry," she observed.

"Here, I'll take care of it." Karyn dabbed a wet swab around Tally's mouth. "You might want to talk to your friend. It's possible she could hear you. People who've awakened from comas sometimes remember loved ones being nearby and speaking to them."

"Okay." After the nurse left, Marla pulled up a chair and sat, grasping Tally's cool hand. "Tally, it's me. I'm here with you. You were in an accident, but you're going to be all right." She smoothed Tally's blond hair away from her face.

Air-conditioning blew into the room. Marla shivered, more from nerves than the ambient temperature. Beeps, clicks, and hissing noises filled the space. Her gaze rose to the monitors, where she viewed the steady rhythm of Tally's heartbeat.

Oh, Tally. Why did you go out last night? Why couldn't you have stayed home? A tear leaked down her cheek. She had to believe things would turn out okay, for her own sake as well as Luke's. If and when Tally woke up, she'd have to deal with her husband's death. A long road stretched in front of them.

Marla didn't know how long she'd sat there until Dalton arrived and put a hand on her shoulder. Her tense muscles uncoiled at his reassuring touch.

"What did Kat say?" she asked him, keeping her face averted to hide her distress.

Dalton signaled for her to join him away from Tally's bedside. When she'd complied, he spoke in a low tone. "Kat got a response on Ken's license tag earlier and wanted to get more information before she called. The accident happened in Davie, which isn't our jurisdiction. Ken was driving down a narrow two-lane road when he swerved onto the swale. Their car flipped over down a ditch and ended up with the driver's side submerged in a canal."

"Why did it take so long for us to hear about it?"

"The rescuers were able to retrieve Tally and Ken from the wrecked car, but they had to wait for daylight to tow it upright. Tally's purse and cell phone were inside. Fortunately, those items were still dry. Kat was about to call us once she clarified their status."

An image played in her mind of the wrecked car where Ken must have been killed. Or had he been merely stunned? Maybe he'd been awake but trapped in the car while water filled his end. Unable to pry himself loose, he would have drowned. A chill swept her nape at the horror of it.

"Who called the cops if it happened at night?" she asked, steering her mind to practicalities.

"A neighbor witnessed the accident. Kat requested a copy of his report."

"I don't understand why this news didn't surface sooner."

His eyes darkened to slate. "New Year's Eve is a busy time of year in terms of accidents. The Davie cops would have had plenty to keep them occupied, and ditto for their rescue teams. The car wasn't towed from the canal until today."

Kat knew how worried they'd been. She should have called as soon as the license tag registered. Marla pressed her lips together, keeping silent on the subject. She'd hoped Dalton's influence would soften the lieutenant by now, but he still couldn't crack her stern exterior. Kat had transferred into his department without his chief explaining how or why. Despite Dalton's subtle inquiries, her past remained a mystery.

Marla should cut her some slack. Maybe she'd hoped to spare them pain by learning if the car's passengers had made it. But wouldn't the police report have mentioned a fatality?

She returned to her friend's side, staring down at her in helpless anguish. The constant clicking and hissing from the ventilator sounded in the background. How frail we are, she thought, surveying Tally's still form with a choked sob. She'd need all the miracles of modern medicine to come out of this unscathed. And poor Luke, who'd grow up without a father.

Marla turned a tear-streaked face to Dalton. "We should get Phil's number from the nurse. Maybe we can pick him up at the airport. It's the least we can do."

"We'll see when his flight gets in. You should get home to the baby. The best way to help Tally is to care for her child."

"I'll want to visit her here, too. I have to talk to Ma about babysitting. If she's not available, perhaps I can call Mrs. Phelps. It's not fair to ask Brianna to give up her vacation time."

"My mother would probably love to pitch in as well. She wouldn't mind driving down from Delray. And we have plenty of leftovers from our party, so you won't have to cook for a few days."

His last remark lifted her spirits. How typical for the man to always think about his next meal.

*****

Brianna had done fine in their absence, getting Luke through another feeding, giving him a bath, and changing him for the night. Marla complimented the teen while wondering where she'd washed the baby. In one of their sinks? She didn't ask, adding the baby's plastic bathtub to her growing list of items to pick up at Tally's house.

Fatigue seeped into her bones as she completed her chores. Finally, she and Dalton had some privacy after retiring to their bedroom.

"Phil got a flight in the morning," he told her while readying for bed. "I offered to pick him up and give him a key to his brother's house. He might as well stay there. And he can drive Tally's car rather than a rental."

"Good idea. I found Tally's living will and power of attorney and faxed them to the hospital."

"Let's hope those choices won't be necessary." He slid under the sheet next to her, turned on his side in her direction, and leaned on an elbow.

"I still can't believe Ken died in a car crash. It's awful, and Tally lying there like a limp doll isn't much better. I'll have to bring a comb next time I visit." Her friend's hair was the one thing in her power to control, and it would help humanize Tally to the staff to make her decent.

"We're here for her. Tally can count on us for whatever she needs."

"I know." Marla curled into him, seeking comfort from his embrace. His warmth seeped into her skin and helped her rejoice in feeling alive.

They stayed folded together for a while, neither one speaking. Marla heard his soft snores and realized he'd fallen asleep. She rolled away, her eyes open and anxiety keeping her awake. Take one day at a time, she advised herself. That's all you can do in a crisis.

And this, too, shall pass, said her mother's voice in her head. With that soothing thought, her breathing slowed and she drifted to sleep.

The baby's cry startled her into full alert mode. "Oh, no. What time is it?" She glared at the clock dial, luminous in the dark. Dalton must have awoken earlier and turned off the lights before going back to sleep. It was two o'clock.

Marla padded into the makeshift nursery where Luke had managed to dislodge one of the towels they'd folded around the bed. Tomorrow she'd have to see about getting a crib. She turned on a lamp and moved to examine the child's diaper. Her finger came away wet. It wasn't time for a feeding, so she changed him and put him back. But he continued to fuss and whimper.

"What's the matter, little guy? Do you miss your momma?" Marla caught his little fingers in her hand. He squirmed and scrunched his tiny face. If she let him howl, he'd wake the household. Instead, an idea dawned on her.

She hurried out, retrieved his stroller, and wheeled it into the room. Then she sat Luke inside, strapped him in, and rolled him down the hall toward the kitchen. It didn't even take ten minutes for him to close his eyes in slumber. Once he was sound asleep, she put him back to bed and then stumbled into her room.

Marla's head felt groggy when she finally woke from an unsettled sleep five hours later. Dalton's side was empty, his sheets ruffled. Had he remembered to give Luke his early morning bottle?

It was seven o'clock. Marla tossed aside the covers and leapt out of bed. So much to do, not enough time.

As she trudged into the bathroom, she contemplated which task to attack first. Her bleary eyes stared back at her in the mirror. Luke's care took priority. She'd call her mother to see if Ma could babysit. Next, Marla considered her work schedule for the day. She'd ask Robyn, the salon's receptionist, to rearrange her appointments so she'd have time to visit Tally.

Dalton greeted her in the kitchen, where he'd brewed a pot of coffee and had a mushroom omelet waiting for her to reheat in the frypan. Luke sat in his stroller, gurgling happily, while Brianna was flipping through *Teen Vogue* at the kitchen table.

"You're a sweetheart," Marla told Dalton, kissing him on the mouth. She poured herself a cup of aromatic coffee and stuck the reheated omelet on a plate. "I gather you fed Luke already. He got up in the middle of the night. I walked him in his stroller until he settled down."

"That's a good technique. We used to do that for Brie when she fussed," Dalton said with a fond smile for his daughter.

Marla's gaze inevitably rose to his broad shoulders and confident posture. He never failed to impress her in a dress shirt, tie, and pressed pants.

"Any word from the hospital?" she asked, unable to eat a morsel until he responded.

"Nope. I'll get the scoop from Kat this morning. What about the baby?"

"Hand me the phone. I'll call Ma. She's always up early." Praying her mother would be free, Marla dialed Anita's number.

"Good morning, *bubeleh*. What's going on? I thought I'd hear from you sooner."

Marla had disbanded the party after telling everyone they had to pick up Luke. "We got a call around dinnertime that Tally and Ken had been in a car accident on Monday night."

"Oh, my God. Are they okay?"

"Ken was killed." Marla's throat tightened. He couldn't be dead, could he? She still found it hard to believe.

"What? That can't be true."

In a choked voice, Marla gave her mother an update. "Dalton is getting Ken's brother at the airport later this morning. I thought to offer my help with funeral arrangements since he's from out of town." *And I've attended enough memorial services to know the local burial places.*

"That would be a nice gesture," Anita replied.

"I'd prefer to stay home with Luke today, but I have clients scheduled. Would you be able to babysit? Brianna offered, but I don't want to ruin her vacation."

"Sure, I can come. I'm so sorry. This is horrible news."

"I know. It's unbelievable. I have to think about Luke, or I'll lose focus."

"Don't worry; I'm here to help. Give me a half hour to get ready, and then I'll be over. We'll get through this together."

That matter settled, Marla stuffed down her breakfast, did the dishes, and put Luke in his makeshift crib for another nap. Dalton dropped Brianna, now free from obligation, off at a friend's house on his way to work. Marla had time to check her email and call the hospital before Anita arrived.

"I just spoke to Tally's nurse," she told her mother, while Anita plopped her purse and reading material on the dining room table.

"How is she this morning?" Anita followed Marla down the hall to the baby's room.

"She needed a unit of blood because her hemoglobin had dropped. Otherwise, she's been stable during the night."

"Hopefully, she'll continue to improve."

"Yes, but we won't know the extent of her head injury until she wakes up. What happens if she needs help on a long-term basis?"

"Worry about one thing at a time. Oh, isn't he adorable," Anita crooned upon spying Luke. "Poor little guy to lose his daddy so young."

"We'll take good care of him. We're not prepared for a baby in the house, though. We don't have the right furniture or the proper supplies in stock."

"Why don't you borrow the stuff from Tally's nursery?"

"Their crib and dresser are too heavy to move. The changing table might fit in our car, and I can see what else is there while I'm at their house. We could end up having Luke for weeks, or even months."

The possibility of her friend not making it leaked into her mind. No, that wouldn't happen. Tally had to survive.

Her eyes misted, and Marla blinked rapidly. She had to be strong. Breaking down wouldn't help anyone.

Anita stroked her cheek. "You'll do fine. I have faith in you."

"I'm glad someone does." Marla reviewed Luke's feeding schedule with her mother, said a hasty goodbye, and rushed to the salon.

She barely had time to stash her handbag inside a drawer before her first customer finished at the shampoo station. A fresh strawberry scent accompanied the woman to her chair, where Marla proceeded to snip and style her hair. Music played in the background on the speaker system, adding a lively beat and competing with the chatter of patrons, the whir of blow-dryers, and the splash of water from the sinks.

Marla didn't get a chance to relate her news to Nicole until lunchtime. She drew aside the other stylist, also her friend and oft-time manager, with a tap to her arm.

"Can I talk to you for a second? I have news. It's not good."

"Sure, what's up, girlfriend?" Nicole trailed Marla into the rear storeroom, where they could have a moment of privacy. She walked with a bounce in her step, which she'd exhibited ever since Marla had introduced her to Kevin Jones, a hunky EMT at the fire department. Nicole's crimson top complemented her warm cinnamon skin, as did the tinted gloss on her lips. In her usual sophisticated style, she'd fastened her ebony hair off her face with a clip.

As Marla repeated the story she'd told her mother, Nicole's mocha eyes rounded in horror. "What? Ken is dead? Oh. My. God. And Tally is lying senseless in a hospital bed? Marla, how could you even come into work today? You should have let us know. We would have covered for you."

"Thanks, but that wouldn't be fair to my clients. Besides, this could be long-term. Tally has a difficult road ahead."

"You'll figure things out. Go to the hospital. I know you want to be there for Tally."

"I want to be there for Luke, too, but I have other obligations. I don't want to disappoint anyone." Marla scrubbed a hand over her face. "Dalton has been great, and so has Brianna. And even my mother has pitched in. I'm sure Kate—Dalton's mom—would want to help out, if I asked her."

"Let me know what I can do. When did Tally plan to go back to work?"

"She hadn't fixed a definite date but said it would be sometime after New Year's."

"What did she intend to do with Luke? Bring the baby along to the dress shop she owns?"

"Actually, she'd mentioned day care. I don't know if she got around to checking places in the area, though."

"That would be a solution. Let me research them for you."

"I'd appreciate it, thanks." After Nicole left, Marla dialed Dalton for an update.

"I picked Phil up at the airport and dropped him off at Ken's house," Dalton's deep voice rumbled in her ear. "I'm on my way to Davie. According to a witness, another car was involved in the accident. It came from behind, sped alongside Ken's vehicle, and appeared to force him off the road."

Chapter Three

Marla gripped the phone tighter to her ear. "The doctor didn't say anything about more people being hurt."

"The other driver fled the scene," Dalton said in his flat detective tone. "The man who called in the accident had gone outside his house to let off some fireworks. He saw the second vehicle begin to pass Ken's car and then swerve into it. Ken must have turned the wheel to avoid a collision. His Acura rolled over down a ditch and landed half-submerged in the canal."

"Maybe the other person was trying to get back in their lane and misjudged the distance. How well lit is that stretch of road?"

"Pretty poorly, from what I'm told. It's in a low-traffic neighborhood that borders a canal without any barrier. The witness says the second car, a dark SUV, sped away. I spoke to the lead investigator. He says tire tracks support the fellow's report."

"If true, the driver didn't even stop to help. Or maybe it was too dark for him to see what he'd done. How fast was he going?"

"I don't have those details yet. I'm heading over to the scene now, and then I'll stop by the station in Davie to see what else I can dig up. Meanwhile, we have another case. A guy was stabbed outside a convenience store last night in an apparent robbery."

"Oh, great."

"Kat's handling it for now, until I get more info about our friends. But a traffic accident in another town normally doesn't fall into our ballpark."

"What about the phone call from work that drew Ken out on New Year's Eve? Why would he even be on a dark road in Davie? Did you ask his colleagues?" Marla squirmed with unease. Something struck her as wrong about this situation.

"Not yet," Dalton replied. "I decided it's better to wait. His office staff will have been notified about his death just this morning."

"You're right. They'll be reeling from the news." Who would take charge with Ken gone? Didn't he own the agency?

"I should focus on Tally's recovery and caring for Luke. Ma is over at the house, but I can always call your mom or Mrs. Phelps if necessary. Nicole is researching day care centers for me. I remembered Tally had mentioned this idea when she spoke about going back to work."

"Sounds like you have things covered. Any word from the hospital?"

"Things were stable at the ICU when I called earlier. I'd like to visit Tally before I go home later. It'll be rush hour, though." She envisioned the traffic on I-95. It would be slow going, and she wouldn't get home until after dark.

"No problem. Do what you have to do, but check in with me before you leave the salon. We'll compare notes then."

Marla hung up with a heavy heart. Prior to this event, she'd often call Tally to exchange updates. She couldn't believe her friend was lying unresponsive in a hospital bed and fighting for her life. Oh, gosh. Had anybody informed the girls at her dress boutique? They knew she was on maternity leave, but this? Even though Tally wasn't at the shop from day-to-day, she stopped by periodically to maintain the business accounts.

Dread pitted her stomach at the notion of informing

them. Hopefully the cops had already done that sad task. Nonetheless, she'd have to contact Tally's staff one of these days.

The salon receptionist peeked her head in. "Marla, your twelve-o'clock is here." She noticed Marla's expression. "Are you all right? I'm sorry about your friend. Have you heard any more news?"

"Tally is stable for now. I'll be out in a minute, thanks."

Marla grabbed a water bottle and took a few sloppy gulps. Her stomach ached, but she didn't feel hungry. It was more like a sick, anxious feeling.

Including Tally's shop assistants, she considered how many people would be affected by the accident. It wasn't just tiny Luke. Both of her friends' work forces would be stunned and saddened.

A dark cloud followed her throughout the afternoon. She regained a sense of control from the normal sounds and smells of the salon. If she thought about Tally, Ken's funeral, or how their office personnel would cope, she'd be bowled over by the repercussions.

"How are you holding up?" Nicole said during a momentary break between clients. The other stylist peered at her with concern, a spray bottle of cleaning solution in her hand.

"I'm worn out already, and I still have so much to do."

"You have a lot of burdens right now. But listen, I took care of one of them. A friend of mine who has a six-month-old has just enrolled him in day care. She says this place is the best in the area, but you'd better get your name in now. They always have a waiting list. Sorry I didn't tell you earlier, but your clients haven't let up." Nicole handed Marla a slip of paper with the details.

Marla flashed her a grateful grin. "Thanks for doing this. It's one less chore on my list. I'll see if I can make an appointment for tomorrow morning to check them out."

She made the call, then cleaned her station while preparing to leave. A desperate urge to see Luke and cuddle him took hold of her, but she shunted that unfamiliar sensation aside. First she had to reassure herself that Luke's mother held onto the thread of life.

Remembering she'd promised to check in with Dalton before leaving the salon, Marla gave him a call once outside. The late-afternoon air chilled her bones. Day turned into night earlier in January, and with the setting sun came cooler temperatures. Glad she'd worn a leather jacket, Marla cradled the phone close to her ear while she headed to her car.

"Hi, I'm on my way to visit Tally," she told her husband when he'd answered.

"I'll fetch Brie on my way home and will take care of dinner." His deep voice sounded like soothing music to her ears.

"Did you visit the scene of the accident?"

"Yes. That road would be dangerous even in the daytime. It's a narrow two-lane drive with a canal on one side. Houses border it on the other side, and it leads to some sort of warehouse district that has an easier outlet. It's not a great part of town."

"What on earth would have brought Ken to that area? Do you really think it was work-related on New Year's Eve? What could be so important?"

"I have no idea, and neither does Sergeant Mallory, the investigator assigned to the case."

"Has he asked Ken's colleagues about it?"

"He's informed them about Ken's death, but that's all. I did interview the alleged witness. The guy swears he saw another car cut Ken off and speed away."

"Does this man seem reliable? It was New Year's Eve. He might have been drinking."

"He seemed earnest, but people's memories are never fully accurate."

31

"Is there evidence on the Acura that another car made physical contact?"

"As I said before, tire tracks confirm the presence of another vehicle. I haven't been to the yard where Ken's car was towed. I'll have to wait until Mallory clears the Acura first. But the vehicles wouldn't have had to touch for Ken to swerve out of the way."

"I imagine his car was totaled. Somebody should notify their insurance company."

"I'll take care of it, unless Sergeant Mallory has already given them a call. He would have obtained that information from Ken's wallet. Their auto policy might provide medical benefits as well."

"What happens to the stuff inside their car?" People kept all sorts of items in their vehicles. Did relatives have to claim these personal possessions after a fatal traffic accident? The notion gave her a shudder.

"Maybe Phil, as next of kin, can go over to the lot while he's here. I'll ask Mallory when I talk to him. I don't want to pester the guy with too many questions right now."

"Has this Sergeant said anything about the possibility of Ken being purposefully forced off the road? Or does he merely consider the accident an unfortunate hit-and-run?"

"He hasn't come to any conclusions yet. As a professional courtesy, he'll keep me informed of any major developments. But we're also personal friends of the victims, which gives me—"

"A conflict of interest." Marla reached her Camry and opened the door. "We'll talk more at home. Love you."

*****

Not much had changed at the hospital when Marla arrived, frazzled from rush hour traffic and the always-hazardous drive north on I-95. Tally appeared pale against the bedding.

Bruises became more evident now that Marla could see past her initial anxiety. Just as well Tally is out of it, Marla thought. She'd be hurting badly if awake.

After a brief consultation with the nursing staff, Marla took a seat at Tally's bedside. The respirator hissed, and other machines beeped a steady rhythm. That was good, wasn't it? Steady was a desirable outcome.

Holding her friend's hand, she babbled on about Luke and how Tally would heal with time. Her voice wound down, getting dry and raspy. She blinked rapidly, her eyes moist.

Please, Tally, be all right. You have to wake up soon.

Not big on prayers, nonetheless Marla closed her eyes and mumbled a plea to the Lord. "She has a baby boy who needs his mother. Please help her get better and not have any residual brain damage."

Tally could wake up with memory loss, tremors, or any number of other ailments. It would be difficult enough for her to deal with Ken's death. Thankfully, imparting that news was the doctor's job.

Marla patted Tally's limp hand before rising to seek her friend's nurse. She found the woman wheeling a medicine cart down the aisle.

"Excuse me," she called, hustling in that direction. "Has Tally's brother-in-law been here at all? He arrived in town this morning." *You'd think he would be concerned enough to come visit.* Marla would feel better if he made the effort to see Tally in person. It would show he cared about her.

The nurse's eyes scrunched, deepening her crow's feet. "I believe you're the sole visitor today, although some man phoned to ask about her. He said he was a friend of the family and not a relative. I told him he'd have to call the doctor for information on Mrs. Riggs' condition."

"Oh? You wouldn't have this guy's name, would you?"

"Sorry, I didn't write it down."

Hmm, which friend of Tally would that be? Marla

contemplated this question during the drive home. Dalton was the only one who came to mind.

She parked the car in the garage and emerged into the brightly lit kitchen. Her shoulders slumped with relief as she hung her keys on a hook by the door.

Dalton, busy at the sink, turned off the faucet. "Here you are. I was getting worried."

"Traffic was heavy. It's always slow this time of day."

He dried his hands on a towel and walked over to embrace her. "I don't like you driving by yourself at night."

"I'm fine." Their unspoken fears about car accidents flickered through her mind. "Where are Brie and Luke?"

"Brianna is on the phone in her room, and Luke is asleep. I stopped off at the baby store and bought a portable crib, so that'll help us out."

"Good thinking." She followed him into their makeshift nursery to see for herself. Sure enough, a maple-colored crib stood against the wall in their guest bedroom. Luke lay inside, his eyes closed in repose. He looked so cute in his sleeper outfit that she had to smile. "What's that thing?" She pointed to the protective padding around the interior.

"It's a bumper. We could probably use more sheets since I only bought one set."

"You'd better make a list of supplies. I'll borrow whatever I can get from Tally's house when I go there next." Leaving Luke to his slumber, she entered the hallway.

"I don't mind buying a few items. You never know," Dalton said in a playful tone. "We might need to furnish our own nursery someday."

"You wish." She swatted him on the shoulder. He knew her feelings on the topic. And yet this time, the idea gave her an unwanted sense of awe and wonder.

*****

34

Thursday was her late day at work, so Marla strapped Luke into his car seat, stuck the folded stroller into her trunk along with the diaper bag, and hopped in on the driver's side. She had a whole slate of errands to perform this morning. First on her list was visiting the day care center that Nicole's friend had recommended.

Located near Sawgrass Mills Mall, the place was farther west than she might have chosen, but the facility was fairly new and the caretakers seemed to enjoy their jobs. While wheeling Luke around, she got a full tour and watched the staff interact with their small clientele. Security was tight, and video monitors ever present.

Since they had room for one more infant under six months, Marla showed her power of attorney and signed Luke up for a trial period. She was glad the director agreed to cancel the contract should Tally awaken and prefer to keep Luke at home.

Would Tally even stay in that house with Ken gone? What kind of life insurance policy did he have? Would it pay off their mortgage? It would be terrible if Tally had to downsize due to lack of funds. Then again, she might choose to move closer to her dress shop or to the day care center.

These issues would have to be dealt with later, when her condition improved.

Marla agreed to bring Luke on Monday for his first day care session. She'd foot the bill for now but hoped Tally would be able to pay her back later. Things could get expensive, between baby care and supplies. No wonder young couples put off having children right away. It wasn't affordable until they'd built up their income stream. Having grandmothers nearby could serve as an advantage in that regard.

Outside, Marla pushed the stroller toward her white Camry. The smell of wood smoke rose pleasantly into her nose. Somebody must have a fireplace going in the vicinity.

Glad she'd had the smarts earlier to put on a warm sweater, she swung Luke from his stroller to the car seat and fastened him in. Oy, it was a shlep to go anywhere with a child.

With Luke secured in the rear, she sat in the car with the motor running and dialed Tally's house number. She'd already checked in with the hospital this morning. Fluctuations in her friend's blood pressure concerned the nurse, but they'd let her know if anything critical happened. Meanwhile, Marla hoped to catch Phil at the residence.

He answered on the third ring, his voice wary.

"Hi, Phil? This is Marla Vail. I'm Tally's friend and Dalton's wife. I was hoping to stop by with Luke to say hello and maybe pick up some more baby supplies."

"Sure, I'm not going anywhere."

Unfazed by the lack of warmth in his tone, Marla set on the path toward his lodgings. Did Phil even care about his nephew's welfare? Was he grieving for the loss of his brother? Marla had never met him in person, but Tally had spoken of him in disdainful tones.

He opened the door, his wheat brown hair ruffled and sticking up in places, his jaw covered by scruffy growth. Phil regarded her with pale blue eyes from behind a pair of wire-rimmed glasses. He wore a plaid shirt open at the collar, faded jeans, and worn leather loafers.

"Hi, I'm Marla. It's nice to finally meet you in person, although I wish the circumstances could be better. I'm sorry for your loss. We'll all miss Ken a great deal, especially his son." She indicated the baby, who made a gurgling noise and offered one of his rare smiles.

Phil's expression softened. "Come on in. This is the first chance I've had to greet my nephew."

Marla sat in the living room at his invitation. She didn't intend to stay too long but wished to break the ice. "Tally mentioned you're a chemist?"

He bobbed his head in an affirmative motion. "That's

right. I work at a lab for a pharmaceutical company. It's nothing earth-shattering, but it pays the bills."

Marla rocked the stroller back and forth. "What got you into the field?"

"I was one of the nerdy kids who liked chemistry in school. Or maybe it was because we had a cool teacher who made things fun. Learning the periodic table was like a game to me."

"Ken is ... was from Miami. You never had any desire to move back to Florida?"

He gave a snort of laughter. "Nope. You can keep the heat and humidity. Where I live, it's less congested. I like the sense of community and the slower pace away from the crowded coastlines. I should have come to see my brother, though. After Dad died, we drifted apart."

If Phil had a steady job, what made him such a flake in Tally's view? From his graying temples, he looked to be in his mid-forties, older than Ken. Was it because he'd never married? Did he drink, gamble, or spend money wastefully? Tally had never pinpointed the reason why she didn't trust her brother-in-law.

Regardless, it wasn't Marla's role to judge him. She summoned a tactful response.

"Look, I realize this is difficult for you, especially being from out of town. But if I can help with arrangements—"

Phil shot to his feet and began pacing. "Thanks, but I've already decided to do a private graveside burial, unless my brother left other instructions. I've found a place with reasonable rates. You wouldn't believe how much funeral homes charge these days."

"Actually, I would. I've researched Pre-Need plans."

Phil gave her a glum look. "I'll get it done as soon as the body is released, but my funds are short. It would help if I could access my brother's accounts."

"Are you listed as signatory? Otherwise, you'll have to request reimbursement from his estate. Please let us know what arrangements you make. Dalton and I would like to attend the burial. Have you given any thought to a memorial service? Ken's friends and business associates will want to pay their respects."

"Tally can take charge of a service when she's ready. Or you can hold one for both of them, if she doesn't make it. From what your husband said, she's not out of the woods yet."

Marla pressed her lips together, dismayed by his casual attitude. She shoved the stroller in his direction. "Would you mind watching Luke while I gather more supplies? Or perhaps you'd rather care for him while you're in town? It would give you a chance to get to know your nephew." She had no intention of handing the child over to him but wished to gauge his reaction.

Phil held up both hands. "Whoa, I don't think so. I'm not the fatherly type. The kid is all yours."

"Fine, then please keep an eye on him for a few minutes." Without a backward glance, she rose and strode toward the bedroom wing.

Which space was Phil inhabiting—the master suite or the guest room? Aware that she had mere minutes to poke around, she dipped into the master bedroom. Her gaze roamed to the king-size bed, neatly made up with a colorful comforter in a tropical design.

Tally and Ken might have been awake on New Year's Eve when the phone rang. Had he taken the call here or in the family room while watching TV? She picked up the mobile unit on his nightstand and scrolled through the caller ID. None of the numbers jumped out at her as being familiar, but that didn't mean anything. The out-of-area calls were likely from telemarketers. If she had more time, she would copy the others, but Phil might wonder what was keeping her.

Besides, Ken's call might have come through on his cell phone, not the house line. Either way, Sergeant Mallory would probably be examining his recent call lists.

She replaced the receiver in its cradle, then surveyed the room. Her glance caught on a crumpled piece of paper in the trash can by Ken's side of the bed.

She retrieved the note and squinted at the hand-scrawled words.

Louise ... Melaleuca Lane ... Bay 6

"What are you doing?" Phil snapped. He stood in the doorway, glaring at her with furrowed brows.

"Um, I needed a pen to write down a list of baby items I'll be wanting. I found a pen and notepad here on the nightstand." Marla waved the paper before stuffing it into her skirt pocket. Hopefully, he hadn't been standing there for too long.

"The kid fell asleep, so I put him in his crib. I figured he'd be more comfortable there."

"I'd imagine so." Praying the baby would nap for a while, Marla swept her arm in a broad gesture. "It's hard to believe Ken won't be coming home. Even if you hadn't spoken to him in a while, he was still your brother. Is there anything here that you might want? I can tell Tally for you when she's awake."

Phil shoved his hands into his jeans pockets and lumbered into the room. His eyes saddened as he replied. "The only thing that means something to me is the Rolex watch he got from our dad. I'd probably like to have it as a keepsake."

"I'll bet Tally won't mind, unless she wants it for Luke. I think Ken wore a Citizen watch, so her son could have that one instead."

An image of Ken surfaced in her mind as though he were still alive and vibrant. His wheat hair was similar to Phil's, except for the latter's side part. The brothers shared the same blue eyes, but Ken's had a deeper hue. Both of them had tall, lean frames. And Ken dressed better by far, but then he had to present a professional front since he dealt with people all day, while Phil worked in a lab.

Marla winced as a new thought surfaced. "I wonder what happened to the jewelry they were wearing in the accident. Would the police have their personal items, or the hospital?" Wouldn't the nurse have handed their belongings over to her and Dalton if the hospital had them? Or were the cops keeping everything as evidence?

"I have no idea. By any chance, do you have a copy of Ken's will or know where it's located?" A pained expression entered Phil's eyes as he pushed his glasses up at mid-nose level. "I've been so busy calling around to various mortuaries that I haven't given it a thought. I'm not expecting my brother to leave me anything, but it would be nice to know."

"I have copies of their documents at home. I'll take a look."

Phil already knew Dalton filled the role as Ken's executor and successor trustee after Tally. Marla had been Tally's choice in the event her husband didn't survive her. They'd both listed Marla as the baby's guardian.

Phil moved to the nightstand and picked up a hardcover book Ken must have been reading. "My brother always did like thrillers. I'm into science fiction myself."

"Tally will have to sort through everything later," Marla said, considering the monumental tasks ahead for her friend. "Meanwhile, somebody has to cancel their appointments, pay their bills, and take care of the house. I should take home her calendar and address book, unless she keeps those on her cell phone. Or would you prefer to take charge of this stuff?" She gave Phil a questioning glance.

The chemist put the book down and faced her. "You're more familiar with their personal business than I am. I'd appreciate it if you would handle these things."

"Would you know if they have a safety deposit box? That could be where they keep their original documents."

"I've no idea. Check their desk and file cabinet. Honestly, I'm hoping to put my brother to rest and then hop on the next airplane out of here. So I'm grateful for your help."

Luke interrupted with a whimper that cascaded into a series of cries. Marla veered into the child's room, where she sniffed an unpleasant odor. "I believe he needs a diaper change," she told Phil, who had followed her. "You'd better empty the garbage afterward so the dirty diapers don't fester in here. We'll have to find out which days trash pickup comes to this street."

After doing her duty and putting Luke back in his stroller, Marla opened the folding closet doors. Inside, she found a stash of diapers, clean bottles, and baby toiletries. "Oh wow, we should have looked in here the other day. Look, there's a portable swing still in its box. I might take that along. Oh, and I mustn't forget the plastic bathtub."

"I saw one in the middle bathroom," Phil said, hovering in the doorway. "Your husband mentioned he might come by for the changing table later. So tell me, what do the doctors say about Tally's condition?"

"You haven't called the hospital?"

"Not yet. I've been busy."

Yeah, right. Selfish jerk. She hoped Tally had hidden her valuables, suddenly not trusting the man to safeguard his sister-in-law's interests. "As Dalton told you earlier, Tally is unconscious with a head injury. Her recovery could be long and difficult once she wakes up."

"I hope she has good health insurance. Speaking of the topic, do you have copies of any policies Ken might have had?"

"You mean, like life insurance?" Marla asked.

"Or accidental death. His auto insurance might provide a benefit."

"I'll have to look through the packet of papers Tally gave me for safekeeping. I don't think it contains insurance documents. Ken's office might have that information."

Marla placed her supplies by the front door before proceeding to wheel Luke into the kitchen. An empty frozen pizza box sat on the counter beside a pile of dirty dishes. It appeared Phil had been helping to clean out the refrigerator, she thought with a cynical twist to her lips. He was making himself right at home but without assuming any of the responsibilities.

What a shmuck. All he cares about is himself.

Then again, he seemed quite interested in Ken's insurance policies. She narrowed her eyes as she regarded the chemist. If Ken had a life insurance policy, who was the beneficiary if Tally didn't survive him? Had the policy been written years ago, before they had a son? Maybe Ken hadn't changed the terms. Could Phil be his heir if Tally died?

A horrible notion came to mind. How did she and Dalton know when Phil's flight actually arrived? What if he'd come to town earlier than he let on? He could have caused the accident that killed his brother.

Chapter Four

Marla discarded the notion of Phil's possible culpability for the car crash as being too paranoid. She'd be wise to focus on practical matters and let the cops deal with the accident.

Inside Tally's home office, she surveyed the furnishings. A computer desk, bookshelf, printer stand, and file cabinet occupied the space with a comfy chair by the front window. A lump rose in her throat. Ken wouldn't be coming in here ever again. Never in her imagination had Marla envisioned sifting through her friends' things like this.

Her mind numb with grief, she froze in place, uncertain what to tackle first. She needed to cancel any impending appointments Tally and Ken had made, so that necessitated finding a calendar. They both could have kept this information on their cell phones, which were presumably in police possession. Hopefully, her friend had a backup somewhere in this room or on their desktop computer.

Somebody should respond to their email, too. Was that to be her job as well? Resentment flared toward Phil, who didn't want to share any of the responsibilities. Then again, he hadn't shirked his brotherly duty of making Ken's funeral arrangements.

The tasks seemed overwhelming, but she had to start somewhere. Pausing by the desk, she riffled through the papers on top. She struck gold upon spying a leather-bound appointment book in a bin among a pile of printed receipts. A further search revealed Tally's address book. Thank goodness her friend hadn't kept everything on her phone.

What about Ken? Where did he keep his records? Maybe more information was available online.

Marla sat at the desk, turned on the monitor, and moved the mouse. Desktop icons popped up on the screen. After clicking on various folders and finding nothing useful, Marla debated what to do next. She might have to let Dalton tackle this part. If they could access Ken's emails, it might hint at who had called him out on a holiday evening.

Or, he could have a laptop where he stored his emails. Since she didn't see one in the house, it might have been in their car the night of the accident or kept at Ken's office. Dalton could find out if a notebook computer was recovered from the wreck.

In the meantime, she shut off the monitor but left the computer turned on to avoid triggering password protection at their next attempt. She rose, considering what else she needed to find. A checkbook would come in handy.

A search through the desk drawers produced the item, although it wouldn't do her much good as yet. Marla would have to present Tally's power of attorney document at the bank in order to gain access to her accounts.

Most people never thought about dying or being disabled and leaving such a mess. With online accounts, it became even more complicated. Everyone should be advised to leave a list of passwords for their heirs and to mention Internet sites in their estate documents. She and Dalton needed to address this issue, too.

Her temples throbbed from the complexity of it all. Luke was what mattered the most, she reminded herself. How well had Ken provided for his son?

A search through the file cabinet didn't reveal any insurance documents. Likely Ken kept that information at work, since he owned an insurance agency.

Clutching the items she'd retrieved, Marla headed for the kitchen. Phil, who'd been stooping in front of the baby and making silly faces, sobered at her arrival. He straightened his spine, quickly wiping any frivolity from his expression. She smiled inwardly. So Luke's uncle wasn't immune to the child after all.

"Please let us know the burial information when you have a date and time," she told him. "And if anything changes in Tally's condition, I'll give you a call."

"Thanks." Phil's shoulders drooped, and his mouth twisted with self-deprecation. "I appreciate your help with everything and in caring for Luke. I'd be no good as a dad."

"You might surprise yourself, but it's a lot of responsibility for a single person."

"No kidding. Let's just say I'm glad you're the designated guardian." He handed her a pile of envelopes. "Here's the mail from yesterday. When I've gone home, somebody will have to come by the house every few days to collect it."

Outside, he helped load the baby things into her car while she fit Luke into his seat.

Marla waved at him before starting the ignition and moving along. They'd all have to move on, she thought morosely. That's what happened when someone died. Life kept going forward, while the survivors struggled to find meaning in the void.

Glancing at the dashboard clock, she decided to make one more stop before bringing Luke home. Some of the answers she needed could be found at Ken's office. Regardless of whether Dalton had visited Ken's colleagues yet, she had news to share with them.

Before long, she pulled into a parking space in front of the standalone building housing his business. Low hedges provided minimal landscaping for this spot near a busy shopping strip. Several cars were parked in front, which could belong to employees.

Marla went through the rigmarole of unfolding Luke's stroller, unstrapping him from the car seat, switching transport devices, and wheeling him inside the structure. She left the diaper bag in the car. Hopefully, this wouldn't take long.

The front office consisted of two desks facing forward, a visitor seating arrangement including potted plants, a coffee table holding magazines, and a counter with a coffeemaker. A water dispenser stood in another corner.

At one desk, a young man wearing a dress shirt and tie spoke into a headpiece. He spared her a quick glance before resuming his conversation. The other employee, a fiftyish blonde with shoulder-length hair, gave her a wan smile.

"Hello, may I help you? My name is Jeri, and that's Ryan," the woman said in a soft Southern drawl.

Marla advanced, pushing the stroller. "I'm Marla Vail. Ken was a close friend of mine. I'm sorry for your loss."

Jeri rose from her chair and rounded her desk. "Isn't that his son? I recognize that cute nose." She bent to tickle the baby's chin. Luke cooed at her, waving his tiny hands. When Jeri straightened, she regarded Marla with moist eyes.

"Are you caring for their child? Poor little guy."

"Yes, I'm serving as Tally's trustee and Luke's guardian."

"This is so unreal. I'm still expecting Ken to walk through the door."

"I feel the same way. It must be difficult for you." Marla paused to swallow the lump in her throat. "I've spoken to his brother and wanted to let you know the plans."

"Guys, you have to hear this," Jeri called to her colleagues beyond an open inner door. "Come on, Marla, let me introduce you."

Marla followed her to a series of glass-partitioned offices. She met Shawna, a mocha-skinned woman with a short bob of ebony hair, and Darryl, a middle-aged white guy who wore his gray hair slicked back from a receding hairline.

"How many people work here?" she asked, eyeing a further inner sanctum with a closed door.

"That's Ken's office," Jeri explained, noting the direction

of her glance. "Aside from the owner manager, five of us staff the place. Ronnie isn't here today. He's our financial planner. So what were you saying about Ken's final arrangements?"

"His brother plans to hold a private graveside burial. Tally will probably arrange for a memorial service once she recovers, so you'd be able to attend then."

"How is she doing?" Jeri tugged at her patterned top, its blue hues enhancing her cobalt eyes.

"I've visited her in the hospital. It'll be a long road to recovery."

Shawna swept her arm in an expansive gesture, a number of bracelets jangling on her wrist. "It's not the same around here without Ken. I can't imagine what it will be like for the boy growing up without his daddy." She swiped a tear drizzling down her cheek.

"Tell me, did any of you call Ken on New Year's Eve?" Marla inquired to rouse them from their grief. "The babysitter said Ken received a work-related call, and that's what made him go out late on a holiday night."

The others shook their heads, while Darryl responded. "The police detective has already asked us that question. We told him no. I don't think Ronnie called him, either. He was busy partying on New Year's Eve." Darryl's deep baritone voice boomed like a radio announcer. He wore a slate gray sport coat over a white shirt and crimson striped tie.

"So how come your office is still open? I'd have expected you to close with your owner gone." Marla hoped she didn't sound insensitive. Dalton had told her the staff was still keeping office hours. Shouldn't they have shut down for a few days out of respect for Ken?

Luke started to fuss, and she rocked the stroller back and forth. It was probably close to his feeding time, or else he needed a diaper change.

"I'm the senior member," Darryl related. "I've taken over as manager until a new guy is appointed, or until we learn who inherits the business. Ken didn't write policies anymore. That's what Shawna and I do. His role was to review our reports along with customer service ratings. Those can wait until a new owner takes over. Do you have any idea when that might happen?"

"You'll have to ask my husband. Dalton is Ken's executor and successor trustee. He's also a detective on the Palm Haven police force, but he doesn't have jurisdiction on the accident since it happened in Davie. The lead investigator is keeping him informed."

That might not be totally true, but these guys didn't have to know it.

Jeri wrung her hands. "We'd considered shutting down, but that wouldn't serve our customers. Meanwhile, we're in a holding pattern. For all we know, the business might be sold, and then we'll be out of our jobs."

"Let's hope that doesn't happen," Darryl said in a firm tone. He scrunched his eyes like a squirrel spying an acorn as he regarded Marla. "So you'll tell us if there's a memorial service? We'd want to come."

"Yes, of course." The baby's cries got louder. "I'm so sorry. Luke needs my attention. Oh, there's one more thing before I leave. Ken's brother wants to know if you have copies of any personal insurance policies Ken might have had."

"I'll check our files, but it will have to be later," Jeri replied. "I have some return phone calls to make to clients, and I've delayed them as long as I can."

"Didn't Ken leave instructions for his wife?" Darryl cut in. "I mean, wouldn't he have told Tally where he kept their important papers?"

"I'm sure he did, except I can't ask her, can I?" Marla retorted. "We'll need to know about all his policies. Also, please check to see if Tally has health coverage through your agency. If so, I'd like a summary of her benefits."

Tally might need to go to rehab after the hospital, Marla thought. Hopefully, her health insurance would cover that expense.

These were things Marla and Dalton needed to discuss for themselves. Death, dying, and disability weren't favorite topics in their household, despite Dalton's work that exposed him to these possibilities every day.

Jeri tapped her arm. "Ken had a generous health care plan for all of us. I'll see if Tally is included."

"Thanks, I'd appreciate it. Tally has her own business, so it's possible she's listed on their group policy." She exchanged business cards with Darryl and Jeri, who seemed to be the senior members of the group.

Jeri walked Marla to the door. "I feel so bad for Tally. We'd like to send flowers, but the ICU doesn't allow them. Should we send them to the brother?"

"No, he plans to leave town as soon as his job is done. Why don't you wait until Tally is awake and moves to a regular hospital room?"

"All right. Please let us know about any change in her condition."

Before Marla could leave, the clean-shaven young man from the other front desk loped over to greet her. "Hi, I'm Ryan Browning. Sorry if I was on the phone earlier."

"No problem. I'm Marla Vail, a close friend of Tally and Ken."

"Yeah, I heard. Ken was nice to give me this job. It's my first position out of college. I still can't believe he's gone."

"I know." Sensing he wanted to talk, Marla gave the man an encouraging smile.

"He took an interest in each of us, asking about our families. And he offered to pay for our education, too, if we wanted to attend seminars. Lately he seemed distracted, though."

Luke emitted a series of cries, stirring restlessly.

"Ryan, let the lady go. You can see the baby needs attention." Jeri pressed her lips together, her eyes a stormy blue.

"In a minute." Ryan grasped Marla's arm and drew her aside. "Ken was a careful driver. He wouldn't take risks on a dark road late at night."

"What are you saying?" She tilted her head to hear better since he spoke in a low tone.

"I heard a rumor that another driver was involved. The cops should dig deeper."

Jeri hustled between them. "Look, the baby is crying. Ryan, you should go back to work. Your next boss might not be so lenient when you waste valuable time."

Marla said her farewells and departed, while pondering their office dynamics. What had Ryan meant to say? Could one of them be lying about the phone call Ken received that fateful night?

She put aside those considerations as other priorities drew her attention. Her path led home, where she fed Luke, changed him, and put him down for a nap. Soon her mother would arrive to babysit. Marla wouldn't get home until after eight since Thursdays were her late day at work.

"Hi, Ma," she called from the front doorway when her mother appeared.

Anita shlepped a hardcover book along with her purse as she approached the entry. She wore a snug pair of navy pants and a matching top with a long gold chain. Viewing her pristine outfit, Marla had a vision of Luke spitting up as he sometimes did with a burp. She'd forgotten to retrieve the cloths Tally threw over her shoulder when she fed him. That was another item to add to her shopping list. Meanwhile, dishtowels could serve the same purpose.

"How's it going?" Anita brushed past her and aimed for the kitchen, where she put her things down on the counter.

"I've been out all morning. It's good of you to come."

"My pleasure, *bubeleh*. Y'all know how I wish you and Dalton—"

"Thanks, I'm aware of your desire for more grandchildren. Talk to my brother Michael about it instead of me. I'm leaving for work."

The lines deepened around Anita's mouth, but she refrained from making a retort that would aggravate them both. "Where's the baby?" she asked in a mild tone.

"Luke is taking a nap. Look, I borrowed this stuff from Tally's house. I'll put it away later."

Anita viewed the supplies Marla had obtained. "I can sort them out for you. Any word on Tally's condition?"

Marla recalled the gut-wrenching call she'd received twenty minutes ago. "The doctor wanted permission to put a chest tube in. Tally has a pleural effusion. That means there's fluid around her lungs, although my mind blanks out when he uses medical terms."

"It's a good hospital. Tally will be all right."

"She might survive, but what then? She could need care for the rest of her life."

"Take one step at a time. You're doing the best you can for her."

"Phil didn't seem too concerned." Marla reviewed her visit with the brother.

"Just as well that Tally and Ken didn't rely on him as guardian for their child."

"Amen to that. Oh, I found something Dalton might need to know." She pulled the scrap of paper from her pocket that she'd obtained at Tally's house and texted him the message.

Melaleuca Lane? he texted back. *That's where the accident happened. Thanks, I'll pass this on to Sergeant Mallory.*

Marla wondered if Ken had been on his way to meet the woman whose name was on the note. Since Tally had tagged along, it was more likely the lady was a colleague than a lover. So how come the people at Ken's office hadn't mentioned anyone named Louise?

*****

Later at the salon, Marla brought Nicole up to date. They stood outside on the pavement by the front window, soaking in the fresh air and a moment of quiet.

"We need to find Ken's estate documents," Marla said. "His will should tell us what he wants done with the business. I'm assuming Tally inherits his personal possessions and financial accounts."

"I thought you had copies of their papers."

"We have their living wills and signed power of attorney documents. Their wills and trusts must be in a separate packet. Dalton and I keep our important papers in our safety deposit box, but Tally and Ken may not have wanted to rent a bank vault. I didn't find a key in their house."

"Why not let Dalton worry about Ken's end of things? You have enough to do between Tally and Luke," Nicole replied, her eyes radiating sympathy.

"Yes, that's true." They chatted about inane topics before resuming work.

As Marla zipped through her late-afternoon appointments, she hoped to hear from Ken's staff regarding his insurance policies or from Dalton about the address she'd given him. Her phone remained annoyingly silent.

By the time she got home at eight-thirty, fatigue weighted her down. The sight of Dalton giving Luke his last bottle for the night in the kitchen perked her up and brought a fond smile to her face. How endearing he looked seated at the table with the baby nestled in his arm. His lips curved upward as he regarded Luke, his gaze holding a soft look she didn't see often.

"Oh, you're home," he said with a quick glance in her direction.

"Where's Brie?" The house was relatively quiet, with no sign of the teen.

"In her room. She got a new book she wanted to read."

"Good for her. I don't even have time to read my email these days. Did you see the envelopes I brought back from Ken's house?"

"Yes, and I didn't spot anything urgent in the pile. How was your day otherwise?" When Luke finished his bottle, Dalton prepared to burp him.

"I couldn't wait to leave the salon when we have so much to do. Can I hold Luke?" she asked, after the baby gave a loud belch.

"Sure." He handed over a dishtowel for her to sling over her shoulder.

The child's warm body felt incredible against her chest. Marla nuzzled his soft skin and planted a kiss on his temple. He tasted so tender, like innocence personified. Rubbing his back, she was gratified when he emitted another noisy burp. She hugged him close, a tangible source of comfort from her overwhelming concerns.

"I put away those supplies you brought from Tally's house," Dalton told her. "Luke is almost big enough to fit in that swing, so I took it out of the box. And I picked up the changing table on my way home."

"Great, we should have enough in stock for now." Her mouth puckered as another thought surfaced. "I need to examine Tally's calendar to see when Luke has his next pediatrician appointment."

"You look tired. Why don't you get ready for bed? You can check her schedule another time."

"There's too much on my mind for me to relax. I'll put Luke to sleep, and then I could use a glass of wine. Maybe I *will* get comfortable before we discuss things. I'll fetch Tally's calendar, and we can look at it together."

Marla poked her head inside Brianna's bedroom along

the way. The teen, absorbed in reading, barely acknowledged her.

"How's Tally?" Brie asked without looking up.

"She's holding her own for now." Marla didn't mention the chest tube Tally had needed to help her breathing. Hopefully, that wouldn't prove to be a serious setback.

"Close the door, will you? I don't want to hear you guys talking."

Marla, shaking her head in bemusement, complied with the teen's demand. A half hour later, she reentered the kitchen. She wore a nightshirt and carried Tally's appointment book. Dalton handed her a glass of red wine.

"I found Ken's estate documents buried in our file cabinet," he said, sitting opposite her at the round glass table. He set a bulging manila envelope on the surface. "You go first with what you've learned today."

"Okay." She related her visit to the day care center, her stopover to see Phil and swipe supplies from Tally's house, and her condolence call to Ken's staff members.

"That Ryan fellow actually said the police should dig deeper?" Dalton repeated with a frown.

"I got the feeling he might have said more if we'd been alone. Darryl and Jeri were the most verbal of the bunch. The other account executive, Shawna Madison, didn't say much. And the financial planner was absent."

His lips compressed. "Go on."

"I asked about Ken's insurance policies. Hopefully they'll get back to me on that topic. Meanwhile, their main concern is who inherits the business with Ken gone."

Dalton tapped the envelope. "All of Ken's personal possessions go to Tally. His financial accounts are in his trust, with Tally's trust as the beneficiary. If neither of them survives, Luke gets everything once he reaches maturity."

"And the insurance agency?"

"Tally is the new owner. If she fails to survive Ken, the

asset is to be sold and the proceeds put in trust for their son."

"Did Ken leave anything for his brother?"

"A gold Rolex watch and ten thousand dollars."

"Phil will be pleased Ken thought of him. What else?"

"There's a charitable donation listed. And, I found a life insurance policy. Tally will get a million dollars through an irrevocable trust."

"Oh, thank goodness." A wave of relief hit her. Tally wouldn't have to worry about finances, thanks to Ken's foresight.

"I have to obtain the death certificates before I can officially step in as successor trustee. I'll check with Phil to see if he ordered extras from the funeral home."

Marla motioned to the papers Dalton had withdrawn from the envelope. "Does Ken say anything about burial plans?"

"Nope. I'm assuming he doesn't have any prior arrangements. Did Tally ever mention the subject to you?"

"We didn't have that talk, unfortunately." Marla leaned forward, hands clasped on the table. "How do *you* feel about it? I'm Jewish, so I need to be buried in the ground. But your religion doesn't have such dictates."

Dalton gave a low chuckle. "I won't be here to care, will I? But I think it would be best if I'm buried next to you."

"We should consider Pre-Need Plans." Her mother had one, and Marla had already vetted the possibilities at a couple of funeral homes during her research on another case. But they'd need a cemetery that took interfaith couples.

"Will you put in the claim for Ken's life insurance?" she asked her husband with a tilt of her head.

"Yes, I'll take care of it. Meanwhile, I spoke to Ken's car insurance adjustor. He said I should sign a notarized release for the vehicle after Mallory lifts the hold on it. I can go over to the yard first to collect any personal belongings that are still inside, along with the license tag. The adjustor will retrieve the car and take it to their company's lot, where he'll appraise the damage. Also, he needs a copy of the police report when it's ready."

"Good, those are a few items off our list. Let's look at their appointments." She opened Tally's desk calendar. "Here's the next doctor visit for Luke. It isn't until February. That should be his six month exam. I see some nail appointments and yoga classes I'll have to cancel. Hey, what's this? Tally has something called *tea circle* twice a month."

"Your guess is as good as mine." Dalton stuffed the papers he'd found back inside the envelope. "Any mention in her calendar about the address you gave me?"

"You mean the one written on that scrap of paper from the trash can? I don't see anything, and there's nobody listed here by the name of Louise. Why, did you check the location?"

Spooks chose that moment to sniff her ankles and nudge her. She reached down to scratch the poodle behind his ears. Lucky yawned from his spot in the family room. She should refill their water dishes before retiring for the night. Lifting her wine glass, she took a sip.

"Sergeant Mallory sent a guy over there," Dalton said, his mouth thinning. "It led to a warehouse at the end of the lane where Ken was heading when he had the accident. The officer found a woman's body inside."

Marla choked and spewed red wine. "W-what?"

"What's more interesting is the hit Mallory got on her fingerprints."

Chapter Five

"Don't keep me in suspense. Who is the dead woman?" Marla asked, having difficulty comprehending what this new development would mean.

"She's an agent for the Florida Department of Financial Services in the insurance fraud division."

"What was she doing in that remote location late at night on New Year's Eve?"

"Her wrists were bound, so I'd guess she hadn't gone there willingly."

"Did you contact her department? They might have more information." Marla cradled the glass of wine in her hand.

"Sergeant Mallory notified them. They said she was involved in an investigation. They'd take care of their operative, and Mallory should keep his nose out of their affairs."

"That's it? You'd think they would be more cooperative." Marla swallowed past a lump in her throat. "How did the woman die?"

"She was shot in the head execution-style."

"How awful. Whoever she'd been investigating must have caught onto her."

"I tend to agree." He leveled his gaze on her. "Based on the note you found in Ken's bedroom, it appears her presence there was known to him."

"Could that be where he was going?"

Nancy J. Cohen

"Obviously. The question is, why?"

"When was the woman killed? Do you have a time of death?"

"The medical examiner estimates she died sometime between when Ken got the call, according to what the babysitter told us, and when he had the accident. But the M.E. has yet to do a full workup on the body."

"So she would have been dead already if he'd arrived at the warehouse."

"True. We have no idea what the caller might have told Ken."

"What do *you* think?" Marla gulped down the dregs of her wine. She didn't care for the implications of this conversation. What had their friend been involved in?

"If Ken knew the woman was there, he was in on her abduction. Maybe he was called to clean up the mess. It's possible he had an accomplice who phoned to say he'd captured the agent on their tail."

"His accomplice? Who do you believe this woman was investigating?"

"Didn't you hear me? She works for the insurance fraud division."

"Dear Lord. You think she was investigating Ken's office?"

"It looks that way, and possibly the owner in particular."

"Do you suppose Tally knew? Was this why she went with him that night, to convince him to do the right thing and turn himself in? But then they couldn't have known the woman had been shot."

"We won't know until Tally wakes up, will we?" Dalton stroked his jaw, bristly from a day's growth. "This just keeps getting nastier."

"It's dangerous to jump to conclusions. We should give Ken the benefit of the doubt."

"You believe he's innocent when things are pointing his way?"

58

"If you're right, then who forced him off the road, assuming the witness's report was accurate?"

"Maybe his accomplice double-crossed him. We need more information."

"It's Mallory's case. And if the woman's department steps in, it could be taken out of his hands," Marla pointed out.

"That won't stop me," Dalton assured her. "These are our friends. We're directly affected by their accident. Besides, I'm Ken's executor. That must give me some legal rights."

"Speaking of legalities, I need to show Tally's power of attorney at the bank to access her checking account. Or should I bring a copy of her trust?"

"I'd think the POA will be adequate unless their accounts are in the name of the trusts. You should ask Tally's doctor for a letter verifying her disability in case you need it."

"Let's go together to see her on Sunday. Did Mallory say when Ken's body would be released?" If the burial took place that day, they'd have to rearrange their plans.

Ken's death still seemed surreal. Marla glanced at the doorway, as though he might walk into their kitchen at any moment. Now he'd never get the chance to build that miniature railroad set with his son he'd mentioned, or to grill his specialty steak for them again. She could almost hear him describing the latest model cars.

"Mallory is hoping the M.E. will give clearance this weekend," Dalton said, staring at a blotch on the table. "They're waiting for more lab results to come in, although preliminary tox screens are negative. It appears Ken died from traumatic injuries and not drowning."

"Thank goodness. How horrible if he'd been trapped underwater while being fully awake."

Dalton stretched his hand across the table to grasp hers. "Luke is his legacy. We'll be able to tell the kid about his father when he grows up."

"I just pray Tally will be there for him. What do you intend to do next?"

He squeezed her hand then let go to lean back in his chair. "I won't interfere with Mallory's investigation, but I'll do my own background checks on Ken's colleagues."

"While you're doing your cop thing, I could come in from the consumer angle. I've met everyone except their financial planner. I'll make an appointment to discuss investments."

"It would be more logical to inquire about long term care policies. I hate to mention this, but what happens if Tally remains disabled? Nursing care would eat through her savings pretty quickly."

Marla bristled at the idea. That wouldn't happen to her friend. "Things won't go that way, and she'll have Ken's life insurance. That should meet her needs, even if she requires live-in care to stay at home."

"Nevertheless, ask about long term care while you're at the agency. Tally might have a policy. It's smart to buy one when you're young and healthy."

"Jeri said she'd look up their insurance plans for me." Marla noticed his glum expression. "Wait, you're serious about us looking into this for ourselves?"

"In my line of work, anything can happen. I have disability and life insurance, but not long term care. I'll bet you don't have coverage, either."

"What does your disability plan do?" She hadn't asked for the details before.

He rose, plucked her empty wine glass from the table, and moved to the sink. "I believe it provides for a monthly income, but it doesn't deal with nursing home payments, rehab, or home care. We'll have to review all our policies."

"Yes, I guess so." She remained mute for a few moments, thinking they wouldn't be having this discussion if not for Tally's accident. Maybe it would be the only good thing to come out of it. Dalton was right in one regard. His job could be hazardous, and he had his daughter's college education ahead. "All right, I'll make an appointment at the agency, and I'll try to speak to Ryan while I'm there. He knows something, but he's afraid to talk in front of the others."

"Be careful. If there's a rotten egg in that bunch, you don't want to rile them."

*****

Friday morning at work, Marla discussed her plans with Nicole. They'd both arrived early and were setting up for their first customers. As she related the latest news, her fellow stylist's expression ranged from horrified to thoughtful consideration.

"Maybe the agent was investigating someone else in Ken's office, and he was cooperating. Why is Dalton so quick to put the blame on him?" Nicole tapped a painted fingernail to her lip. Her brow scrunched, and her brown eyes reflected contemplation.

Marla unwound the cord from her blow-dryer and plugged it in. "Ken was on his way to that warehouse. He must have known the woman was there."

"Oh, yeah? Who does Dalton believe called Ken out on New Year's Eve? One of his colleagues in crime?"

"That's right. He had to be colluding with someone else."

"And this person shot that poor woman? You said she died sometime between when Ken got the call and when he had his accident. So she was alive when the phone call came through."

Marla stared at her friend. "Yes, that sounds logical."

"Was there evidence of a struggle? Did the woman try to escape, and the captor killed her by accident?"

"Dalton said it was execution-style. We don't have the details."

"How's Tally doing? If she'd wake up, I'll bet she has some answers. Any change in her condition?"

"She's still breathing, so that's good news. I hope she isn't in danger from Ken's cohort. If this person believes Tally knows anything, he could come after her next." Marla's heart lurched at the notion. This case kept getting more complicated.

"Can Dalton suggest to the investigator that they put a guard on her?"

"I'll mention it to him, but he doesn't want to get in Mallory's way. Dalton said he'll do a background check on Ken's colleagues, while I make an appointment to talk to them about long term care policies. He has life and disability insurance through work, but neither of us have an LTC policy. Think about Tally. What kind of mental capacity will she have when she wakes up? She might need care for the rest of her life."

"That's a terrible thought. Let's hope she'll have a clear mind once the brain swelling goes down and her body heals."

"Amen to that. In the meantime, I'll have an excuse to visit Ken's office again."

"Have you been over to Tally's dress boutique? I imagine the staff has heard about the accident, but you could see if she'd mentioned anything to them about her husband's business affairs."

"I'm not free until Sunday, and we want to visit Tally then. Plus, Sunday should be family day. We need to spend some time with Brianna."

"Is Tally's place open on Monday? You could go then."

Marla nodded, her mind formulating a plan. "I'll drop Luke off at the day care center, do my errands, and then I can visit Tally's boutique and Ken's insurance office. I won't let this rest until we get some answers. Dalton can use his resources, although he and Kat have another case to work on. That's going to be occupying his time."

"Kat knows what this means to you both. She'll cut him some slack."

"Let's hope so. She hasn't used the coupon for a

complimentary cut I sent her for Christmas. That woman has a hard shell to crack."

"Who's taking care of Luke today? Is he doing all right?"

The front door bell chimed. Nicole hastened to plug in the implements at her station.

"Brianna offered to watch Luke. She's happy to earn extra money by babysitting."

"How is she doing with her driving lessons?" Nicole smiled, aware of how those went over with Dalton.

"We need to give her more practice this weekend. She'll be taking her test in two more months. Hmm, I wonder if Dalton and I should consider merging our auto policies."

"You might get more discounts that way."

"I'll give our company a call. Maybe they supply long term care policies, too. It would be helpful to get another quote for comparison. Oops, here comes my first customer. Gotta go."

*****

By the time Marla drove home at the end of the work day, Dalton wasn't back yet. She tried to relax and focus on Luke for the evening. A phone call to the nurses' station at the hospital reassured her that Tally was hanging in there. It didn't help that she felt guilty for not visiting more often.

To make up for her negligence, she played with Luke. His antics both delighted and entertained her. She could watch him for hours, especially when he gave her a rare smile or stared at her with his big blue eyes. It still astounded her how this tiny being depended totally on her for sustenance, but the responsibility didn't faze her. Instead, she looked forward to being with him every day.

Could she do a better job of maintaining vigilance with a child this time? Remembering the tragedy in her past, Marla tightened her mouth. Tammy's loss had been her fault. She'd been babysitting for the toddler when the phone rang. Tammy's parents had told her to expect the call. Marla had been only moments in the kitchen, but that one instant was all it had taken for Tammy to amble outside and fall into the backyard swimming pool.

Marla's heart thumped at the memory. She would do whatever it took to ensure Luke's safety. Nothing would happen to this kid while under her care.

The day care center had her nervous, though. There you were dependent on strangers. And what happened when you sent your child to school on a bus? That must be even scarier.

Her mind zipped ahead. Brianna was learning to drive. An inkling filtered into her brain of the anxieties that afflicted Dalton. It never ended. As babies grew into adults, you continued to worry about their welfare. That's what love is, she realized. It bit so deep that it hurt. Yet you couldn't go through life fearing the possibility of loss, or you'd miss the joyous occasions. What was the quote? "It's better to have loved and lost than never to have loved at all."

Luke's face cracked a smile, and Marla's innards melted a bit more. How could she deny herself the chance to have her own child? She wouldn't be facing the perils alone. Dalton and Brianna would be there along with their mothers, like they were for Luke. And her travel plans? They could be adjusted for a family.

Her expression eased as she thought of them taking a trip together. Had Dalton ever gone anywhere significant with his daughter? She'd have to ask. But now wasn't the proper time, with Tally's life in the balance and Luke needing her focus.

Sometime during the night, she felt Dalton sink into the mattress. She rolled over to face him and stroked his arm.

"Hi," she murmured, her voice tinged with sleep.

"It's late, sweetcakes, and I'm beat. Go back to dreamland."

"I'll dream about you." Her eyelids closed, and she drifted off.

Saturday morning, Marla checked her email and then got ready for work. Dalton had already left for his office to work on his case.

Brianna stumbled into the kitchen, having set her alarm so she could watch Luke after Marla left the house. The teen had fixed her hair in a ponytail and wore pajamas with happy faces. Her gaze swung to Luke sitting in the baby swing Dalton had put together.

"You're too cheerful this morning," she grumbled after Marla greeted her. She headed to the fridge to pour herself a glass of orange juice.

"I appreciate you getting up early to babysit. Do you want breakfast?"

"It's too early to eat. I assume you gave Luke his bottle?"

"Yes, he's good until his next feeding, and he has a clean diaper." Marla finished putting together a bagged lunch and stuck it in her purse.

"Okay. We'll be fine until Grams comes over later. Dad said if he gets home early, he'd take me driving again."

"That's good. You need all the practice you can get. I'm off all day tomorrow, so we can give you more hours behind the wheel. We'll go see Tally in the afternoon."

She scrapped those plans, however, when Dalton called her later at work.

"Ken's body has been released. Phil set the burial for Sunday. He couldn't get a time until the afternoon, and then he wants me to drive him to the airport."

"When will we visit Tally?"

"My mother said she would babysit. We can go to the airport together and then swing up I-95 to the hospital. Brianna can stay home with Mom."

"Let's not forget to ask Phil for the house and car keys." She couldn't believe he hadn't been to see his sister-in-law. The jerk. At least he was doing his duty for his brother.

*****

The graveside service went relatively quickly with no one else in attendance other than Ken's one relative and two friends. His office staff would have come if invited, Marla ruminated, seated under the awning erected by the cemetery staff. The fresh smell of turf entered her nose along with a cool breath of January air. She'd worn a skirt out of respect and was glad for the leather jacket she'd had the foresight to wear. Dalton and Phil sat on either side of her, while a hired minister intoned the prayers. It didn't feel right without Tally there.

She eyed the coffin in its simple maple design. Ken didn't deserve this end, but who did? Accidents were brutal. They took loved ones without warning. You didn't have the chance to say goodbye.

Marla sniffled, wiping her nose with a tissue, especially touched when Phil got up to share a few memories of his brother's childhood. His voice cracked at one point, as though he wasn't impervious to emotion after all. Perhaps he just hid his feelings well.

Dalton took her hand and squeezed it. His confident presence, tall and imposing in a black sport coat, gave her reassurance. She couldn't imagine doing this for him one day.

In a somber mood, they drove Phil to the airport without indulging in the usual funeral feast. Before leaving, he handed over the keys he'd used during his visit.

"Thanks for your support," he said, hefting his carry-on bag. "I never thought I'd be burying my brother this way." His face reflected his sadness, as did his slumped posture.

Marla gave him a quick embrace. "Car accidents are horrible. One minute you're here, and the next you're gone. It's worse for the survivors."

He nodded his agreement. "Keep me informed about Tally's progress, will you? I hope she'll be okay. And I'm happy their kid is in your care. You'll do right by him."

After he departed, Marla and Dalton headed north on the highway toward the hospital. She felt better that Phil had wanted to hear about Tally. He might not accept any responsibility toward his remaining family, but maybe deep down he did care for them.

"Why do you suppose Mallory didn't come to the burial?" she asked to divert her morose thoughts. "Don't detectives usually attend a victim's funeral to gauge the reactions of the guests?"

"This wasn't a public event. And technically, Ken isn't a victim." Dalton kept his hands on the wheel and his eyes on the road.

"No? What about the witness's claim that someone forced Ken off the road?"

Dalton's jaw tightened. "I'd like to know if the CSI techs found traces of paint from another vehicle on Ken's car, but Mallory isn't sharing those details."

"We're best friends with Ken's wife. He's probably right to keep a tight lid on things when we have a personal interest in his case. You're lucky he tells you anything."

"I'm getting heat from Kat to focus on our investigation. It appears the robbery murder might not have been so random after all. The dead guy received threats beforehand."

"See? You need to focus on your job. I'll learn what I can with my methods. What about your background checks into Ken's office workers?"

"It's hard to tell from looking at their bank accounts. A couple of them get deposits on a regular basis, but that could be their commission from customers' insurance premiums. I don't have the authority to question them without stepping on Mallory's toes."

"Did either of you ever trace the call that Ken allegedly received that evening?"

"Mallory did share that information. The call was made to Ken's cell from a burner phone."

Marla had seen enough TV shows to know a burner phone was a prepaid cell phone usually disposed of after use. "So that's a dead end. What about the office staff's phone records? Anything suspicious there? Any criminal activity in their pasts?"

"If somebody at Ken's place is involved, they're covering their tracks pretty well."

"I'll take that answer as a negative." She shifted in her seat, watching the passing scenery on the highway. Strip shopping centers, homogenous housing developments, and industrial centers ceded one into the other in a nonstop congested corridor. Palm trees and other tropical greenery broke the monotony.

"Things don't add up in my estimation," Dalton admitted, "but we need more hard facts. If only Tally would wake up, she could fill in the blanks."

*****

Tally wasn't in any condition to talk when they reached the hospital. She lay as still as a mannequin under the sheet covering her slender body. Marla got permission from the nurse to comb her hair. Although the hospital staff did a good job of keeping her clean and tidy, Marla felt better running the comb through her friend's blond locks.

Tears leaked from her eyes as she sat by the bedside. Dalton had gone to consult with the doctor. Tally's chest tube had been removed, having done its job. She was receiving antibiotics through her I.V. to prevent pneumonia and nutrients through a feeding tube. The medical staff had started weaning her off the paralytic agents that kept her calm. If she couldn't breathe on her own, they'd gotten Marla's agreement to do a tracheotomy.

Marla swallowed her tears and cleared her throat. "Hey, Tally. It's Marla. I'm here with you. You're in the hospital, but you'll be okay. Dalton and I are watching Luke, so don't worry on that score."

Tally's eyes moved under her closed lids. Was she dreaming? Her cheekbones looked prominent in her pale face, her mouth partially open. She appeared as though at any moment, she might wake up.

Marla put the comb away and perched on the edge of the bed. She grasped Tally's free hand that wasn't stuck into a pulse monitoring device. Sadness weighed on her and made her hollow inside. *I don't know if I have your strength, Tally. Give me some sign that you're in there.*

Nothing happened. Marla reached for a tissue from her purse and dabbed her eyes. She wouldn't help anyone this way.

Sounds and smells filtered into her awareness. Steady beeps and hisses competed with the clank of metal carts and chatter from the nurses' station. Cool air blew into the cubicle, keeping the atmosphere at a chilly level while an antiseptic tinge pervaded the place.

"The doctor says she's doing better," Dalton said upon rejoining her. "He thinks she might have a chance for a decent recovery down the road."

Marla winced at the thought of the rehab and medical bills in Tally's future, but those would be worth it if she'd regain full consciousness along with her memory.

"What else did he say?" she asked, rising to her feet.

"Just that she'd been lucky to be on the dry end of the vehicle when it landed half in the canal. I told him about the burial today."

"Yeah, she's really lucky." Marla shook her head at the statement. Tally would be lucky to be alive, if she came out of this in one piece with her mind intact. But then she'd have the pain of grief to face. Nobody lucked out on accidents like this one.

Dalton must have sensed her need for comfort, because

he drew her into his embrace for a quick hug. "The nurse gave me some interesting information," he said, stepping away. "You'd asked about the friend who had called regarding Tally's condition. The person's number came from a four-zero-seven area code. That's Orlando."

"What does that mean?"

"I don't know yet. It could originate from another burner phone."

"I assume you'll try to trace it?"

"I will, but don't get your hopes up. I have to be careful how much time I spend on this stuff."

"Kat knows Ken was a close friend. She should be more lenient."

"All the more reason why she thinks I should steer clear of this case."

She peered at him, aware of nurses and other personnel walking past but ignoring them. "Have you learned anything more about why she'd asked for a transfer to your district?"

"The chief said Kat is here until she heals, but he won't elaborate."

"Do you know where she worked before? Maybe you have friends there you can ask about her."

"Word would get around if I made inquiries behind her back. She does a damn fine job, so I'm not pushing the issue. Oh, I told the doctor that you need a note regarding Tally's incapacity. He'll leave one at the nurses' station for us to pick up on our way out."

"Thanks, I would have forgotten if you hadn't mentioned it." She had too much on her mind. Hopefully, tomorrow she could take care of some of these tasks. Since the salon was closed on Mondays, she had the entire day free. And with Dalton's activities on the case being limited, she'd have to use all her skills to learn the truth.

Chapter Six

Monday dawned with a balmy breeze and warmer temperature. Marla enjoyed the weather as she took the dogs for an early morning walk. It was glorious out, with impatiens and other flowers blooming while the north shivered under an Arctic blast. She loved living in Florida, especially at times like this. And despite the tragedies that happened in the daily news, life went on. So it did here as well, she thought, strolling past their neighbor's house.

Alan Krabber who'd lived next door was gone. The former homeowners' association president had been murdered in his house, which subsequently had been sold by his nephew. A young couple had moved in who weren't fazed by the place's history. Marla walked past and waved at Susan Feinberg one house over. Susan was putting her kids in the car to take to school.

A pang of envy hit her. She and Susan were the same age, and yet the other woman already had two school-age kids.

Marla could have her own children instead of being a surrogate to Tally's child. Was it too late? Had she lowered her chances for a healthy pregnancy?

She should make an appointment to talk to her gynecologist. She'd been on the pill for so long that the hormones might have adversely affected her body. It could take months for her levels to adjust if she went off the meds. Not that she was seriously considering the notion, but it wouldn't hurt to gather information.

71

After Dalton left to drop Brianna off at the school bus stop on his way to work, Marla bundled Luke into the infant car seat. Today was his first time at day care. Her nerves taut, she hoped she was doing the right thing.

She needn't have worried. Once they arrived at the day care center, the seasoned staff took over. Luke's face puckered as Marla turned away after delivering him into their capable hands. His resultant wails trailed off by the time she reached the door. Thank goodness. Otherwise, she'd have felt guilty leaving him there.

After completing her errands, she returned home and called Ken's insurance agency.

"Hi, Jeri," she said into her mobile unit. "This is Marla Vail. I'd like to make an appointment with Ryan to discuss long term care policies. Tally's condition has made us aware that we might need one someday." Ryan was the young man who'd seemed to have something to say to her.

"Hey, Marla, it's good to hear from you. How is Tally, the poor dear?" Jeri asked in her soft Southern drawl.

"She's making progress, thanks. And her son is doing well. He's so adorable."

"Bless your heart for taking care of him. You'll need to speak to an account executive to discuss an LTC. When do you want to come in?"

"This afternoon, if possible."

"Shawna has an opening at one o'clock. Would that work? Ryan will be here, but he doesn't do sales."

"Yes, thanks, I'll see you then." She'd figure out some way to corner Ryan while there.

She hung up while considering how the insurance field was rife with fraud. Any number of possible scams reared their ugly heads. Each day, it seemed some new way to swindle people came to light. One of Ken's colleagues could have been his partner-in-crime.

Jeri, the fortyish blonde, was a more likely candidate

than Ryan, the youngest member of the group. The two customer service reps were responsible for billing and claims. Could Jeri be collecting insurance premiums and putting them in her pocket? Maybe Ken got alerted by a customer who'd said his policy had lapsed but he had paid his bills. Or perhaps Ryan was padding his customers' policies with endorsements they hadn't ordered. He'd been the one to warn Marla earlier, but that could have been a smoke screen.

Then again, an account executive could be involved. Shawna and Darryl both sold new policies, prospected for clients, and ran the referral program. They seemed sincere, but either one of them might have reasons to need money. She shouldn't discount the financial planner, either. He could be selling bogus investments. She'd have to make it a point to meet the man.

Jeri stood to greet Marla upon her arrival early that afternoon. They shook hands, while Marla gave a nod of acknowledgment to Ryan at the next desk over.

The young man's eyes gleamed, as though he wrestled for an excuse to talk to her. She surveyed the dark brown suit that matched his hair. From the superb cut of his clothes, he could have been working in a menswear shop instead of an insurance office. He probably made more money on commissions from customer policies than he would in a clothing store, though. And yet, it seemed a waste for him to sit behind a desk all day when he appeared so spiffy. Maybe he believed in the adage, Dress for Success, and hoped to move up in the world.

"I didn't expect to be back so soon," she told Jeri, refocusing her attention. "As I said, Dalton and I are interested in a long term care policy. Sadly, we buried Ken yesterday in a private service. He wouldn't have needed an LTC if they had one."

"Your husband notified us that Tally inherits the agency," Jeri said, biting her lower lip. "What do we do until she's ready to take over?"

"We carry on as usual," Darryl announced as he strolled into view. He wore a navy suit that contrasted to the icy blue of his eyes. "I hope she'll consider me for the role of manager since I'm already acting in that capacity."

Jeri harrumphed, then turned to Marla. "She wouldn't manage the place herself, not when she has another business to run. Isn't that right?"

"Yes, Tally owns the Dressed to Kill boutique. If she decides to keep the agency, she'd have to appoint someone else to take charge."

"Is there any more news about the accident?" Darryl stroked his jaw as he regarded Marla from the inner doorway.

"Sorry, I haven't heard much else. Have you?"

"Unfortunately, no. The detective on the case has been here asking some pointed questions. I don't care for his tone."

"What do you mean?"

"Like, we're guilty of causing the accident. How absurd. What would any of us have to gain? Ken was a good boss. We miss him."

"Amen." Jeri sank into her seat and grabbed a tissue from a box on her desk. "Where's the baby? I'd hoped to see him again. I feel so bad for him losing his daddy."

"Luke is having his first experience at day care. I should get moving so I can pick him up on time. Is Shawna available?"

Darryl peeked into the inner sanctum. "She's just getting off the phone. Come on in."

Marla proceeded inside to the account executive's workspace. Shawna rose to shake her hand while Marla admired the woman's makeup, especially the gold eye shadow that complimented Shawna's warm mocha skin.

"I love your nails." Marla pointed to her gold metallic polish with little angel appliqués. A quick survey of Shawna's bookshelves showed a collection of angel figurines amid various family photos. "I see you're into angels. And are those two cute kids your children?"

"Yes, they're a handful." A smile flitted across Shawna's face.

"Your husband is a handsome guy. What does he do?"

The smile vanished. "His firm downsized, so he's looking for new employment. What can I do for you today, Marla?"

She must have touched upon a sore subject. Had the man been laid off or fired from his job? Either way, it put more pressure on Shawna to earn bread for the family.

"I'm here to learn about long term care policies. I'm not even sure what they do. How is this different from disability insurance?"

Shawna answered once they'd both taken seats. "Disability gives you a monthly check so you can pay your bills. Long term care provides coverage for chronically ill individuals, people with Alzheimer's disease, or other conditions where you need help caring for yourself. But don't think it's just for old people. Adults between the ages of eighteen and sixty-four make up forty percent of those needing long term care services. You never know when something is going to strike, whether it's a disease or an accident. It's best to be prepared."

Marla visualized Tally lying limp in a hospital bed. "Most of my friends don't want to think about these possibilities. That includes Pre-Need funeral plans. We're all going to get sick or die at some point in our lives. Why wait for our loved ones to make those decisions when we can do it now, and it's more affordable?"

Shawna tapped a painted fingernail on her desktop. "Absolutely. Nobody wants to dwell on what might happen to them. Even if you've saved a nest egg, it would go pretty fast if you had to pay for nursing home care or a live-in home health aide. It saves your children from having this burden someday. Or, if you have no kids, it brings peace of mind that you have the means to get care in your old age. You can't rely on Medicare. It doesn't provide long-term solutions, nor do most other policies."

"How do you become eligible for benefits?" Marla asked, feeling ignorant on the topic.

"You have to be certified in writing by a doctor that you're unable to perform a minimum of two ADLs, or activities of daily living, for at least ninety days. Or you have to require supervision due to cognitive impairment."

"Activities of daily living? What does that mean?"

Shawna stared at her as though she'd grown a hair out of her nose. "The six ADLs include dressing, eating, toileting, bathing, mobility, and continence."

"Okay," she said, not quite sure what they all meant. "So does this cover you only if you're in a hospital or nursing home, or also if you're able to live at home?"

Shawna folded her hands on the desk. "The nursing care portion covers a nursing home, assisted living facility, Alzheimer's or hospice facility. The community-based care covers treatment in your home by a licensed nurse, therapist, or home health aide. It may include homemaker services, but only if done by one of these people at the same time they're providing health care. A Care Coordinator will decide what level of care you need."

"How long do these benefits last?" Marla pressed her lips together. What if Dalton ever had a stroke and was permanently disabled? Or if he got shot in the line of duty? Or if one of them was in a car accident like Tally?

Shawna rolled a pen on her desk back and forth. "You can select a one year limit, three years, five years, or longer. Naturally, the longer the term, the higher the premiums will be. In addition, do you want a cost-of-living rider? This helps you keep tabs on inflation by providing for annual increases in the daily benefit at a rate of five percent compounded each year."

"That sounds like a smart choice."

"Also, consider how much daily benefit you might need.

Like, do you want one hundred dollars or one hundred and fifty? Do you want the same amount for community based-care as for a nursing home facility, or less?" Shawna slid back in her chair, reached inside a drawer, and brought out a brochure. "Here, this explains our qualified long term care plans. Qualified means the premiums are tax deductible medical expenses. Also, the benefits are not taxable."

Marla put the brochure in her lap under her purse. "How often do these premiums have to be paid?"

"It's an annual payment, unless you choose our monthly payment plan. You're smart to consider this now while you and your husband are healthy. People who wait until they're in their sixties and have some ailments aren't as likely to get a policy, or else it will cost a bundle. I can give you an estimate based on your age."

"I'm thirty-seven and Dalton is forty-six."

The account executive did a calculation and rattled off some numbers. "That's simply an example. The actual premium would depend on which variables you choose."

"So with a sixty day elimination period, a ten year term, a one hundred and fifty dollar a day benefit, and an inflation rider, it would cost us each less than two thousand dollars per year. That's not bad." She and Dalton could easily afford that amount out of their annual budget.

Shawna gave her an indulgent smile. "Why don't you and your husband look over that brochure? You can make an appointment to come in together and fill out your applications."

"Will we need medical exams?"

"The underwriters will make that determination. Since you're so young, it'll depend on the responses you give on the health questionnaire."

"This is great information. Thanks so much. By the way, was Jeri able to find any information on Ken's policies? Like, did he have this kind of coverage for Tally?"

A forlorn look spread over Shawna's face. "Unfortunately, no. Tally is covered under our group health policy. Her auto policy has medical benefits, too. But they didn't have LTC plans. I believe Jeri called your husband with these details."

"Dalton mentioned Ken's life insurance, but he must have forgotten about the rest. What other policies does Tally have?"

"She has life insurance, but its benefit amount is a lot less than Ken's. They added it after Luke was born. A woman may not think she contributes much, but add in the loss of her work income plus the cost of hiring a nanny, and it's a considerable sum."

"Would you know if Tally has a separate group health policy for her employees?"

Shawna tapped a finger on her desk. "If she has only two or three people working in her shop, she might treat them as independent contractors. Have you spoken to the staff? They could tell you about their insurance coverage. I imagine they're upset about Tally's accident."

Marla's skin flushed with guilt. "I haven't been there yet. It's on my agenda for today."

"It's scary how fast our lives can change, isn't it? I still expect Ken to walk through the door, say hello, and pour himself a cup of coffee like he did every morning. It's not the same around here. He had a strong presence that we all miss."

"It must be difficult to deal with his absence along with the uncertainty of what will happen to your jobs."

Shawna put on a brave face but her eyes showed grief and a modicum of doubt. "We're carrying on as best we can. It's not easy with investigators breathing down our necks. First it's the police detectives, and then someone from the Florida Department of Financial Services shows up. I don't understand their involvement."

Marla gave her an oblique glance. Hadn't anyone told these guys about the dead woman in the warehouse, and that

Ken was presumably on his way over there? If not, it wasn't her place to reveal this information.

"What did they want?" she asked in an innocent tone.

"They asked questions and searched Ken's desk. The state finance folks wouldn't normally be involved when an agency owner dies. They must know something we don't. Otherwise, I can't imagine why they'd be interested in our office."

Oh, no? Somebody forces Ken off the road. A dead body is found. He's implicated in a case of insurance fraud by virtue of the victim's identity. Was he also an accessory to the woman's murder?

Marla was surprised the authorities hadn't interrogated his colleagues more thoroughly. Did they believe Ken was a minor player in a bigger operation? They could have been hoping he'd lead them to the kingpin, unless he occupied that role. Having a baby might have tipped the financial scales where he was concerned. Kids were expensive to raise. Had he devised a scheme to make more money?

"According to the babysitter, Ken allegedly received a work-related phone call the evening of the accident," Marla said. "Are you certain it wasn't anyone from here?"

"Oh, please. The cops must have checked our phone records to verify our statements. Nobody from our place made that call."

So why do you look so uneasy? Did Shawna suspect that her fellow workers weren't being truthful? Or did the account executive have something to hide?

Marla crossed her legs, seeking a topic that would help her learn more about them. "Tell me, how well do you guys know each other outside of work? Do you socialize after hours?"

"We'll go out for a drink sometimes or have lunch at a restaurant to celebrate a birthday. Jeri and Darryl have more in common with each other."

"In what way?"

Shawna gave a snort of laughter. "Isn't it obvious? They're middle-aged white folks. Ryan is a kid who's green behind his ears. He's got potential, but he's weighted down by his mamma, poor thing."

"What do you mean?"

"The lady has Alzheimer's, and he's her only child. His father is deceased. So the burden of care falls on him."

"That must be tough." And expensive, too. Was he using his parents' savings, or did most of his salary go toward his mother's caregivers? Maybe he wasn't as well off as he appeared. "Does he have a girlfriend? I presume he's still single."

"Ryan doesn't share that part of his life with us. I found out about his mother when I overheard him talking to someone on the phone about her."

Marla vowed to speak to the guy on her way out. "Tell me about Darryl. Is he married? I've noticed his family pictures show two young people but no older woman who might be his wife."

"He's divorced. Those two are his son and daughter."

"He seems to like boats, judging from the photos of yachts on his wall."

"That's because he dreams of owning one someday. Darryl loves going to boat shows." Shawna spoke in a derogatory tone, as though she felt better choices could be made with leisure money.

Marla racked her brains for something else to keep the conversational ball rolling. "I'd like to meet the financial planner. When does Ronnie come into the office?"

Shawna shoved her chair back and rose. "You'll have to make an appointment to see him. Shall I check his schedule for you?"

"Let's wait until Dalton and I review our assets. We'll need to plan for the future."

"Oh?" Shawna's gaze dropped to Marla's belly as she stood and prepared to leave. "You're not—?"

"No way. Thanks for the information on the long term care policy. I'll show this brochure to my husband."

In the front office, Marla noted Ryan had a free moment, so she took the liberty of dropping into the chair opposite his desk.

"Hey, I wanted to have a word, if you don't mind."

"Sure, what can I do for you?" The young man darted a glance at the entry. Jeri had stepped outside, where she was visible through the window speaking on her cell phone.

"If my husband and I decide to apply for a policy with your agency, I'd like to know your team has our best interests at heart."

"Of course, we do. We're here to serve your needs. You can't foresee what might happen, so it's best to get the broadest range of coverage you can afford."

"What led you into the insurance business?"

His mouth tightened, and a pained look entered his eyes. "I got firsthand experience. My father died when I was twelve. If not for his life insurance, our family would have had difficulty keeping our heads above water, so to speak."

"How did your mother manage? Are you her lone child?"

"Yes, I am. I'd always missed having a sibling, but it would have been even harder on her. She got a job in a fancy department store as a buyer, and I became a latchkey kid."

Marla pointed to his suit. "Is that where you got your taste in clothes? You dress so well, you could be a model."

His teeth gleamed white as he grinned. "It's important to convey the image of success in the business world." Ryan's wristwatch pinged, and he paused a moment to press a button on it.

Marla squinted to get a better view. Was that one of those computerized watches? It appeared Ryan liked wearable technology as well as fancy suits. He had expensive tastes.

"What are your goals?" she asked out of curiosity. "Do you want to rise up the ranks at this agency?"

"That's one step I'd like to take, but I don't plan to work at this job forever. It's just a start for me."

She plunged into the opening he'd provided. "How about working for the state's Department of Financial Services? Wouldn't that be an advance from this office?"

The crease lines deepened on his brow. "Funny you should mention them. Their department reps came by to question us, but they wouldn't reveal what's going on."

"Do you have any theories?"

He gave a furtive glance at the inner doorway. "Ken was mixed up in something, but they were tight-lipped about it."

"I thought you knew more. You warned me off the other day."

"Not about Ken. I think he was—" Ryan cleared his throat as Darryl strode into the front office. His voice raised a notch in pitch as he carried on. "As I was saying, based on my personal experience, I decided that when I grew up, I'd help other people make provisions for their loved ones. Most folks don't face the reality that someday they'll either die or be disabled. They don't share their final wishes, nor do they set up trusts in the event they're incapacitated."

"That's so true." Marla gathered her purse and rose. She wouldn't accomplish anything more at this point. "Thanks for your input. It's good to hear a younger person's viewpoint about these issues."

Darryl gave her an inquiring glance. "Did you get what you needed?"

"Oh, yes. I'll be discussing these policies with my husband. We'll be in touch."

Outside, Marla paused on the walkway to retrieve her sunglasses and car keys. Jeri stood off to the side, talking in an urgent tone.

"I don't care what it takes or how much it'll cost. I want

Cassie to see a specialist. There has to be something else they can do. I won't allow my child to suffer this way."

Marla, tempted to linger, sensed Darryl's gaze glaring at her through the window. She stepped onto the asphalt, but not before startling Jeri. The older woman gave her a frightened glance and then walked farther along the sidewalk to complete her conversation.

Marla moved on to her next errand, while considering what she'd learned. It appeared that each one of Ken's employees had a reason to need extra income. How far would they go to get it?

Chapter Seven

Tally's boutique was located in a modest shopping strip anchored by a popular home goods store. As Marla approached Dressed to Kill from the parking lot, she wondered what to say to the staff. They might be angry she hadn't called sooner, but she'd wanted to wait until Sergeant Mallory had notified them about Tally's accident.

Marla stepped inside the air-cooled interior, recognizing Stacy Maria Scranton standing by the cash register. Tally had recently appointed the fortyish woman as manager. At Marla's entrance, Stacy put down the papers in her hand and walked over to give Marla a quick embrace.

"Hey, Marla. I was wondering when you were going to stop by."

"Sorry it's taken me so long, but I've had to deal with caring for Luke."

"How is the baby?" Stacy stepped back to regard her with sad hazel eyes. The older woman wore her autumn red hair in a short layered cut that complemented her facial structure.

"I've enrolled Luke in day care so I can go to work." Marla hoped he was doing okay. She resisted the urge to call and check up on him.

"Tally had mentioned enrolling him when she returned to the shop. Have you spoken to the doctors about her condition?"

"Yes, I have." Marla filled Stacy in on Tally's medical progress.

The two of them appeared to be alone. Racks of clothing filled the store along with shoes and accessories. Marla bought new outfits here each season to support her friend. Otherwise, she shopped in less expensive places. How many employees worked there in total? And why hadn't she asked Tally for those details before?

Maybe it was because she did most of the talking when they were together. Tally was an excellent sounding board for her crime-solving escapades. Marla had never considered that meant Tally listened more than she spoke. If Marla had been a proper friend, then perhaps Tally would have confided in her.

"Who notified you about the accident?" she asked Stacy. "Was it Sergeant Mallory?"

"That's right. He came by in person. We were shocked to hear Tally and Ken had been hurt in a car wreck. With a new baby at home, Tally often didn't check in for days at a time."

"Ken was more than hurt. He didn't survive," Marla pointed out.

"It's so horrible. I can't believe he was killed." Stacy covered her face with her hands.

"What else did Mallory say?"

It took the shopkeeper a moment to respond. She lifted her head, her eyes moist. "He asked us questions about Tally's recent activities. I can't imagine why, since Ken drove the car that night."

"As lead investigator, Detective Mallory has to cover all the angles. Dalton and I have been overwhelmed since this went down, but that's no excuse for my neglect."

"Tally is a close friend of yours. I can understand your shock at the terrible news," Stacy said in a soft tone meant to convey sympathy.

"That's putting it mildly. Dalton and I have taken on roles we'd never expected to play. Dalton is Ken's executor, and I'm Luke's guardian. Phil—he's Ken's brother—flew into town for the burial, but he left soon afterward. He wants nothing to do with his nephew's care."

"That's a shame." Stacy went behind the cash register counter and sank into a folding chair. She gazed at Marla with a despondent air. "So what happens to us? Will Tally be capable of taking charge again? We've all been managing as best we can under the circumstances."

"The doctors say she has a good chance of recovery. I'm focused on taking care of Luke and maintaining her household affairs for now. Is there anything coming up business-wise that I should be told? I'm also her trustee and have power of attorney."

"Yes, there's the landlord's request." Stacy's crow's-feet deepened as she frowned.

"What do you mean?" Marla moved closer to where Stacy sat and leaned against the counter. A pleasant citrus scent drifted into her nose. Tally always said sales improved when a store smelled enticing.

"Mr. Weaver wants to sell this shopping strip, but Tally is the only lease holder who won't relocate, even with his incentives. His buyer has given him an ultimatum for getting all the tenants to agree."

"So Tally was obstructing the owner's plans? Could you provide his name and contact info for me? I should probably get in touch with him."

Stacy provided the data. "I agree with Tally. Our customers know this locale. Plus, the home goods store is free-standing, and they don't have to move. We get a lot of walk-in traffic from them that we'd lose if we changed locations."

"I'll talk to the guy and see what other options might be available." Why had Tally not mentioned this problem? Because Marla had been too busy talking about herself?

Stacy rose and rounded the counter to face her. "The newspaper report said another car might have been involved in the accident. I'm wondering if someone pushed them off the road on purpose. It just seems so unreasonable for Ken to be driving recklessly with a new baby at home. Consider the landlord issue. And then there's Iris Caswell. She was quite unhappy when Tally let her go last month."

Marla stared at her. Could these theories hold any truth? "Do you know why Tally fired this girl?"

"Iris had been relating a sob story to customers who felt sorry for her and gave her money. That woman is an out-and-out liar. She'd put Pinocchio to shame."

"Does she have any violent tendencies?"

"We don't do criminal background checks on our employees, so I wouldn't know. But Iris is the type to bear a grudge in silence and let it simmer."

"Can you look up her phone number for me? I might want to talk to her as well as the landlord." What if their assumptions had been wrong? Dalton believed Ken's partner-in-crime might have turned against him and forced his car off the road. But what if Ken hadn't been the intended victim? That idea brought all sorts of new possibilities to mind.

"Tell me, did Tally ever mention a ladies' tea circle to you? I brought her calendar home so I could cancel her upcoming appointments, and I noticed she'd been meeting with this group twice a month."

Stacy regarded Marla with a puzzled expression. "She didn't mention it to me. Maybe it was a recent thing, after she had the baby. You know, it would give her an excuse to get out of the house and chat with other adults. New mothers often feel stressed when they're confined at home."

That could be true. Marla should ask Mrs. Phelps. Tally would have had to hire a babysitter, since these meet-ups took place during the day, unless she'd brought Luke along. And when was the next one scheduled? Marla should go in order to meet the women. It meant adding another chore to her busy to-do list.

She heaved a weary sigh and then asked one final question. "Did Tally seem agitated or mention anything unusual the last time you spoke?"

"Sorry, no. She babbled on about the baby. Luke was the most precious thing to her."

"Were you aware she'd taken a trip to Sunny Grove recently? I noticed the entry in her appointment book. I'm wondering what that was all about."

"It's news to me. I thought you were close friends with her, Marla. How come you don't know these things?"

"It seems we weren't as close as I'd believed." She couldn't keep the regretful note from her voice. "So will you continue to manage the store until Tally is on her feet again? I can help with finances if necessary. I do my own bookkeeping for the salon."

"I'll be fine, but thanks for offering." Stacy's gaze turned nostalgic. "I used to manage an office up north back in the day. Working in a dress shop is more fun and far less aggravating. Or at least, it used to be before Tally's absence."

"How many people work here altogether?"

"There are four of us, plus Tally. We need more staffing in the afternoons and evenings, so the other girls don't come in until then. I prefer mornings as I'm an early riser, and it's quieter. I can work on my knitting and watch the game shows." She pointed to a TV mounted on a wall that was turned on but silent with closed captions.

"Please let me know if you have anything to add, and I'll do the same." Marla handed over a business card while vowing to interview the rest of the staff another time.

"We're worried sick about Tally and would appreciate updates on her condition if possible. I'm glad Luke is in your care. Give him a kiss for me."

"I will. And don't worry too much. Both Luke and Tally are being well cared for, and that's the best we can do for them at this time."

As she drove away, Marla wanted to think over their conversation, but she had too many other errands to do. One item on her list was a stop at the baby store. Supplies might be cheaper at a big chain than where Dalton had been buying them.

She'd visited the huge emporium a couple of times before to buy gifts for friends. It had been a while, and Marla hesitated inside the place wondering where to go. Row after row of toys, videos, and games dazzled her senses along with bright overhead lights and loud music playing the *Star Wars* movie theme.

Weren't the shelves arranged according to age groups? The colorful items to her left as she moved ahead appeared to be toddler age, too old yet for Luke. On her right, rows of dolls met her gaze. She paused, scanning the Barbie and baby dolls and Disney princesses.

Memories of her own childhood flooded her. She'd loved to do her dolls' hair, while her friends had changed their outfits. The clothes were fun, but not as much as creating different hairdos. Even then, she'd shown an interest in styling hair. She'd preferred the bigger dolls to work on, though, not the skinny ones with unrealistic figures. She patrolled down the aisle until she came to a larger set called American Dolls. Now those were more her style.

She spied a collection of miniature kitchen sets and sped ahead to examine them. What fun. She imagined herself playing with those fake foods and cookware. Toddlers today had so many choices. Another aisle held a display of brightly colored toys with buttons and dials. Some of them taught the alphabet or offered number games.

These items were way more advanced than anything she'd had as a child. Did anyone even play board games anymore? Computers were part of a kid's life today from the get-go.

How did a new mother decide what to buy? Did she consult other new moms, or choose toys based on her own childhood experiences? Certainly Marla would have to get the latest Mr. Potato Head. Who didn't grow up with that one? She smiled as she envisioned an older Luke playing with the various parts. He'd be a joy to watch as he gurgled with delight and showed off the result of his efforts.

A deep yearning filled her chest. Someday soon, she'd have to give Luke back to his mother. Would visits to him, or seeing her niece and nephew only on holidays, be enough? Would a life filled with work truly satisfy her?

She'd always wanted to travel, but wouldn't sharing those experiences with a family be more meaningful?

Marla wasn't ready to answer those questions. Along with the joy came the risk of pain. She didn't know if she had the strength to overcome that crippling fear.

Her gaze slid to the boy toys across the aisle. What did Dalton do as a child? Did he like Ninja Turtles or Superman or sports heroes? An image of him sitting cross-legged on the carpet at home and playing with a son came to mind. She clenched her jaw, unwilling to explore those feelings. This wasn't the right time. But then, when would it be?

Anyway, she'd come here with a mission. Where were the diapers, formula, and other baby items?

She had almost decided to leave when she spied car seats and strollers toward the rear. Finally! She searched each aisle until she found the diaper section.

Shelves full of different brands offered a variety of choices. Now what? Should she stick to the type Tally preferred, or try something more economical? Her eyebrows lifted as she assessed the average price. *Forty dollars for a pack of diapers? Ouch.* She identified other goods they could use and winced at the cost. Children were an expensive proposition.

You raised them, loved them, gave them everything they needed, and then they left in the end. If you were lucky, they stayed in contact and maybe came home for the holidays.

But wasn't that the point? You wanted them to become self-reliant adults. This cycle had been repeating itself since the early days of humanity. But what heartache accompanied the innate drive to see life continue?

These days, traffic accidents took more lives of young people than the rampant infections of years past. Dalton worried every time Brianna got behind the wheel to practice driving. Wait until she got her driver's license in March. With Tally's accident hitting home, he'd be doubly anxious. Yet there were always things to worry parents. You had to push it aside, enjoy the moment, and carry on with optimism.

A waft of cool air hit her from an air-conditioning vent, and Marla realized she'd been standing frozen in front of the diaper section. She grabbed a package and moved on to acquire the rest of the supplies on her list. Her heart softened as she regarded a display of pacifiers. Maybe she should get one for Luke. He'd be teething soon and might like something to suck on.

She left the store with a long receipt of credit card charges. Baby Luke was worth them. Eager to see him again and cuddle his little body, she headed to the day care center.

He'd done well on his first day, according to the staff. His face brightened when he spotted her, and a happy gurgle escaped his mouth. Marla scooped him into her arms.

During the drive home, she thought about Ken's car. Had Dalton gained access to his wreck yet? There might be clues inside as to Ken's purpose in leaving home. She'd ask Dalton about it at dinner.

He broached the subject first, waiting until they were seated at the kitchen table. "Sergeant Mallory released Ken's car today. I went over to the yard to meet his insurance adjustor. The vehicle will be written off as totaled. The check can go into his estate."

"What about their personal possessions?" Marla passed him the plate of pecan-encrusted tilapia she'd prepared.

Brianna sat in the other chair, digging into her garlic mashed potatoes.

"I grabbed what I could find. It was a mess." He swallowed, his Adam's apple visible. "Ken's door was mangled. I could see why the rescue team had trouble removing his body. Tally was fortunate her side remained dry and fairly intact."

"She still whacked her head when they rolled over," Marla reminded him.

Her attention shifted to Luke, sitting in his infant seat. Although still a bit wobbly, his neck was getting stronger every day. He made baby noises, his big blue eyes staring at her. His hand gripped a toy she'd bought, a series of colored rings that he could bite on when he started teething. She had to give him a bath yet before putting him to sleep for the night.

"Dad, have you heard any more about the other car involved in the accident?" Brianna asked. She tickled Luke, who chortled in response.

"There's only the witness report and the tire tracks. Mallory is working the murder of that woman in the warehouse. If someone called Ken out there that evening, it had to be an accomplice. This is the person we need to find."

"What have you learned about Ken's work force?" Marla queried, eager to tell him about her sojourn to Ken's office.

"Not as much as I'd like. None of them have any background of criminal activity. And the state finance department is being markedly silent about their investigation."

"You're assuming their agent was in town for that purpose." She summarized her interviews with Ken's staff. As her mind flashed back to her visit, she straightened her spine. "I saw a matchbook on Ryan's desk. It didn't register earlier, but it's for a bar on the beach. I still feel he has something to tell me. Maybe we should check the place out."

Dalton spread his hands. "Sure, why not? If there's a

rotten egg in that bunch, better to find the person now. It would save Tally from more trouble down the road."

"We could go on Friday, when Ryan is likely to be there," Marla suggested.

"I have plans for that evening," Brianna piped in. "Sorry, but I won't be able to babysit."

"That's okay, honey. I'd prefer not to bother my mother, either," she told Dalton. "Ma is leaving on her cruise in two weeks. It isn't fair to monopolize her time."

"Her boyfriend has grown children," Dalton said. "He'd understand."

"Speaking of Reed, you never did tell me what you found out about him." They'd just met their mother's new boyfriend last week, and Marla had asked Dalton to check up on him.

"He's widowed and has two sons. I think he really likes your mom. But you're right. We shouldn't lean on her too much. Why don't you call Mrs. Phelps? She's familiar with Luke."

"Good idea. In the meantime, I'd like to attend Tally's tea circle on Thursday. The women meet in the afternoon, according to her calendar. I'll ask Robyn to clear my work schedule. There's a time and place listed, but that's all. I have no idea who belongs."

"Huh, nobody who has a day job, if they meet during a weekday. Where is it?" Dalton asked, helping himself to a second portion of fish.

"At a café in Boca called Cuppa Joy. I looked them up online. They offer the usual café fare, plus fixed-price meals for different ethnic tastes. It actually sounds kind of interesting."

"Did you call to see if you need to add a reservation? The group must reserve a number of seats ahead of time."

"I'll do it in the morning. I wonder how Tally heard about them, and how long she's been going."

Dalton gave her a perceptive glance. "You're miffed she

didn't mention it to you. Maybe she wanted to do something new and different on her own."

"You've known Tally since high school, haven't you?" Brianna asked Marla. The teen pushed her empty dinner plate away and retrieved her homework from a nearby backpack.

"That's right. We grew up in New York State and were BFFs until college." Marla sagged in her seat as memories invaded her mind. "Tally applied to NYU. She wanted to get a job in fashion merchandising after she graduated. My parents had bought a condo in Florida and were wintering there, so I headed south to University of Miami. I majored in education to become a teacher, which was more my mother's ambition than mine."

"Did you and Tally keep in touch with each other?" Brianna's brow furrowed, as though she were contemplating her own departure for college in a few more years. She'd already mentioned her desire to attend school in Boston, a notion that displeased Dalton.

"Yes, we did," Marla replied, eager to share her history with Tally. "During the first summer, we both came home and hung out together. Our parents belonged to a swim club in Westchester, so we either went there or cruised the shopping malls. During the second summer, Tally seemed preoccupied, but I had my own problems by then."

"That's when Tammy died," Dalton said in a soft tone meant to soothe.

"I dropped out of college. And a year later, I married Stan." He'd been the attorney she hired after Tammy's parents threatened to sue her for their toddler's death. Marla hadn't wanted to trouble her parents, as her father wasn't well. How she had earned the money to pay the lawyer's bill was another shameful episode in her past.

"Where did Tally and Ken meet each other?" Brianna inquired, gripping a pen in one hand. Her school notebook lay open on the table.

"They met at NYU. Ken came from Florida, and he meant to return home after earning his degree. He wanted to work in the insurance business. His family had been through a hurricane, and the experience had gotten him interested in disaster claims. Plus, he missed the south and the slower pace of life."

"So he proposed? And Tally was willing to give up her dreams of living in the city to move to Florida?" Brianna clicked her ballpoint pen on and off.

Marla glanced away. Hadn't she told Dalton and Brianna this story before? It brought back painful memories, but maybe slogging through them would help something surface that might be relevant today.

"They planned to marry after graduation," she continued, "but Tally's mother, who was divorced, became ill. Tally stayed home to care for her until she died. After settling her mother's estate, Tally moved south and married Ken. She was twenty-three. I was already married to Stan at that time."

"Was that when you first met Ken?"

"No, I'd visited Tally in college and got to know him then. Tally asked me to be maid of honor at their wedding. It was a quiet affair, since she still mourned her mother's loss. She used her inheritance money for the dress shop. Both she and Ken focused on their careers during their first ten years of marriage."

"How did Tally like Stan? Did you ever get together as couples?" Unable to sit still, Brianna doodled in her notebook.

Marla smiled inwardly. Brianna would be great on the debate team, which she'd said she wanted to join next year. The acting classes she took now were only to improve her public speaking skills. It appeared she'd picked up interviewing techniques from her dad as well.

"We renewed our friendship, but the guys merely tolerated each other. Tally could see I was unhappy. It didn't help that my mother adored Stan. What's not to like about a rich, Jewish lawyer? But he was a control freak. Everything I did had to meet with his approval. Tally saved me from him."

Dalton rolled his eyes. He'd heard this part before, but Brianna hadn't. Marla wanted to explain it to her, so Brianna would avoid the same mistakes.

"Tally suggested I go to cosmetology school. She knew doing hair was a passion of mine. After graduation, I worked for a year in a salon. During that time, I gained confidence in myself and initiated divorce proceedings. I used the settlement money from Stan to start my own business."

"So you owe Tally a lot," Brianna concluded. "If not for her, you might still be married to Stan. Didn't he resent her interference?"

"If so, he didn't show it. Besides, wife number two came along to distract him. A guy like Stan attracts women like conditioner to shampoo."

"But Tally and Ken seemed happy together?"

"That's right. They were vested in their careers and did some traveling. Then Tally decided she wanted to have children. She had trouble getting pregnant, and Ken was nervous about the financial strain of raising kids. He put money into that gemstone mine and didn't tell Tally about it. You remember," she said, tilting her head toward Dalton.

He drummed his fingers on the table. "Yeah, we were concerned about why he was acting secretive at the time. Fortunately, that North Carolina mine paid off when they hit a lode. But you'd said Tally seemed preoccupied during your sophomore summer," he told Marla. "Could she have been worried about her mother's health?"

"Tally did mention her mom, but with a hint of bitterness rather than concern. I'm not sure what happened between them, but you may have a point. Maybe her mother refused to heed the warning signs, and Tally was angry with her over it. But that doesn't seem like enough to explain Tally's behavior. There could have been other issues bothering her."

"Sometimes the past unlocks a key to the present," he suggested.

Marla might have pursued his enigmatic statement, but Luke's whimpers indicated he needed a diaper change. Besides, it was past his bath time.

She rose and carried the dirty dishes to the sink, where it was Brianna's chore to wash them that night. Then she scooped up the baby and hefted him toward the bedroom wing.

Later, she'd consider why Tally had seemed estranged that summer. Was she worried about her mother's health, or was something else on her mind that she hadn't shared?

Chapter Eight

Thursday rolled around before Marla knew it. Work and duties at home had kept her busy in the interim. She looked forward to a respite with a few hours off that afternoon.

The café where the tea circle ladies were set to meet was located on a side street off Glades Road in Boca Raton. Marla pulled into the parking lot, noting the crowded spaces. Business must be good at this place.

She scanned the two-story structure after emerging into the cool January air. The restaurant appeared to be downstairs in a converted house. Tables were set on a covered front porch, but most patrons sat indoors for warmth.

With her purse tucked under her arm, she strode inside, thinking she'd get lunch if the tea circle was a bust. She paused just beyond the entrance to examine the interior. The spacious room held white-clothed tables with fine china settings and vases of fresh flowers. Antique portraits decorated the walls, while classical music played in the background. Marla sniffed a pleasant cinnamon scent and decided she liked the cozy atmosphere. Waiters entered the dining room from a kitchen at the rear, where a side staircase had a Private Only sign blocking access.

Most of the tables held up to four people, except for a circular table near the bay windows in front. Although it was set for eight, only four chairs were occupied. Did that mean the group expected more people to arrive? Marla had called ahead and had been reassured adequate seating would be available.

She approached the women seated there and gave them a broad grin. "Hi, is this the tea circle? I'm Marla Vail. My friend, Tally Riggs, told me about you, and I was hoping to join."

A brunette with a tapered bob and a pleasingly round face glanced toward the door. "Is Tally here? We haven't heard from her lately."

Marla, taking the comment as an affirmative response, plopped into a chair next to the woman. She arranged her purse strap across the seat before facing the other patrons. From the filled teacups at their place settings, she surmised they'd already helped themselves from a large porcelain teapot on the table.

"Tally has been in an accident. Nobody notified you?"

"No, is she all right?" the same woman said, her eyes wide.

"She's, um, recovering. Tally had told me about this group, and I'd been meaning to come. I hope you don't mind my barging in like this."

The lady on her other side tapped her arm. "We're glad to have you," she said a smooth tone. "I'm Rissa Kyle, by the way."

Rissa wore her red hair parted in the middle with loose ringlets that looked movie-star perfect. Marla tried not to examine her roots too closely. She suspected she'd see extensions in that mass of locks. The plum color on Rissa's pouty lips complimented the lavender top she wore over a flowery skirt. Her skin stretched taut, a little too taut to be natural.

The other women introduced themselves. On Marla's right sat Edie, the brunette. Marla appreciated her welcoming smile.

Deanne was a stick-thin woman whose straight black hair hung down her back. Her blunt-cut bangs gave her an older-era vibe belied by her youthful face. The stark style made her countenance appear even narrower. With her prominent nose and gaunt cheekbones, she'd make a good witch at Halloween. Her low, throaty voice added to the impression.

Bridget wore her bleached blond hair in a curly, chin-length cut with side-swept bangs. Her blue eyes regarded Marla warily, as though she viewed her as a competitor. She wore a heavy layer of mascara, a western-style shirt with fringe over a tight pair of jeans, and an aura of disdain.

"So tell us why you're interested in joining our group, Marla." Rissa's brows arched. "Are you bored at home? Hoping to meet new friends? Looking for something different and exciting in your life?"

"Yes, what do you do?" Deanne chimed in.

"First, I'd like to learn more about this circle. How did you get started?" Marla leaned back as a waiter appeared.

"Tea or coffee, miss?"

"I'd like coffee, please. Regular, with cream on the side."

"It's our tradition to have tea," Bridget remarked. "Green tea is full of healthy anti-oxidants. You should drink at least one cup a day."

"Oh. Is that what's in the teapot? That'll be fine," she told the waiter. After he'd poured her a cup and left, she regarded the others expectantly.

Rissa addressed her question. "I started the group and advertised it online as a meet-up for ladies. We meet twice a month and rotate the site. Each of us takes a turn hosting and finding a location."

"So you don't always meet here?"

"Heck, no. In recent times, we've been to a chocolate factory, a yoga studio, and a vegan restaurant. It's fun to try new places. Our single requirement is that they have to offer refreshments and give us a tour, if applicable."

"Sounds like fun. I can see how it would appeal to Tally. So you're not all new moms looking to get away from the kids for a few hours?" Marla had thought this might be a variation of the mommy and me theme, but minus the infants.

"Good God, no." Bridget snorted with laughter. "Tally might be a new mother, but we've been around that block already. How about you?"

Marla almost choked on a sip of tea. "I'm married, but I don't have children of my own. My husband's teenage daughter is enough for me to handle. It's a second marriage for us both," she explained. "So then, what's the purpose of this group? To get together and schmooze?"

"To make new friends and share opportunities," Rissa replied with a meaningful glance at Bridget. The two of them exchanged a secret smile.

Marla hoped she hadn't stumbled into the wrong kind of group. But then, Tally wouldn't have belonged, would she? "What kind of opportunities do you mean?"

"We're always looking for flexible ways to earn money, or where to go to get work done," Bridget said in a snotty tone. "When we get to be a certain age, we have to keep up appearances. And having some money filter in on our own helps us fund that maintenance."

Marla's inner sense told her an undercurrent ran through this conversation, but she wasn't getting it. Were they discussing face-lifts and Botox treatments? Tally didn't need it. Her friend still had the bone structure and looks of a model. So why had she joined? For the friendships alone? Had her feelings of closeness to Marla evaporated to the extent that she needed to go elsewhere? Had Marla been too self-absorbed to notice?

"You didn't mention what you do most of the time," Deanne persisted. Her espresso brown eyes aimed darts at Marla meant to make her disgorge information.

"I'm a ... housewife." She'd been about to say "hairdresser" but didn't feel these women worked for a living. They might not appreciate her social status. "My husband is employed in the security field, and he earns enough that I can stay home. I keep busy with my activities."

Oy, she sounded like an airhead. But that must have pleased Rissa, because the lady on her left gave her a crocodile smile. "How lovely. Or how boring, depending on how you look at it. We prefer the term domestic managers, don't we?" she queried the group.

Bridget stared down at them. "*My* husband is CEO of a Fortune 500 company. We have an apartment in Manhattan as well as a summer place on Nantucket Island. I'm heavily involved in charitable functions. We support many worthy causes, if you're interested in volunteer work."

"I donate my time to the Child Drowning Prevention Coalition," Marla admitted.

"Speaking of kids, the Florida legislature finally passed that bill allowing people to rescue children or pets from locked vehicles in the summer heat, without incurring civil penalties." Edie's face flushed as everyone's attention diverted her way.

Bridget's mouth thinned. "That's a good move on their part. You should be glad, after what your husband did."

"Bridget, shut up." Edie fidgeted, clearly uncomfortable with the turn of conversation.

The blonde addressed Marla. "He left Edie's elderly mother in his car and locked it with his remote. Then he went into Target, where he got caught shoplifting a bunch of electronics. The cops found the mother-in-law alone in his car panting and barely alive."

"He just meant to go inside for a few minutes," Edie said. "As for those gizmos, he forgot to stop by the cash register on his way out."

"Oh, sure, Edie. Like he forgot to put the money in the right account at work. He's in the clinker where he belongs. You're lucky to be rid of him."

"That's not true. He's a good husband. They wanted to make an example of him, when they should be putting the murderers and rapists away instead."

"Girls, let's not get nasty," Rissa intervened. "We're supposed to be here to support each other."

"Tell me more about the bill that passed," Marla said to Edie to change the subject.

Edie clasped her hands in her lap. "I got involved after my mom nearly died. Little children are the main concern. You read in the news every week about how some kid has suffered heatstroke and died a horrible death from being trapped in a car. Florida is second to Texas in the rates of child deaths due to this cause."

"I don't understand. How can any parent leave their child unattended inside a car?"

"Beats me, but not every mom or dad is as vigilant as we are. Or, kids might be playing outside, and they climb into the trunk thinking it's fun. They get locked inside accidentally, and no one knows where they are until it is too late. Young children are at higher risk because their bodies heat three to five times faster than an adult's."

"That's terrible. I can barely tolerate getting into a car in the summer before the a/c kicks in. It wouldn't take long for body temperatures to rise to critical levels if you were stuck inside." Marla gripped her spoon, imagining how difficult it would be to breathe in the suffocating heat. For a child trapped in a car, minutes would be all it would take. What a torturous way to go.

Edie's eyes blazed with zeal. "I belong to the Safety First Alliance. It's an organization aimed at educating the public about these hazards. Tally said that after she'd had her baby, she couldn't understand how anyone could lose track of their kids for even one minute."

Marla's hurt freshened. When had she and Tally become so distanced? Preventing accidental deaths in children was important to her, too.

"I'm interested in learning more," she said. "What can be done in terms of prevention?"

"People have to be educated never to leave a child alone in a car," Edie stated. "Doors should be kept locked so kids can't get inside on their own, and the remote or keychain should be stored in a child-proof location."

"That seems logical. What else?"

"Drivers can put an item in the backseat that they'll need at their destination, such as a briefcase or purse, as a reminder that their child is in the car with them. It's easier to forget you have your kid there when your routine is changed. Personnel at day care centers can also be alerted to call the parent if the child isn't dropped off at the expected time."

"I used to keep a stuffed animal in our son's car seat," Deanne said with a pout, as though any lapse of judgment was beneath her. "After I'd put Jake inside, I would sit the doll next to me in the front. It helped me remember he was there. You can't be too careful. Mothers have left their children in the car to go inside a gas station and pay the bill or use the bathroom. All it takes is a few minutes for the interior of a car to heat to lethal levels when it's hot outside."

"Carjacking is a threat when you leave your kid alone, too," Rissa remarked. "That's another reason not to disappear with a child inside your vehicle."

"What happens to the parents?" Marla asked. "I can't imagine living with that amount of pain." Yes, she could. She'd been through a similar experience. It stayed with you forever.

Edie opened her mouth, the words pouring from her like a water faucet. It appeared they'd pushed her hot button. "Under Florida law, it's illegal to leave a child under six years old unsupervised for more than fifteen minutes, or unattended at all inside a vehicle. But the laws vary from state to state."

"Don't think these are deadbeat parents, either." Deanne tucked a strand of long hair behind her ear. "I read about a case where the father went to work and forgot to take his sixteen-month-old daughter, who was in the car, to day care.

He was a public defender, and the mother was an assistant state attorney. So it can happen to anyone."

Marla's stomach churned. She could well imagine the horror those parents faced.

"We also educate people about helpful technology," Edie added. "For example, you can put a sensor on the baby's seat buckle that will send an alarm to your remote if you move a certain distance away. Not a lot of parents know these options exist."

"Okay, you've convinced me," Marla said. "It's a worthy cause. Sign me up."

"You'll be glad. We do more than warn parents about heatstroke. Like, power windows are a hazard to young children. Or parents will move their car in the driveway, not realizing their child is playing there. Kids themselves might set the car in motion. They should be taught never to play in or near a vehicle."

"Don't forget your pets," Bridget inserted. "I can't imagine leaving my Fluffy alone inside a hot car, but people think nothing of locking their dog in there while they go grocery shopping. Even cracking a window open isn't going to help during the summer."

Marla got short of breath thinking about it. "So what else does your tea circle do besides talk about important issues in the news?"

Bridget tittered. "We gossip about each other, what else?"

"Or we complain about our husbands," Deanne said in a wry tone.

"Four of our group members didn't show up today, and at least two of them said they were coming." Bridget glanced among them. "You'd think people would be more reliable."

"Kitty had a last-minute job," Rissa told her.

"Oh, yeah? Why her, and not me?"

"Her particular skills were requested, from what I understand."

"That isn't fair. I could use the money."

"Now don't get petty, Bridget. There's enough work for everyone."

Marla cut in. "Do you two work for the same company?"

"In a way. It's a home-run business," Rissa said. "You might be interested in joining us if you're looking for some adventure."

"I'd love to hear more," Marla replied, sensing this was an appropriate response. "I need to get out of the house and stretch my wings. That's why I came today."

"Oh, really? How far are you willing to go, darling?"

"That depends on what I'd stand to gain."

Rissa studied her fingernails painted with a swirl design. "How much did Tally tell you about us?" She spoke in a casual tone, but Marla noticed the tightening around her mouth.

"Very little, actually. Tally said the group was fun, and you met in different places. She'd joined to make new friends." Marla hoped the lie didn't show on her face.

"Poor thing was getting bored staying home alone all day with her baby."

Before Marla could reply, the waiter arrived with a three-tiered serving plate that held crust-less sandwiches and blueberry scones. A platter of pastries and individual yogurt parfaits with fruit completed the meal. Glad she'd eaten a light breakfast, Marla helped herself. Deanne ate sparingly, choosing the fruit and sandwiches and avoiding the sweets.

"Do all of you live in Boca?" Marla asked, during a quiet interval when they were busy eating and sipping tea.

"Yes, at least the three of us do. We're on the east side of town," Rissa said, as though that was the better location.

"*We* have a villa on the water." Bridget paused with a teacup halfway to her lips. "You'll have to come see it sometime. We've been featured in various high-end architectural journals."

They wouldn't be impressed by her house, Marla thought. Her mentality wasn't suited to a Boca Babe's lifestyle. She couldn't imagine what Tally got from this group. An escape, perhaps? But from what? She had a wonderful son and owned a popular boutique.

This last gave her pause. Could Tally have been scouting for a new store location? Was she actually considering her landlord's imperative to move?

"Where do you plan to meet next?" she asked. "It's two weeks from today, yes?"

Rissa gestured to her. "Give me your email, and I'll let you know."

Marla reached for her purse to hand out her business cards before realizing that wouldn't be wise. She related her email address and phone number out loud while the others typed the info into their cell phones. She got their data in exchange.

What had Tally been thinking? Marla wondered for the umpteenth time during the drive south. Was this merely a playful escape for her friend, or was there a point to it? Had Tally even told the group members that she owned a dress shop? Having a real job seemed an anathema to them. And why did Marla sense that something else was going on here? Did Tally discover what it was, or had she been part of it?

Marla had the women's phone numbers. If she had any spare time, she could always make individual dates to sound them out on her terms.

But for now, other items filtered into her mind. She planned to stop off to see Tally in the hospital, and then she'd go to the salon for the rest of the work day. Tonight was her late shift.

At the ICU, Tally's condition hadn't changed much, or at least it didn't seem so to Marla. Her friend lay as still as before, her blond hair spread against the white bed linens. The overt bruising had faded, so that was good. And she seemed to have less tubes and devices attached. The best news was that Tally was breathing on her own.

Marla spoke to the nurse, who said Tally's vitals had stabilized and the brain swelling had subsided.

"When will she wake up?" Marla asked in a strangled tone, standing outside the cubicle.

"She's moving around more now. We're optimistic about her chances. The doctor has ordered physical therapy to keep her joints mobile."

"I'm glad she won't need a tracheotomy," Marla managed with a wan smile. "If her brain swelling is down and she's off the meds, why is her coma persisting?"

The nurse patted her shoulder. "Your friend's body is still healing. These things take time. She could wake up tomorrow or weeks from now. It might be sudden or a gradual regaining of her senses. There's no way to tell."

"Thanks, I'm grateful for everything you do for her." After the nurse left, Marla scraped a chair over to Tally's bedside and took a seat. She discussed the tea circle group and her visit to Tally's shop, where people were concerned about her.

Marla's throat clogged with unshed tears, and she broke off after reaffirming that Luke was loved and safe.

Taking action to learn more details about the accident was one way she could occupy her mind. So Friday night, she and Dalton questioned Mrs. Phelps again before heading to the bar where they hoped to encounter Ryan Browning from Ken's insurance office.

The babysitter arrived with an air of confidence. She breezed inside their house, the scent of cleaning fluid accompanying her. Her golden blond hair, arranged in a soft layered cut, looked freshly touched up. She wore a slash of pink lipstick on her smallish mouth. It blended well with her rose pants set that looked like cruise wear for the older generation.

Lucky and Spooks accosted the woman in the front hallway. Dalton controlled the dogs with a sharp command. The poodle barked his greeting, while Lucky pranced back and forth and salivated. If they behaved, they knew a treat would be forthcoming.

"Sorry about the dogs. If they bother you, we can lock them up." Marla led the way into the kitchen. Brianna had gone to sleep over a friend's house to work on a school project.

"No bother. I love animals. Any cats?"

"Not here. We're dog people. We've just taken the dogs out, so they should be okay until we get home."

"Where's Luke? I've missed the little boy." The sitter plopped her purse down on a granite countertop. Her sharp blue eyes scanned the area like a squirrel searching for nuts.

"He's been bathed and put to bed. Thankfully, he's sleeping through the night now." Marla gave her a tour of the house. At the temporary nursery, she halted. Luke's baby smell emanated from the room.

An odd reluctance to leave him grabbed her. Could she trust this woman?

Tally had employed her, so she must have checked the lady's references. But how did Tally hear about her? Marla asked the sitter this question after handing her a list of emergency phone numbers back in the kitchen.

The older woman's mouth eased into a smile. "Our housing community has a newsletter. She read my name in the section where neighbors give referrals to service people."

"So you'd been babysitting for a while?"

"That's right. When my husband passed, I needed to occupy myself. Our kids were grown and out of the house but still single. I'm hoping to have grandchildren someday, but in the meantime, helping young mothers in the neighborhood gives me a purpose."

"How long had you been living there?"

"We moved into the area four years ago. The house was a downsize for us since we didn't need a big place anymore. Neither of us cared for condo living, so we bought a three-bedroom home."

Mrs. Phelps opened her purse on the counter and stuck the list of phone numbers inside. She withdrew a bottle of hand sanitizer and squirted liquid on her palms. Rubbing her hands together, she regarded Marla with a patient air, as though she were used to this line of questioning.

"Do you have any cleaning spray? I'll do some light housekeeping while I'm here, if you don't mind. I like to keep busy. It helps me stay awake."

"You'll find our supplies in the laundry room." Marla indicated the closed door off the kitchen dining alcove. "We keep a container of dog treats in there, too, if you should need them." The dogs had quieted, resting in their favorite spots in the adjacent family room.

"What time should I expect you home?"

Marla glanced at Dalton, who'd been tapping his foot impatiently near the garage entrance. "We won't be out late. Shall we say by eleven?"

They'd looked up the lounge online. The beachside bar had live music starting at eight on Fridays. If Ryan planned to hang out there, it was either to unwind directly after work or to maybe pick up women once the place got rocking.

"How is Tally doing? Is she conscious yet?" Mrs. Phelps peered at her, the lines deepening between her brows.

"No, but the doctors say she's improving. I'm praying for her recovery. Luke needs his mother."

"I still can't believe this happened. I'm sorry I couldn't make the husband's funeral. I'd taken another job, and the couple had gone out of town. I was sleeping over to take care of their kids."

"Don't worry about it. Ken's brother preferred to have a private service."

Dalton walked over and draped an arm across Marla's shoulder, as though sensing her grief. "We've met his work colleagues. None of them called him that night, or so they said. Did Tally mention any other information when she told you about that phone call?"

Mrs. Phelps shook her head. "Didn't the cops try to trace the caller?"

"Yes, but that proved to be a dead end."

"Too bad. I can't conceive of who else might have drawn him out on a holiday like that, can you?" Mrs. Phelps squirted her hands with sanitizer again, as though forgetting she'd already done it. She rubbed her palms together with an absent air.

"We know where he was headed," Dalton added, observing her with keen eyes. "Ken drove his car down a dark street bordering a canal. At the far end was a warehouse."

"Oh, my. That's a strange place to go on New Year's Eve."

"Tell me about it," Marla murmured. Where was Dalton going with this? Was he provoking the sitter to see if she knew about the dead agent at Ken's alleged destination?

Dalton's cell phone rang. Startled, she glanced at him. Who would call them on a Friday evening? Oh, no. He didn't have a new homicide case, did he?

"It's Sergeant Mallory," Dalton said upon viewing the screen.

A sigh of relief whooshed past her lips. Thank goodness her husband wasn't being called to a fresh murder scene.

Or was he?

Chapter Nine

"Hello, Sergeant Mallory. What's up?" Dalton gripped the cell phone by his ear. His eyebrows raised as he listened. "That's good to know. Thanks for sharing this information with me. I'll be in touch."

He hung up, regarding Marla with a baleful glare. "Can we have a word?" They stood aside, and he lowered his voice. "A lab report came in. Paint from another vehicle was embedded on the driver's door of Ken's Acura. The lab techs identified it as belonging to a Lexus GS model. It has a platinum-colored exterior and is a match for the tire tracks. That car is worth at least fifty thousand dollars."

Marla's heart thudded with excitement. "Never mind the price tag. This confirms the witness's story that another car was involved. What's being done to locate it?"

"Mallory has contacted the local repair shops. It's likely the Lexus has sustained paint damage, too."

"Has he notified the Department of Financial Services where that woman worked? Maybe they can help with a state-wide search."

"What woman?" Mrs. Phelps cut in.

Marla gave her a sharp glance. Had the sitter meandered close on purpose?

Dalton responded, his tone wry but his gaze eagle-sharp. "We found a woman's body in a warehouse at the end of the street where the accident took place. Ken might have been on his way there when he was waylaid."

Mrs. Phelps clapped a hand to her cheek. "Good Lord. A body, you say?"

"The victim worked for the insurance fraud division. She'd been shot execution-style. We suspect she may have been investigating Ken's agency."

Mrs. Phelps sank into a kitchen chair. "What does this mean? He wasn't meeting someone from work like he'd said?"

"A colleague from his office might still be involved. Maybe they ran a scam together, and Ken's partner double-crossed him. Anyway, it's Detective Mallory's case, not mine. Marla, we should be going."

"Okay, I'm ready." She collected her purse while doubts assailed her. Was it safe to leave Luke with this woman? Tally had trusted her, but should Dalton have done a more thorough background check? Then again, you couldn't investigate every babysitter from your neighborhood. That would be a bit paranoid.

Marla frowned as another idea hit her. "Say, did you babysit for Tally back in October when she went out of town? I saw in her calendar entries that she'd visited Sunny Grove. Dalton and I were on our honeymoon then, and Tally must have forgotten to mention this trip to me."

Mrs. Phelps's brow wrinkled in puzzlement. "Sorry, I don't remember her leaving for any length of time. I must have been otherwise engaged, or else her husband watched the baby. How do you know she and Ken didn't take Luke with them for a short getaway?"

Her suggestion confounded Marla. "I didn't think of that option. You could be right. It's too bad Ken's cell phone got damaged in the accident, or we could have cross-checked his calendar."

"Mallory has contacted Ken's service provider and requested his cell phone records," Dalton said in a helpful tone.

"That's a logical move on his part, but will he share the results with you?" Marla tapped her chin in thought. "Ken may have backed up his data manually to his home computer in addition to the Cloud. I do that on a regular basis for my iPhone as an extra precaution. Sergeant Mallory has only confiscated Ken's work unit to date."

"Yes, but he may want their personal machine now that there's evidence someone caused the accident."

"How do we know this person didn't merely bump Ken's car as a warning? The other guy couldn't have known he would veer off the road and end up with his side of the Acura submerged in a canal."

Mrs. Phelps shooed them toward the garage door. "Look, would you two mind continuing this conversation elsewhere? Your voices will wake the baby."

They complied and soon headed east toward Fort Lauderdale Beach. Dalton focused on the road ahead, crowded with weekend revelers. Traffic proceeded in a slow but steady stream.

"We should link our security system to a baby monitor," he suggested. "It would allow us to view Luke on our cell phones."

"Great idea. I'll see if the video cam in Tally's house is portable. I should look for a high chair while I'm there. Luke will be getting steadier at sitting up soon, and he'll need to start on solid food."

"We could be introducing solids to him already. Do you have a baby blender?"

"A what?"

"It's a kitchen appliance that allows you to grind food. You know, liquefy the stuff."

Oh, yeah. Just what I want to do when I come home from work—grind up some cooked carrots and peas to make baby mush. I don't even like those veggies.

"No, thanks. I'll buy baby food in a jar. Tally can do all

the grinding and blending she wants when she comes home. I'm not the Earth mother type. I don't think breast feeding would be my thing, either."

"Have you been thinking about it?" He gave her a wishful glance.

"Let's not go there. This isn't about me."

She wondered how his deceased wife had raised Brianna. Had Pam been the perfect mom who'd made everything from scratch? Would Marla be deficient in Dalton's view if she did things differently? With her work schedule, convenience mattered more to her than prevailing feeding practices.

Parenting took an entirely new skill set than what she'd practiced as a babysitter years ago. How could she even contemplate going down that road?

Instead, she focused on the one in front of them and revived her theme from earlier. "Do you suppose the car accident was meant to be a fatality?"

"We won't know until we catch the other person involved." Dalton's expression hardened. "Mallory said there was some sort of odd residue on the warehouse floor. He's having it analyzed."

"That could be helpful. What else has he learned?"

"He's identified the weapon used by the killer but hasn't recovered it."

Marla didn't inquire about the type of gun. Despite Dalton's attempts to teach her weapon skills, she had trouble differentiating among the various firearms. She should make more of an effort to pay attention to his lectures when he took her to the shooting range.

"Any hints from the dead woman's colleagues about her mission?" she asked.

"They're running silent. I'm thinking they don't know who else is included in the scam." He raked his fingers through his hair in a gesture of frustration.

"Sounds like the leads are rather thin."

"The killer is covering his tracks, but we'll get him. Or rather, Mallory's team will have the honors."

She heard the resentful note in his voice. "You wish this were your case, don't you?"

"Of course I do. Tally and Ken are like family to us."

"Maybe we feel that way, but I'm not so sure they did."

Dalton gave her a knowing glance. "You're not happy Tally kept secrets from you. But she entrusted you with Luke, sweetcakes. Even though she chose to keep part of her life private, she gave you her most precious possession."

"I suppose. But there's no question we've drifted apart. She started in with that New Age stuff a while ago. At least she doesn't go to the drumming circle anymore, and she'll eat chicken now, if not red meat."

"She's a new mother. That's a whole other ballgame."

"So why didn't she join a mommy and me play group instead of the tea party circuit? And why not tell me about it?"

"Maybe she wanted to strike out in a new direction. People change, and friendships come and go."

Marla shook her head, confused as to where she stood in her friend's view. Was it wrong of her to expect Tally to remain her BFF? Had it been a one-sided opinion of late? True, their interests had been diverging, but they had business ownership in common. Or had Tally seriously been considering selling out to her landlord and staying home to raise Luke? She wouldn't have mentioned day care centers in that case, would she?

Dalton was right in one regard, though. When it came down to life's ultimatum, Marla was the one person Tally trusted above anyone else.

*****

The bar at the beach had valet parking. Marla emerged from their car and smoothed down her jeans. She wore a corduroy jacket over a pullover sweater, glad for the extra cover when a cool breeze stirred her hair. At least the cold spells in South Florida only lasted a few days.

She paused inside the lounge to study the contemporary motif. Clear columns holding aquariums stretched toward the turquoise-painted ceiling. A polished wood bar lined one entire wall, its stools crowded with patrons. Small round tables filled the rest of the space, while at the far end, a guitarist strummed his instrument. A disco ball threw colored lights on the walls, designed with murals of undersea life.

"May I help you?" asked the hostess in a black dress enhanced by a garish crystal necklace.

"Are any tables available?" Dalton replied with a frown.

No doubt the loud noise bothered him. They both preferred more intimate restaurants to bar scenes. Marla tuned out the background chatter, guitar music, and the clink of glassware.

"Inside or out?" The hostess indicated a collection of tables spilling onto the sidewalk. These had an ocean-view across the street, but at nighttime, you couldn't see much.

Marla would rather be seated indoors where it was warm. "We'll take a table in here," she said, gesturing toward the interior. They had a better chance of spotting Ryan there, too.

"I can take your names for now, or you could grab those vacant seats at the bar. It's bound to get more crowded once our headliner musician starts at nine."

"Fine, we'll take what's available." Dalton steered Marla by the elbow to the only available seats in the house. "Do you see Ryan anywhere?"

"No, but it's early yet. He might still show up."

"Let's hope he comes soon. I don't like having my back to the door."

They hopped onto a couple of tall stools. Dalton ordered a beer on tap while she requested a glass of Chardonnay.

They were on their second round when she spotted Ryan stepping across the threshold.

"We're in luck. Here he is," she said, nudging her husband.

Dalton withdrew a twenty-dollar bill from his wallet. "I'll pay for the drinks while you approach him. Pretend we're bar hoppers for the night."

"Oh, yeah, like Ryan will believe us. We're too old for this crowd." She noted some middle-aged guys there, doubtless on the prowl. The mostly twenty-somethings filling the lounge made her feel out of place.

She got up and sauntered toward their target. "Hi Ryan, imagine running into you here."

His eyebrows lifted as he registered her presence. "Marla, I wouldn't have expected to find you in this place."

"Dalton and I needed a break from baby care. You'd mentioned this hangout, so I thought we might check it out."

"I'd mentioned it? I don't recall ... hey, isn't that Detective Vail?"

"We *are* married," she reminded him. "I believe he interviewed you about Ken."

"So what is this? Another interrogation? I'm not the one you should be questioning."

"That's exactly why we want to talk to you. I gathered you meant to tell me something at the office. We aren't within hearing range of your colleagues now. You can say whatever is on your mind."

Once they'd taken seats at a suitable table, Ryan leaned forward. "Why is there an investigation going on? Beyond a traffic accident, I mean."

"I thought you might have some insights to offer us," Marla said, crossing her legs. "You'd warned me not to dig too deep."

"That's because this whole thing is so strange. Ken gets a call from a colleague on New Year's Eve? To my knowledge, it wasn't one of us."

"How can you be so sure? You don't keep tabs on everyone."

"No, but what reason would they have? Likely Jeri spent that evening at home with her daughter, Cassie. I suppose the girl could have had a crisis, and Jeri called Ken for advice."

"What sort of crisis?" Marla took a sip of white wine from the glass she'd brought from the bar.

"Cassie has a health condition. Jeri doesn't talk much about it. She's always upbeat and has a good word to say. It would help if she would open up so we could offer support."

"She's married, isn't she? Maybe her husband stayed home with their daughter that night while she went to meet Ken."

Ryan folded his hands around his ale glass. "She lives in Coral Springs. Why would she meet him in Davie?"

"Perhaps she needed money, and Ken offered her a loan. Or maybe they were partnering in something else, and an urgent issue came up that demanded action." The news of the insurance fraud investigator's death hovered on her tongue, but Marla couldn't give that information away if Ken's office staff hadn't been told.

Ryan's eyes narrowed. "You might be right about the partnering, but I'd look at Darryl rather than Ken. He and Jeri have had some heated discussions lately. I couldn't hear what they were saying, but I could see them through the glass partitions."

"Do you suspect those two of colluding together?" Dalton interceded. He'd let Marla take the lead, but she could tell he was getting impatient from the way he tapped his foot.

"I don't know." Ryan shifted restlessly. "I just think it's weird what happened to Ken. Lately in the office, he'd been acting withdrawn. And when the others were gone, I caught him looking through their desks. He could have discovered something that got him killed."

Or maybe Ken wanted to see if any of his colleagues knew what he was doing so he could better cover his tracks, Marla thought.

"Where can I find Jeri if I want to visit her aside from the office?" she asked. "I'll encourage her to talk about Darryl. Or as you said, it might ease her burdens to talk about her troubles at home. I'm a good listener."

Then again, was Darryl merely a smoke screen that Ryan was casting their way? Could the younger man be the guilty party, trying to throw them off track? Her glance dropped to his cell phone, which he'd laid on the table. Clearly, Ryan was fond of technology. He'd probably know more about burner phones than his older co-workers.

"Jeri and her husband always go to breakfast at TooJay's in Coral Springs. It's their routine on weekends," Ryan replied with an earnest gleam in his eyes. "You might have better luck at sounding her out. I don't know why she's so embarrassed to mention her daughter."

"The girl could have chronic problems that need costly care. You should be familiar with disabling illnesses. Shawna mentioned your mother has Alzheimer's, and the responsibility for managing her affairs falls to you."

His face flushed, and his lips flattened. "That's right. I don't hide it. I owe my mom a lot, and it's important to me that she's well cared for. It hurts to see her deteriorate. Alzheimer's is a terrible illness."

"I've no doubt that's true. So how do you get by?"

Ryan regarded her steadily. "I'm good at my job, so I make enough money to support us both. This is exactly why I advise older folks not to drop their policies. Lots of people feel they're getting up in age. Why should they keep paying on that long term care or life insurance policy? Yet they're approaching the very years when they'll need them."

"Do you get commissions on each policy or referral?" Dalton inserted, pushing back a lock of hair that had fallen onto his forehead. He parted it to the side, but one stubborn curl kept flopping forward.

"Depends on the type of policy. I'm ready to move up to

account executive. I realize I'm relatively new at my position, but I've got the chops to bring in new sales. My talents are being wasted at the front desk."

"Did you ask Ken for a promotion?" Dalton asked him.

"The boss was aware of my plan to move up the ladder, but Darryl and Shawna aren't going anywhere soon. Their sales records make them valuable assets. I'll have to change agencies if I want to advance."

So Ryan's job pitch had been rebuffed. Did he knock Ken off to create a vacancy? "Tell us more about Shawna," Marla said in a coaxing tone. "She seems competent in her role."

Ryan twisted the silver ring on his right hand. "She's going through a hard time right now. Her husband is out of a job, and they have two kids in private school. I don't know how they're making ends meet. Maybe they're dipping into their nest egg."

"Can't you borrow on a life insurance policy? Does she have one with your agency as part of her benefits package?"

"Well, yes. That might be what Shawna and Ken were arguing about when I saw them together. It looked like a heated discussion from their facial expressions."

"When was this?"

"About a week before the accident. He was showing her a printout. I didn't hear what they said, but Shawna seemed upset." The young man leaned forward and fixed his gaze on Dalton. "So tell me, why are you really here? Do you know what happened to Ken?"

"His car was deliberately forced off the road. We have the make and model of the other vehicle. What kind of car do *you* drive?" Dalton asked, his expression giving nothing away about his opinions.

"I have an Audi S5 Coupe. But I still don't get it. What was Ken doing in Davie late at night on New Year's Eve?"

"When we find out, we'll let you know. Or vice versa."

"Okay with me. Meanwhile, I'll keep my head down and

my mouth shut at work. Now if you don't mind, I see some chicks over there who are eager for my company." Ryan shoved his chair away from the table and stood.

Marla and Dalton followed suit. "Thanks for talking to us," she told the young man. "If you hear anything significant, please give one of us a call. You have our numbers."

"Yep, I believe I do." Ryan sauntered away, leaving them both staring after him.

During the drive home, Marla contemplated what they'd learned. "We should visit TooJay's in Coral Springs on Sunday to look for Jeri."

Dalton, hands on the wheel, nodded his agreement. "I still don't trust Ryan. He's eager to cast blame on everyone else."

"Blame for what? I wish the victim's agency would tell us what she was investigating. That would be immensely helpful. And why they aren't sending in another agent to take over the case? Have they been haranguing Mallory about his findings?"

"I don't think they've intervened. Maybe someone higher up has put a lid on the subject. They might figure Ken is out of the picture now."

"But if Ken had an accomplice, you'd think they would want to pursue things further."

"I agree. It doesn't make sense."

"Who works in that department? Like, what are their divisions, and who's at the top?"

"I'll look into it. I'm not familiar with their organizational structure." Dalton pressed on the brake pedal as the light ahead turned yellow.

"So what else did we learn tonight? Was this trip worthwhile?" Eager to return home to Luke and relieve the babysitter, Marla clasped her hands in her lap.

"It was helpful. We know more about the personal lives of Ken's staff."

"Ryan drives an Audi. That's not the car you're looking for, but it doesn't get him off the hook. He has expensive habits."

"I've noticed. His shoes alone must have cost several hundred bucks."

"Do you believe he makes enough money to cover his expenses and his mother's?"

"That would depend on how much of his mother's medical care isn't covered by her insurance. I have to be careful about digging too deep. Mallory will get pissed if I step on his toes. I don't want to tick him off, or he'll clam up."

"You'd be a valuable resource if he would use you as a consultant."

"But I'm also biased. Ken was my friend."

Marla fell silent, unhappy with his limitations on the case. Aware of his frustration, she didn't want to fuel his fire. So she focused her mind on more personal thoughts.

Her hand slid over to caress his thigh. "We used to go out more often before we got married. That bar scene reminded me. What's happened to us?"

"Do you really have to ask? We have a baby at home now along with a teenager and two dogs. The noose of domestic life has tightened."

"Yes, but Luke isn't ours. We'll have to give him back to Tally when she wakes up, assuming she's well enough to return home."

Marla loved Luke, but he wasn't theirs to keep. Caring for him gave them a taste of what it would be like to have their own child one day. It no longer seemed like such an onerous responsibility. And Dalton's analogy wasn't quite accurate where she was concerned.

Had it been so long since Marla's divorce to Stan that she'd forgotten how restricted she'd felt being married to him? Life had become infinitely better with Dalton. She'd describe it more like domestic bliss than a rope around her neck. Being married to Stan had stifled her. Dalton encouraged her to soar.

"Maybe I'd rather stay home with you than gallivant around town," she said with a sexy smile.

"Likewise. But I don't ever want you to feel confined. It doesn't bother me when you go for a girls' night-out, for example, or if you want to join your colleagues for a drink after work."

"I know, and that's another reason why I love you."

When they arrived home, Mrs. Phelps greeted them at the inner garage door. "Did you have a nice evening?" she asked from the kitchen while packing her supplies.

Dalton handed over her payment. "It gave us a break from routine. We're not used to having to call a babysitter, so we appreciate you being available."

"If only Tally would get better, she could take care of the little guy. You'll let me know if her condition improves, won't you? I'm worried about her. The outcome might have been quite different had it been her end of the car in the canal instead of Ken's."

"Yes, Luke is fortunate he still has his mother." Marla didn't rejoice over this fact. Ken was dead. The outcome was bad either way you looked at it.

"Let's hope Tally is in her right mind when she wakes up. Otherwise, Luke might become a permanent fixture in your household."

"God forbid. Tally will be well again, you'll see."

The sitter's words reverberated in her head as she got ready for bed. How did the driver of the other car know what would happen when he bumped into Ken's Acura? He couldn't have predicted the rollover accident. Nor could he have foretold which end of the car, if any, would end up submerged in the canal. This entire incident bothered her on some subconscious level, but she couldn't pinpoint why.

She didn't want to bring it up when Dalton stretched his length beside her and tickled the sensitive skin on her underarm. They were alone except for Luke, who was sleeping peacefully next door. So she turned toward her husband and allowed him to divert her attention.

Chapter Ten

By nine o'clock on Sunday morning, TooJay's in Coral Springs was already packed. Smells of garlic and brewed coffee reached Marla's nose as she and Dalton elbowed their way through the crowd waiting in line for seats. They were looking for Jeri Cresthaven from Ryan's office and might not stay if she wasn't there.

"We're meeting a friend," Marla told the hostess. She breezed past to scan the patrons in the spacious restaurant. A moment later, she poked Dalton's arm. "Look, there's Jeri. She's alone in a booth, although she might be waiting for her husband to join her."

Jeri nursed a cup of coffee but hadn't been served her meal yet. She wore a sad, resigned expression as Marla moseyed over.

"Hey, Jeri, fancy seeing you here. Would you like company, or are you expecting someone?"

Jeri gave her a surprised glance. "Why, Marla, what are you doing in Coral Springs? Don't you have a TooJay's closer to where you live?"

"Yes, we do, but we're planning to visit the farmer's market after breakfast, so we thought we'd stop in here along the way. My mother is watching Luke so Dalton and I could have a few hours to ourselves." Brianna hadn't been available. She'd made plans with a friend, and Marla didn't want to disrupt her schedule each time they needed a babysitter.

125

"Ethan, my husband, is home watching our daughter, bless his heart. Sunday is our aide's day off," Jeri said without elaborating. "Hello, Detective. Why don't you both join me?"

"Mrs. Cresthaven, it's good to see you," Dalton said with a curt nod as they slid onto the bench opposite her in the booth.

Jeri grunted, as though she thought otherwise. "How did you know where to find me? And don't tell me it was a coincidence."

"Dalton did his research," Marla hedged, unwilling to compromise Ryan for tattling on his colleague. The waitress bustled over with menus for the newcomers.

"What else did you learn?" Jeri asked, her gaze narrowing.

"You have a heavy burden to carry with your daughter's illness. I'm so sorry."

"Don't be; we're managing. On Sundays, Ethan stays with Cassie so I can have some alone time."

"What about your other children? Do they help out?"

"One daughter is in college, and the other one is busy with her friends. She stays home for us on Thursday nights. That's our date night. And John, my stepson ... well, he can't be bothered. He's in his own world."

"Cassie's care must be expensive. I hope your health coverage is adequate." Marla, having made her meal choice, put down her menu.

"Your husband works for a tech firm, doesn't he?" Dalton asked, shifting his position to stretch his legs. "I'd expect he has a family policy."

"Neither of our health plans covers long-term care. Who thinks someone so young is going to need it? Cassie didn't get sick until ten years ago. She's twenty-one now. We can keep her as a dependent for a few more years. Then she'll have to get her own policy, and good luck with that."

Marla digested this information. Had Jeri been working

for Ken when her daughter became ill? Or had she applied for the job when two incomes became necessary?

Jeri stirred her coffee, moving the spoon round and round, her eyes glassy. They'd better change the subject. This line of conversation was agitating her, and they still had more to learn.

Marla sat back when the waitress arrived to take their orders and fill their coffee cups.

"How is Tally doing? Has anything new happened since I saw you last?" Jeri asked after the server left. No doubt she felt this was a safer topic than her personal problems.

"She's breathing on her own and moving around. Those are good signs. She could come out of the coma any day." Marla added cream to her coffee and stirred the brew.

"I'm worried she might want to sell the agency rather than holding onto it and appointing a manager. A new boss might not want to keep us on."

"That's a valid possibility. Maybe you should make a contingency plan."

"How is the agency doing?" Dalton asked in an idle tone. "Was Ken having any financial problems in terms of the company?"

Jeri glared at him. "If anything, revenue was up. He gave us generous bonuses at Christmas."

"That must have pleased Shawna," Marla said. "I understand her husband is out of work. When did that happen?"

"It's been over six months now since he got downsized. I'd feel sorry for her, but she wore a new bracelet to work the other day. She said it was David Yurman. He's her favorite jewelry designer, so I doubt she'd wear a knock-off."

"Was it her birthday? Maybe she got it as a gift."

"Her husband wouldn't have bought it, not when they're dipping into their savings while he's looking for a job. So I'm thinking she may have a honeypot on the side."

"A boyfriend?" Marla's mouth gaped.

"Why not? I've heard her on the phone when her voice gets all soft and syrupy. She doesn't speak that way to the hubbie."

"You haven't seen her around the office with a strange man, have you?" At Jeri's shake of the head, Marla's gaze caught Dalton's. The boyfriend could be a bad apple, making Shawna do things she might regret. Dalton's imperceptible nod told her he'd look into it.

"I haven't met Shawna's husband," Jeri added, "although I've seen his photo on her desk. She keeps her social life private."

"Where does she like to hang out on her time off? Does she have a favorite spot where she goes to relax?" Marla asked to keep the ball rolling.

Jeri jabbed a finger in the air. "Check out the nail salon, sugar. Have you seen the expensive acrylics she wears with those fancy designs? I'll bet she spends a lot of time in that place, not to mention money she can't afford. The woman should do her own nails if she needs cash for the household budget."

Their breakfast arrived, and they fell silent while eating. Marla debated what else to say. At her side, all she could hear was Dalton's munching. He seemed more interested in the food than the conversation. But he had a knack for listening and observing verbal cues. Often he'd come up with insights beyond her scope.

"You indicated you're worried about the agency's future," Dalton managed between bites. "What if Tally decides to keep the place and promote Darryl to manager?"

"I wouldn't mind working for Darryl, although he can be a prick sometimes. I doubt he'll be as inspiring to work for as Ken." Jeri stuck a forkful of veggie omelet into her mouth.

"Why not?" Marla bit into her smoked salmon bagel sandwich. She chewed and swallowed, the taste of salty fish lingering on her tongue.

"He's not much of a team player. You can tell by the way he jumps on a potential sale to score a higher ranking. Darryl's out for his own gain."

"You're saying he's more competitive than Shawna?"

"Oh, yeah. And he has an attitude, like people owe him. I wonder what dirt he had in his files that made him scurry to clean up his data when we heard about Ken's death."

Dalton's shoulders stiffened. "That was his reaction to learning his boss had been killed? He went straight to his computer?"

Jeri gave a vehement nod. "I thought it was peculiar. But he's always been an odd ball of cotton. You know that his wife left him? I'm wondering if it's because she found out he's gay."

"Is that true?" Dalton asked.

"I've gotten that impression, but if so, he hasn't come out. We all have our secrets."

Yes, you do, Marla wanted to say but didn't. "How does he spend his spare time?"

"Darryl loves boats. He rents one at the marina near Bahia Mar whenever he gets the chance. The man wants to own one of those fancy yachts someday. Have you seen the photos on his office wall? He attends all those boat shows. Even with commissions, I don't see how he'll ever afford one, let alone pay the dock fees and maintenance."

They dissolved into small talk, Marla chatting about her hair salon and baby care. Jeri offered advice, not that Dalton hadn't been through the experience once before.

"When are you two going to have your own?" Jeri asked with a smile. She'd pushed away her empty plate and reapplied her rose lipstick. The color matched the top she wore over a pair of black jeans.

Marla's skin warmed. She didn't dare glance at Dalton. "We're still talking about it."

"She's talking. I'm ready." Dalton pointed to his chest.

"Caring for Luke is giving me practice," Marla admitted. "It helps me see that I'm able to juggle work and home life. I can't understand how single mothers manage things with all they have to do."

"It's amazing what you can get done when you have no choice," Jeri mentioned in an emphatic tone. "How did Tally plan to go back to work?"

"I believe she meant to enroll Luke in day care, so I hope she won't mind that I've taken the initiative. He had his first experience there on Monday."

"Yes, so you said when you visited our office that day. Be prepared to get sick. Children pick up all sorts of germs from other kids."

"Oh, joy. Thanks for the warning."

Dalton reached for the check after the waitress left it on the table. "I'll get the tab. Thanks for talking to us, Jeri."

"I hope I've been helpful. What does the other detective have to say about the case?"

Dalton's mouth thinned. "There's evidence another car purposefully bumped Ken's Acura and caused him to veer off the road."

"No way. That's terrible. Can you trace this other car?"

"Sergeant Mallory's team is handling it. Marla and I are working on the motive angle. Why would someone want to harm Ken?"

Jeri's gaze darkened. "As I said before, Mr. Vail, everyone has secrets."

*****

"What do you think? Is Jeri hiding something she doesn't want us to know?" Marla mused during the drive back to Palm Haven. Dalton hadn't said a word since they'd left the restaurant.

"If so, we'll figure it out. We have other concerns in the

meantime." He stared ahead, his jaw firm. He seemed more focused on his inner thoughts than on the light Sunday traffic.

"What's on your mind, then?" she asked, annoyed that she had to pry it from him. Why was it always the woman who had to get her man to open up?

"How long are you going to vacillate on extending our family? Either you're for it, or you're not."

Marla's muscles tensed. She should have known Jeri's innocent inquiry would fuel the torch. "Dalton, we've only been married for a year. Can't I get adjusted to our new life first?"

"What is there to adjust? It's a second marriage for both of us. You knew what to expect. Brianna would love to have a baby brother or sister."

"She'll be going to college soon. She won't even be home to watch a sibling grow up."

"That's not the point. She knows it would make me happy. I'd venture to say, our parents would be overjoyed as well. And despite the age difference, Brianna wouldn't be alone some day when we're all gone."

"Are you feeling pressured by your mom, is that it? She wants more grandchildren?"

"No, that isn't why I feel this way. I see how good you are with Luke. You'd make a wonderful mother. You're already great with Brianna."

"Let's not discuss this topic right now." Marla burrowed into her leather seat. She'd been considering going off the pill, but his response irritated her. She knew this decision affected everyone in their families. However, it was her body and her life, and Dalton should respect her choices.

Staring out the side window, she decided a change of subject was in order.

"We shouldn't go home right away," she said in a pleasant voice meant to suggest a truce. "It's Sunday. If we're going to catch Darryl, he's more likely to head over to the

131

docks on his day off. At the very least, we can talk to other boaters and see if it's the right place where he hangs out."

From the corner of her eye, she saw Dalton's lips flatten into a taut line. He wasn't pleased by her evasion. Well, too bad for him. He'd known coming into this marriage how she felt about having children. It shouldn't come as a surprise when she stuck to her resolve. And even if her viewpoint was softening, he hardened her shell every time he pressured her like this.

"You're right; let's do it," he replied in a curt tone. He turned east at the next major intersection, and they headed toward the beach.

Marla attempted to make small talk to lighten his mood as they cruised down Las Olas. She pointed out some new restaurants along the way. By the time they reached the Bahia Mar area, he'd loosened up.

They found a parking space in a lot close to where the Jungle Queen boarded tourists for its cruise down the Intracoastal Waterway. The marina was busy, crowded with charter boat customers, yacht owners, fishermen, and visitors looking for some action on the ocean.

Outside, a briny breeze freshened her lungs. Glad her arms were covered, Marla straightened the V-neck sweater she wore over a pair of black denims. Dalton strolled beside her, his figure imposing in a long-sleeved shirt tucked into blue jeans. Nearby, a pelican sat atop a post at the water's edge, while seagulls soared into the sky with raucous cries.

"Who should we ask about Darryl?" Marla tucked her arm into Dalton's to show him her affection hadn't waned over their argument.

"Let's try that booth over there where they do daily rentals." He led the way, his long stride guiding them in that direction.

"Darryl Trent?" The bearded guy at the reservation stand wore gold hoop earrings, a bandana around his head, and tattoos on both muscled forearms. "We have a reservation for him. He's going out at one o'clock. Are you his guests? If so, I'll need to see some I.D."

"We just want to talk to him." Dalton leaned forward to be heard above the clacking noises from sailboats and the whine of machinery from a motor vessel, where a deckhand worked. "He's checking in at one, or is that the time he casts off?"

"He'll be at the booth then."

"He's a regular at this place?"

"Oh, yeah, the dude loves his boats. He can't wait until he can afford one of his own."

"Does he have a plan for making that happen?"

The fellow spread his hands. "How would I know, man? Hey, how did you say you knew him?"

"We're acquaintances. Does he come alone or have company when he goes on these jaunts?"

"He's always got a hot-looking chick with him, although a couple of times he's brought a pretty boy toy along. I can't figure out which way he goes, if you know what I mean."

"Thanks for the info. We'll come back in a while." Dalton turned to Marla. "We have a few hours to kill. What do you want to do?"

"Let's go across the street to the beach. We can take a walk and then relax at those picnic tables, since we didn't bring any folding chairs."

At Fort Lauderdale Beach Park, the thud of a ball from the basketball court reached her ears. She sniffed the remnants of barbecue fuel from blackened grills scattered under the shade of palm trees. The public parking site had a lineup of cars waiting to get in. On Sunday morning, this place filled up fast. Tourists didn't care about the chilly weather. Unlike the natives, they waded into the water year-round.

Far to the horizon, Marla could make out a freighter on the sparkling sea. The water glittered like diamond chips in the rising sun, its glare hurting her eyes. Wishing she'd worn a hat, she adjusted her sunglasses. They turned left to stroll along the sidewalk bordered by a low wall with a white wave design. The scent of coconut oil from suntan lotion wafted into her nose.

"I'm sorry," Dalton said abruptly. "I shouldn't push you to make a major decision or to change your mind about things. We both went into this marriage accepting each other's baggage and our plans for the future."

"I wouldn't call your daughter a piece of baggage, and plans can be modified. I just wish people would stop pressuring me."

"You made it clear how you felt about having kids before we wed. It's my bad."

"No, Dalton, don't apologize." She took his hand and squeezed it. "I didn't anticipate how I'd feel with a teenager in the house, or a baby for that matter. Taking care of Luke has opened my eyes to new possibilities. I've been meaning to have this conversation with you."

She walked along, eyeing the strangers who passed them. This wasn't a dialogue she'd meant to have in public, but so be it.

"I'm thinking about going off the pill," she confessed. "I've been on it for so long, that even if we decided to have kids, it might be difficult."

Still holding her hand, Dalton peered at her with laser-like intensity. "Are you truly entertaining the idea? Because it would be a life-altering event. There would be no going back."

"I know, and I still want to travel and visit Bora Bora someday. That's been my dream vacation since forever. But the Caribbean is closer and can substitute for now. We could go places together as a family." She paused. "Plus, I was afraid having children would conflict with my career, but now I see having kids and going to work are not mutually exclusive. That is, if you don't mind day care centers and babysitters."

"Or we could hire a nanny. With two jobs, we can afford one."

"I'm not fully sold yet." She dropped his handhold. "I need to let the idea stew in my brain a bit longer, so no promises."

"Okay. Whatever you decide, you can count on my support." He stopped, put his hands on her shoulders, and kissed her soundly in front of passersby. "I love you, and it's wrong of me to put my needs before yours. I'm happy with the way things are, if that's how it will be."

"We'll see. Look, the Goodyear blimp is already in the air."

"Sunday is primetime for advertisers. A plane pulling an ad is sure to follow."

Their attention diverted to the beachgoers and the patrons at open-air cafés across the street. They moved on to safer topics until it was time to return to the marina. They arrived a half-hour early in case Darryl showed up ahead of schedule.

Their target appeared as they hovered by the rental booth.

"Hey, guys, what are you doing here?" Darryl gazed at them in surprise. He'd forsworn his business attire for a sport shirt and shorts with boating shoes on his feet. He wore a baseball cap on his gray hair.

Dalton regarded the blonde in a bikini on the account executive's arm. "We were hoping to speak to you in private."

"Is that so? I'll do the paperwork for my rental, and then you can have a few. Babe, why don't you wait on that bench over there? I won't be long."

"We were wondering what you can tell us about Ryan," Dalton began, when the three of them stood under the shade of a coconut palm on a grassy swale.

Not far away stood the familiar Bahia Mar resort, its white structure an icon in the area and the mecca for the Fort

Lauderdale Boat Show. Valet parking at that stellar event cost sixty dollars per day. Was this the crowd Darryl emulated to join?

Darryl kicked at a pebble on the ground. "Ryan is a good kid. He's personable with our clients, returns phone calls promptly, and gets the job done. I don't see him staying in that position for any length of time."

"What's the alternative?" Dalton asked.

"He'll jump ship as soon as a better offer comes along."

"You don't think he covets your role or Shawna's?"

"We're not going anywhere, so he'd have to seek a promotion at another place. His position is better suited to someone like Jeri, who's content to get a salary with benefits and do the job. Ryan is on a career track. He makes no secret about it."

"I understand his mother has Alzheimer's disease. How can he afford to take care of her and own an expensive car?" Marla inquired. "I notice he has the latest tech gadgets, too."

"Maybe his old lady has savings? I've never asked. As for the car, how do you know he owns it? He could have a lease."

"That's true." She gave Dalton a thoughtful glance. "We were wondering if Ken found any irregularities among those two. You know, Jeri has an ill daughter. They both have the duty of caring for a loved one."

Darryl glowered at her. "Ken wouldn't tolerate any discrepancies in the books, if that's what you mean. And they're not responsible for sales."

"No, but aren't they in charge of billing, policy endorsements, and claims?"

"So what if they are? Do you have proof there's something wrong going on? The other detective took Ken's hard drive. What did he discover from it?"

"Detective Mallory won't share those details." Dalton watched a bird skim the water, dive down, and surface again with prey in its beak. "Ryan said you and Jeri had been having some heated discussions lately. What was that about?"

Darryl's face turned the color of a sunburned tourist. "Jeri is a peach. She really needs her job. She's doing what she has to do for survival."

"Meaning what?"

"One of our clients complained that a couple of endorsements had showed up on her policy that she hadn't ordered. Ken asked me to look into it. This wasn't the first such complaint, either. I noticed Jeri was the one in charge of those renewals."

"So you're saying she padded their policies?"

"Hey, you didn't hear it from me, man."

"Did you confront her about it?"

"Yes, and she said they'd been genuine mistakes. She'd been distraught over problems at home and had mixed up one client request with another policy holder."

"Did you believe her?"

"Look, I told Ken my findings and left it at that. I like Jeri and advised her to be more diligent in the future."

"And Shawna? Ryan saw her arguing with Ken the other day. Ken was waving a printout at her."

Marla leaned inward so she could hear more clearly. A constant clatter from creaking boats, noisy tourists, and squawking seagulls sounded in the background.

Darryl shifted his position so he stood in the shade looking away from the sun. "I told Ken she was stealing my customers. Shawna knows her track record will never equal mine, so she's tried to boost her sales ratings by calling my clients back before I could get to them. Like, she'll never be as good as I am."

"How did Ken react to your accusation?" Marla asked, picking up the conversational ball.

"He promised to check into it, but I doubt he bothered. He often overlooked my contributions."

"Jeri admired a new bracelet Shawna was wearing the other day. It looked like a David Yurman piece, and those can be expensive. Her husband wouldn't have given it to her if he's out of a job."

Darryl laughed as though she'd told a joke. "Shawna likes her bling, and Ronnie knows it."

"Ron Crawley, the financial planner?" Dalton cut in, his tone sharp.

"That's right. Your investigators haven't learned she's seeing him on the sly? For shame, Detective."

Marla arched her eyebrows. This was news. Did Sergeant Mallory know? And was their affair relevant to the case? Ken wouldn't have fired her over it, would he?

"If we want to talk to Shawna, where can we find her? At the nail salon, perhaps?" The ocean breeze blew a strand of hair across her face. She tucked it behind an ear, aware the wind had picked up. A paper advertisement scuttled along the asphalt, ending up splayed against a concrete post.

"Shawna works out at a gym near where she lives in Pembroke Pines. It's one of those big chains," Darryl told her. He glanced at the blonde, tapping her foot with an impatient expression as she waited on the bench. "Sorry, I have to go. Why all the questions, anyway? Shouldn't the accident investigation be finished by now?"

"There's proof another driver forced Ken's vehicle off the road," Dalton said, observing the older man's reaction.

"What? Who would do such a thing?" Darryl tilted his head, a perplexed look in his eyes. "I don't understand. First you say Ken got a call from somebody at work when none of us phoned him that night. The investigator checked our alibis and our cell records. Now you're saying this was a deliberate attempt to harm him? Were you able to trace that call?"

"Mallory had no luck in that regard. This case is his jurisdiction. We're merely concerned about our friend Tally."

Darryl gripped his arm. "Is she awake yet? We're all on

pins and needles at the agency waiting to see what she'll do with the place. She should appoint me as manager."

Marla's husband shook him off. "She's still in a coma. It's too premature to consider that option."

"Let us know the minute she comes around, would you? We'd like to send flowers."

"Of course, we will," Marla said in a soothing tone. "Come on, Dalton. We should go. The man's date is waiting. Which one of these boats is yours for the day, Darryl?"

He pointed to a sleek motor vessel. "It looks small but will give us a good ride. Someday, I'm going to own one of these babies." His gesture encompassed a luxury yacht where a fellow lounged on the rear deck. From the purposeful activity of his friends on board, they were getting ready to cast off.

It was a beautiful day for cruising, with fluffy white clouds in the sky and a stiff breeze. What a different lifestyle. And it's so not for me, Marla concluded, switching her purse strap to her other shoulder.

After saying their farewells, she and Dalton strode toward their car. She inhaled the fresh sea air as her tension ebbed.

They'd accomplished a lot that day. Would they have time to track Shawna for a last interview?

Nancy J. Cohen

Chapter Eleven

Dalton looked up Shawna's home address and all the sports clubs within a five mile radius. They proceeded to visit each one until they found a place where she had a membership. It took a flash of Dalton's badge to gain the information, but they finally hit gold.

It being a Sunday, the gym was packed. They'd be lucky to find her there. Starting at the top level, they searched the sea of faces and struck out. They worked their way down, where Dalton spied her among the treadmill tyrants. Shawna wore earbuds hooked to her phone. As she noted their approach, she ripped the buds from her ears and glowered at them.

"What are you two doing here? Have you come to ruin my day off?"

Marla issued a friendly smile. "Hello, Shawna. Where's your family? Is your husband babysitting the kids?"

"They're old enough to be home on their own, but yes, he's there with them. Sunday is homework day, and it's his turn to help out."

"Do you have a minute to talk? I'm sure you remember my husband, Dalton."

Shawna skewered him with a glare. "Is this about Ken? If I recall, you're not officially on the case. That would be the other guy from Davie."

"You're correct," Dalton stated. "But we have news to share. Are you willing to answer some questions in return?"

"I suppose." Shawna grabbed a towel and her gym bag

140

and followed them to a quiet corner near the weights section. "So, what's up?" the slim dark-skinned woman said, while Marla admired her makeup. She did her eyes nicely, and that crimson shade on her lips matched her tank top.

"We have evidence the car wreck wasn't an accident. Another vehicle was definitely involved. Do you know anyone with this model?" Dalton showed her a picture on his cell phone.

Shawna squinted at the photo. "Nope, sorry. Why are you even asking me? Is it because of the alleged phone call from a work colleague that drew Ken out on New Year's Eve? All of us at the office have denied contacting him that evening. How do you know the babysitter wasn't lying?"

"Sergeant Mallory obtained Ken's cell records from his carrier," Dalton explained. "He did receive a call that night, but the source couldn't be traced."

Marla cut in, unable to stay quiet for long. "That means the caller could have been anyone. Take Darryl, for instance. He seems eager to be appointed manager. He's not so desperate that he'd orchestrate an accident to create the opportunity, would he?"

Shawna stiffened, her scornful glance implying Marla had gone afoul of reason. "Darryl might be ambitious and think the world owes him, but he's not a bad guy. He lets off steam by spouting his opinions. If he resented Ken for not giving him more credit, he didn't act on it."

"I got the impression Darryl believes you're stealing his clients. Did he tell Ken? Is that why Ryan noticed you and Ken arguing one day?"

"Excuse me? You've been talking about me behind my back?"

"We're interviewing everyone associated with Ken. He was our friend, and we want to know the truth about what happened to him." Marla tried a different tack. "Jeri said you'd acquired a lovely bracelet recently. Who gave it to you? Was it the agency's financial planner, by any chance?"

"How do you know about Ronnie and me?"

"It's not much of a secret. Did Ken learn about you guys? Maybe that's why he was giving you a dressing down. He was warning you to steer clear of workplace romance."

Shawna's mouth formed a pout. "You got me there. I suspect it was Darryl who tattled on me. He may feel I'm stealing his customers, but it isn't true. I'm following up on leads that he allows to lapse. His head is in the clouds half the time. Or I should say, he's dreaming about the big-time boat he wants to buy."

"How can he expect to afford it? Is he socking away his commissions? It must be easy for him to save money since he's single."

"Huh. He pays alimony to his ex-wife who left him. She got a better lawyer."

"Do you know why they split up?"

Shawna wiped her neck with a towel while a nearby guest grunted on the weight bench. "I can make an educated guess. When Darryl isn't admiring boats on the Internet, he's viewing naughty photos. You know what I mean."

Ugh, no wonder he and his wife had separated. The woman must have discovered his passion for porn sites. Did Ken catch him at it and threaten to fire him? Or worse, tell the authorities? Would that give Darryl a reason to kill Ken?

"Did Detective Mallory take a look at anyone's computer in the office other than Ken's?" Dalton asked, rubbing his jaw. His face held a thoughtful expression.

"Not really. Should I have mentioned this stuff to him? I mean, I don't want to get anyone in trouble."

Of course you don't, Marla thought, *because if you rat on your co-workers, they might do the same for you. Oops, they already have.*

Shawna glanced between her and Dalton. "What is it you're not telling me?"

"We still have no clue as to why Ken was on that road," Dalton admitted. "Who might have lured him there?"

"I'd like to find out as much as you, Detective."

The insurance fraud team must be keeping a tight lid on their agent's death, Marla figured. Dalton hadn't mentioned it to Ken's colleagues. Presumably, that would be Sergeant Mallory's job. But he appeared to be keeping mum on the subject as well. What was really going on? Was this bigger than any of them realized?

Being kept in the dark didn't help. Mallory shared some of the details, but not all. And they were merely friends of the victim, now that Ken's case wasn't considered accidental. Were they calling it a vehicular homicide, or what?

"We have to think of Tally and her baby now," Marla told the other woman. "The agency will be hers when she wakes up. She'll need to make an informed decision about what to do and who to keep in her employ if she decides to stay on."

"And it's your job to fill her in?" Shawna leaned against a wall and folded her arms, mimicking Dalton's posture.

"Her husband was killed. The person involved could still be someone from your office."

Shawna shot upright, her expression fierce. "That's a terrible thing to say. Every office has interpersonal conflicts. It doesn't mean we'd stoop to murder. You might as well call it by the right term. And why did Tally go with him? She left her baby late at night to run out on New Year's Eve? They were lucky to get a sitter last-minute on a holiday."

"That's true. Maybe Tally wanted to see where Ken was actually going."

"Could he have been having an affair with someone?"

"If so, why would he allow Tally to accompany him?"

"Good point. Or maybe you're looking at everything the wrong way." Shawna collected the bag she'd dropped on the floor.

"Meaning what?"

"Tally wasn't meant to go with him. She jumped in the

car on a whim, from what you've told me. Perhaps the phone call was meant to get Ken out of the house, leaving Tally home alone with little Luke."

*****

Could this notion be true? Marla wondered during their drive to the hospital to visit Tally. Could Ken have been lured away on purpose? If so, her friend might be in danger. But who would want to go after her, and why?

She asked herself these questions again at Tally's bedside, where Marla combed her friend's limp blond hair. Dalton had gone to ask the nurses if there had been any more phone calls from strangers inquiring about Tally's condition.

Tally appeared peaceful, as though she were merely sleeping. Most of the monitoring equipment had been removed. Now she just had a feeding tube, intravenous line, and catheter. Marla was careful to avoid the healing bruise on Tally's head. If only her loving care would rouse Tally and bring her back to awareness.

She placed the comb inside the bedside table drawer and pulled up a chair. "Hey, Tally, it's me. I've fixed your hair, but if you keep on like this, I'll have to bring in a dry shampoo next time." Her throat clogged, and she paused to squeeze Tally's hand. "Luke is doing fine at our house. He's such a darling. I may not want to give him back."

She prattled on, while wondering what Dalton was learning. Did Tally need a guard? Would Mallory even consider their theories?

It wasn't her husband's ballgame, and all they had were suppositions. Hopefully, if Tally was a target, she'd be considered neutralized at this point. Before she woke up, though, Marla had better figure out who might want her out of the way.

"I think this idea about Tally being a target is a long

shot," Dalton said as they headed home toward Palm Haven. His hands on the wheel, he focused his attention forward on the traffic. The report from the nurse had indicated no further phone calls from strangers.

"I'll admit it's illogical, considering the dead insurance fraud agent at the end of the road. But we shouldn't overlook the possibility." Marla wished they didn't have such serious matters on their minds. She'd rather admire her husband's tall form and steadfast manner. A warm glow filled her that had less to do with lust and more to do with the sense of strength he gave her.

He noticed her eyes on him and gave her a reassuring grin. "At least nobody else has been calling about Tally, if you can rely on the nurses. I put a bug in their ears to keep a watch on her and to notify security if anyone unknown approaches her cubicle."

"That's good. I need to speak to those ladies in her tea circle. It's hard for me to understand why she joined them, other than to make new friends."

"Isn't that reason enough? Maybe she felt the need to break out of her mold and do something different. She doesn't have to include you in every activity she does."

Ouch. That arrow hurt, but he was right. Why should she expect Tally to tell her every detail of her life? It could be that having a baby made her reassess her needs and reach for something new.

Marla lifted her chin and firmed her resolve. "The members gave me their contact info, so I can arrange to meet them individually. And it may help for me to visit their recent meeting places to see what gossip I can pick up. What angle will you work on?"

"I can run criminal background checks on the group of women."

"How's your other case going? The robbery victim?"

His expression brightened. "Kat nearly has that one sewn

up. We should have enough any day now to nail the guy who did it. I'm staying out of her way until she asks for more help, but she's got it covered."

"It must be difficult for you not to step on each other's toes," Marla remarked with a degree of resentment. The female detective hadn't made things easier for Dalton.

"We're supposed to be working together. Sometimes, I have to remind her," he replied in a terse tone.

"That sounds like Darryl, according to what Jeri told us. Maybe Ken chastised him because he didn't play with the team."

"Don't the insurance reps work on commission?"

"Yes, but you'd think they would help each other. Like, maybe one of them is better at selling homeowners' insurance, while the other guy gets more auto policies. That sort of thing. Ken would have known their strengths by examining their sales records and certifications."

"And their weaknesses. I wonder if he was planning on letting any of them go."

"How could you find out?" Marla asked.

"Mallory has Ken's hard drive from work. If he's found anything that relates to one of the employees, he isn't sharing."

"This must be so frustrating for you."

"I have a personal interest in the case. I can't blame Mallory for keeping a tight lid on it. He might have the state financial department breathing down his neck, too. I wish he'd at least throw me a bone in that direction."

"What did you find out in your research on them?" Her nose tickled from the dust in the car. She grabbed a tissue from the glove compartment and sneezed into it.

"The Chief Financial Officer holds the top post. It's an elected position for four years. Nathan Rice is the current CFO. I understand he's aiming for the governor's seat."

"I've never heard of him, but I'm not into politics." She

stuffed the crumpled tissue into her purse for disposal later. Dust motes glittered in the sunlight streaming in from the windows.

"Among his other duties, the CFO is responsible for licensing and oversight of insurance agents and agencies. Their department has fourteen divisions that perform the actual work. The Insurance Fraud Division is the law enforcement arm responsible for investigating fraud, whether by individuals, insurance agents, or insurance companies."

"Who's head of that one?"

"Director Liam Kelton is in charge. He has an assistant director. Beneath them are several bureaus. For example, the Bureau of General Fraud is run by a chief in Tallahassee and is further divided into various field offices."

"It sounds complicated." Marla disliked politics unless it affected the causes that mattered to her. And even then, she preferred a summary to a point-by-point news report. She massaged her temples that had begun to throb from all the details. "So who did the dead woman work for?" she asked out of curiosity.

"Her name was Louise Harrison. She worked out of the Fort Lauderdale field office."

"Have you been in touch with them?"

"It's not my case. You know I've been trying to play nice and go through Mallory without annoying him."

"We should let him do his job. He'll be upset enough when he learns we've been poking around Ken's business connections." She stared out the window at the passing scenery. They'd switched to the turnpike and were closing in on Mount Trashmore, judging from the odor in the air. Black birds circled overhead, eager for the meal they spied below. Marla wrinkled her nose until they'd passed that segment of the highway.

"You've given me an idea," Dalton said in an eager tone. "We haven't considered who else might have had a grudge against Ken. A disgruntled customer or a former employee could have wanted revenge."

"We won't find out unless we can access his work computer, and that's not available to us," Marla reminded him.

"How about the one in his home office?"

"It might still be there if Mallory hasn't confiscated it. I haven't checked lately."

"Then we should swing by Tally's house."

Marla phoned her mother to say they'd be later than expected. All was well with Luke, so Anita said they didn't have to hurry home. Nonetheless, Marla vowed to look for an experienced sitter in their neighborhood. It would be easier than relying on family members or calling Mrs. Phelps each time they needed someone to watch the baby.

Come to think of it, why did Mrs. Phelps seem to be free so often? Didn't she babysit for the neighbors in her community as much as she claimed?

"I'm glad Ma is able to look after Luke, but we shouldn't take up so much of her time," she told Dalton. "Don't forget, we have to pick up Brianna on our way home, so we need to be quick. By the way, did you give Sergeant Mallory a key to Tally's house?" She offered Dalton a breath mint from a container in her purse.

He took one and popped it into his mouth. "Nope, Mallory got a key from Phil when he was here. You'd think the guy would call to ask about his nephew's welfare or Tally's condition, but I haven't heard a word from him. Have you?"

"No, I'd have mentioned it if he'd called. The man is a jackass who only cares about himself. That's why Tally and Ken didn't trust him to handle their affairs."

*****

Twenty minutes later, they approached Tally's house, silent without its occupants. The front windows stretched like vacant eyes, reflecting the hollowness of the place. As Dalton pulled into the driveway, sadness draped over Marla like a salon smock with lead weights sewn inside.

She emerged from the car and neared the front door with a heavy heart. Tally should be home, bustling around her happy family.

Please, please, wake up and be normal, Marla prayed as though Tally could hear her. She swiped at her moist eyes as Dalton unlocked the door. His gaze hardened, as though he shunted his feelings behind a professional mask.

Once inside, they veered to the den where the couple kept their lone desktop computer. It looked dead, and when Dalton pushed the power button, nothing happened. A quick examination told him the hard drive was gone.

"Damn, Mallory must have taken it." Dalton looked disappointed even though they'd known this was a possibility.

"Ken might have backed up his documents to the Cloud. We could sign in from our computer at home, but we'll need his passwords," Marla suggested.

"Even if we found them, we don't know what backup program he used."

"Why don't you look in the drawers and see what you can find? Did you ever contact his cell phone provider and ask about cloud storage there?"

"Mallory has that information, and he isn't sharing."

And you don't want to butt in on his territory, she surmised. "Take a look around. I'll collect the mail in the meantime."

Dalton glanced up when she returned to the study. "Are there any bills that need immediate attention?"

"We can sort through the envelopes later. I left them in the foyer. Did you find anything of significance?"

"Nothing useful in here, and I checked Ken's nightstand

as well. Mallory must have taken anything potentially helpful to the case. Is there anything else for Luke that we can bring home?"

"I took most of the portable stuff the last time I was here, but look for a high chair. What do you plan to do about Ken's things?"

"Let's leave those decisions for Tally when she wakes up."

While he headed toward the nursery, Marla wandered into the kitchen to check the refrigerator. Phil must have cleaned out the remaining perishables, but condiments still remained along with longer-term items.

The pantry was full of foodstuffs, too. Most of them could keep, but if Tally didn't awaken soon … *No, don't think that way. We'll leave things as they are for now.*

One shelf held part of Tally's extensive cookbook collection. Marla examined the volumes with fond memories. They'd taken a French cooking class together back in the day. Tally enjoyed reading vintage cookbooks for their personal commentaries about life in an earlier era, while Marla chose regional ones that showcased an area's specialties. They'd often shared recipes, or at least they had done so before Tally swore off red meat and other foods Marla considered staples in her diet.

Tally had veered in another direction then. She'd joined a drumming circle, studied Reiki healing, began yoga classes, and started espousing the mystical powers of rocks and crystals. Since Ken's gemstone mine investment proved to be fruitful in the long run, this last wasn't so difficult to understand.

Recently, Tally had seemed to drift away from these interests and back toward more mainstream views. Maybe Luke had given her life renewed meaning. Or else she'd still felt the need to stretch, and that's why she had joined the tea circle. It gave her a new outlet and a fresh identity aside from Luke's mom.

Marla cast aside these thoughts to conduct a brisk search through the house. When neither she nor Dalton turned up any useful clues, they left. She brought the pile of mail but needed the couple's online codes more than anything. Too bad Tally hadn't kept a printout hidden somewhere.

"I'll stop by the bank tomorrow," she said. "They should be able to tell me which bills are automatically deducted from their checking account. Then I'd like to reach out to the tea circle members to get to know them better."

Dalton frowned. "I'm favoring the trail in the other direction. It's more logical Ken was involved in an operation that came under scrutiny and led to the fraud investigator's death."

Marla conceded his opinion made sense but wasn't ready to give up on their other options. She'd have to wait until the next day, though, to pursue matters further.

On Monday, she awoke prepared to take Luke to day care, go to the bank, and follow her own leads. Luke, however, had different plans.

The baby cried, refused his bottle, and felt hot to the touch.

Alarmed, Marla rushed to consult Dalton. He was in their bedroom getting dressed for work. "Luke may be sick. Come and take a look."

He followed Marla into their temporary nursery and put a hand to the infant's forehead. Luke's face scrunched, and he emitted a howl that shook his entire body.

"Did you change him already?" Dalton asked, a worried crease between his eyes.

"Yes, and he doesn't seem hungry. I brought him back to bed when he refused to eat."

"It feels like he has a fever. Where's the thermometer?"

"Did we bring one from Tally's house? Or do you mean the one that we use?"

"No, it's a thing you put on their foreheads."

"Let me look at the latest supplies I brought back." She retrieved the bag from their guest closet and rummaged through it. "Do you mean this item? It comes with directions and says you stick it in the ear."

"Yes, that's a newer device. Give it to me." He took a moment to do a reading. "One hundred and two."

She cast him a panicked glance. "What do we do?"

"We have to get his temperature down, but we don't have the proper meds in stock. It's been fifteen years since I've done this, don't forget. They probably have better methods these days. Call the pediatrician."

"Could Luke be teething? Doesn't that cause elevated temperatures?"

"Not like this. I'll run to the drugstore and get you something to soothe him until you see the doctor." He stuffed his wallet in a pants pocket and buttoned his sport coat.

"That's okay. You have to get to work. It's better to see what the pediatrician recommends. Don't kids get strep when they're young? Luke might have caught something at the day care center."

"The doctor will probably do a throat swab. They see stuff like this every day."

Oh, great. And if it turned out to be a strep infection, Marla and Dalton had been exposed. This was one of the unfortunate hazards of parenthood.

Nervous about being alone with a sick child, Marla nonetheless shooed Dalton away to work. She'd have to learn to manage on her own. As soon as office hours opened, she called the pediatrician's office and was grateful they could fit her into their morning schedule.

At ten o'clock prompt, she checked in at their reception desk. She had to show documents regarding her authorization to care for Luke. The staff hadn't heard about Tally's accident. One of them called the hospital to verify Marla's story, while another lady made copies of the papers along with her driver's license. Marla felt like a criminal who'd stolen a child. However, a kidnapper wouldn't bring the baby to his pediatrician's office.

She took a seat in the waiting room as directed by the receptionist and gave an anxious nod to the other mothers hanging out in the sick section. The normal kids, present for healthy check-ups, congregated in a separate area.

When it was their turn, a nurse took Luke's weight, measured him, took his temperature with a digital ear thermometer, and then led Marla into a treatment room. Luke fussed the whole time, while Marla felt helpless in her ignorance. How did new moms learn what to do?

A wave of relief hit her when the doctor finally entered. She was a young woman with reddish-tinted hair and a friendly smile. Her white lab coat differentiated her from the staff with their cartoon-character scrubs. The doctor greeted Marla and introduced herself.

"I'm so sorry to hear about Luke's parents."

"Thanks. I never expected to fill this role," Marla confessed.

"You said Luke's father died in the car crash and his mother was injured?"

"Yes, Tally is unconscious in the hospital. She'd listed me as successor guardian and trustee if Ken didn't survive her."

"How horrible. Aren't there any close relatives?"

"A brother-in-law, but he's a bachelor who isn't interested in being saddled with a baby."

The doctor's brow wrinkled. "I thought Tally mentioned that her father lived in Florida. Surely he could pitch in to help his grandson?"

"You must be mistaken. Tally's parents are deceased."

"Really? I didn't get that impression, at least not about her dad. Something she'd said during her last visit … well, never mind. Tally is fortunate you're here for her. What are her chances for improvement?"

Marla's eyes inexplicably filled with tears. "Who knows? She's getting better physically, but mentally is another issue."

"Let's hope she comes out of the coma soon. Luke needs her. So what's wrong with the little guy?"

"He woke up fussing and hot to the touch this morning. I called your office right away."

"Has he been in contact with anyone who's sick?"

"I started him at day care last Monday," she said with a modicum of guilt.

The doctor gave a knowing nod. "That will do it. Did you give him any medicine this morning? His temp is still up there."

"No, I wasn't sure what to do. He doesn't seem to have any other symptoms. He's restless and not very hungry, but I suppose that's to be expected."

"It's important to keep fluids in him. Let's take a look."

A nurse came in to hold the baby while the doctor did her exam. The lady physician murmured soothingly to Luke as she checked him over.

"Seems like a virus to me," she told Marla, while washing her hands at the sink. "I don't see any signs of strep, but the nurse will do a swab just to be sure. Call us if he develops any other symptoms or gets worse. I'll leave you some prescriptions at the front desk."

"Thanks so much, doctor." Marla refastened his diaper, pulled on the baby's clothes, and strapped him into the carrier she'd brought along.

When the swab came back negative, Marla gave a sigh of relief. That was one good thing in their favor.

At the exit, the receptionist gave her several medications and a tube of teething gel, plus a set of written instructions. While grateful she didn't have to make a separate trip to the pharmacy, Marla winced when the acquisitions came with a hefty bill.

"Will you be filing for Tally's insurance?" she asked the desk clerk.

"Yes, we'll take care of it. In the meantime, please sign here that you're responsible for any unpaid amounts."

Marla complied. She'd already given the co-pay upon arrival. Aware that Luke had an appointment for his six month visit coming up, she didn't schedule a recheck. If his condition worsened, she'd bring him back sooner.

Would Tally's coverage be changed with Ken gone? Or did she have her own health policy to supplement his group plan? Whose coverage provided for Luke's care? Darn, she should have asked at the doctor's office.

Back at the house, she wrote down the time for his medication dosages, changed his wet diaper, and put him in his crib. At least he didn't have strep. This must be some random virus he'd caught. She phoned the day care center, which she'd notified earlier, and gave them the verdict. Then she called her mother.

"I used to wipe you and your brother down with rubbing alcohol when you got fevers. It evaporated on your skin and helped to lower your temperature," Anita said.

"They don't do that anymore, Ma." Marla sat in her study on speaker phone, eyeing the mountain of Tally's unopened mail on her desk.

"The important thing is to keep the baby hydrated. Do you want me to come over?"

"No thanks, I'll manage, and I wouldn't want you exposed to his germs."

"What will you do about work tomorrow?"

"I'll have to stay home. Tuesdays are our slow day, anyway." Nonetheless, she'd have to ask her receptionist to reschedule clients, but who knew how many days she'd be out?

What did other mothers do? It would have been helpful had Tally joined a mommy and me play group instead of the tea ladies. Then Marla could have asked them for advice.

"If this doesn't break out into a full-fledged cold, it might be a short-term thing. I'll come there tomorrow so you can go to work." Anita's commanding tone brooked no argument.

"I hate to rely on you again, Ma."

"Nonsense. That's what I'm here for, although it would be gratifying if it were *my* grandchild."

"Oh, don't start."

"Just saying. Expect me around eight-thirty in the morning."

Marla had little time to be annoyed by her mother's remark as ministering to Luke occupied her for the rest of the day. She managed to get some of her household chores done, call Dalton with a quick update, and catch a nap in the intervals between Luke's feedings and medication schedule. He fussed in discomfort, while she wished she had more ways to help him. Poor guy could only pucker his tiny face and cry.

She lifted him from his crib and cuddled him as though that would help, but then she realized her body heat might make him warmer. Wheeling him around in his stroller might be more useful. She tried that tactic and was relieved when it eased his distress.

It wasn't until later when she picked up her cell phone to call a friend, needing to hear an adult voice, that she noticed a text message waiting for her. It came from Ryan's mobile number that she'd programmed into her phone.

Call me. I found something.

Her pulse accelerated. She phoned him back but it went to voice mail. Maybe he'd respond to a text.

A return message came through: *Can't talk. Will catch you later.*

She pictured Ryan at his desk in the insurance office. What was going on that he couldn't mention in front of his colleagues?

Chapter Twelve

Marla told Dalton about Ryan's call when her husband walked through the door around four o'clock. "I wonder what he has to say," she concluded.

"You'll find out when he calls you back." Dalton emptied his pockets on the kitchen counter. "How's Luke?"

"The medicine is helping, thank goodness, although he's still fussy. I tried some of the teething gel the doctor gave me. Why are you home so early?"

"I thought you might need a hand. Besides, Kat made an arrest on the robbery case. She's got enough evidence to put the guy away."

"That's good news." Marla followed him to the bedroom where he went to change. His manner seemed subdued. "What is it you're not telling me?"

He tossed his jacket onto the bed. "Kat has asked for a transfer back to her former precinct. She finally told me what was eating at her."

"No kidding. Well, don't keep me in suspense." She knew working with Kat hadn't been easy for him. The lieutenant had been a closed book from the moment she showed up, silent over her reasons for a transfer and his chief not revealing why it had been granted. Sinking onto a corner of the bed, Marla waited while Dalton changed into jeans and a sport shirt.

"From what I gathered, her partner died on their last case

together, and she blames herself." Dalton paced as he spoke, his expression grim. "She became personally involved with a suspect, and the man pulled a gun on them when her guard was down. Her boyfriend fatally shot the partner, and Kat killed him before he could turn the weapon on her."

"That's horrible."

"She was suspended from duty pending an internal affairs investigation. She wanted to resign but was convinced to go for therapy instead. Then when they reinstated her, she got the mayor to grant her a temporary transfer. She's still dealing with the emotional fallout."

"Kat should have told you sooner. It might have affected her performance."

"But it didn't. She kept her cool."

"Yeah, like an ice queen. I hope she melts when she goes home. Those mental barriers have to come down sometime if she's to forgive herself."

"You, of all people, should know we learn from our mistakes. It takes time to heal."

"You're right." Marla had moved on from her personal misdeeds.

"I'm glad she's made peace with herself and is ready to return to her own people." Dalton went to lock his firearm in their home safe, located in the master closet.

"So what happens with you?" she asked upon his return. "Will you get a new partner?"

"I don't need one. Captain Williams wants me to assume more administrative duties." He scowled at the notion. "Langley has passed the exam and made sergeant."

"Good for him. But will they hire more people? I mean, your department gets short-staffed around the holidays when everyone wants time off."

"I'll continue to share the call schedule and the investigative work, but I can delegate the more mundane tasks. That isn't a bad thing."

"Your powers of observation are second to none. You pick up on details that your colleagues might miss."

He regarded her with a fond smile. "My expertise will still be available. I'm hoping I can get home earlier each evening, unless there's a hot case for us to work on."

"That's always a plus." Luke's whimper drew her attention. "Oh, dear. It's not quite time for his next medicine dose. His fever might be spiking again."

Dalton stood by as she checked the baby's temperature in the nursery. Luke would need the medication again. Feeling bad for him, she stood over the crib and tickled his tummy. A colorful mobile twirled lazily overhead. As they watched Luke's facial expressions in fascination, Dalton's hand grasped hers.

"Any more thoughts about—"

"I made an appointment with the gynecologist."

"O-kay. When were you going to tell me?"

"I did say I'd been thinking about it. There's nothing to report until I see the doctor."

"No problem. Just wondering."

She let go of his hand and turned to him. "And no promises either. This is a good trial run for us. It's helping me get used to the idea, but I'm not totally sold."

*****

Marla didn't go back to work until Wednesday, when Luke was well enough to return to day care. She hadn't felt comfortable allowing Anita to come over and be exposed to his germs, so she'd called off her mother's visit. The illness had lasted a couple of days and went away as suddenly as it had appeared. It made Marla realize that if she chose this path for her future, she'd have to create more flexibility in her schedule.

It was hard saying goodbye to Luke that morning. He gurgled at her and wriggled his little body. She felt sure he must recognize her as his caretaker by now. She kissed his little fingers where he lay in a crib before turning away.

During the drive to her salon, she wondered how Dalton would get along without Kat there as back-up. She meant to ask him if he'd been able to get in touch with Ryan. The young man had never called her back, and Marla's other attempts to reach him got his voice mail. It was damned odd that he didn't even respond to her text messages.

Ryan hadn't shown up at the office yesterday, either, as she'd tried that number on Tuesday. Darryl answered and said Ryan wasn't feeling well. He had called in sick.

A mantle of unease settled upon her. She should have heard from him by now. So when Dalton called at mid-afternoon, she stepped aside to answer.

"Bad news," his somber voice declared. "We found Ryan Browning's body this morning. He'd been shot."

"What? Where?" Ice sluiced through her veins as shock overtook her.

"He lives in the Hibiscus Estates subdivision. His gardener knocked on the door after doing the lawn, and it swung open. Someone had left it unlocked. Ryan's body was inside."

"Oh. My. God."

"Ryan must have let in somebody he knew. There weren't any signs of forced entry."

Marla's sense of reason returned. "Likely he stumbled onto something that got him killed. If only I'd answered the phone when he first called…"

"I'm heading over to his office now to talk to his colleagues. I'd like to know which one of them took his call about being sick. We can verify it on their phone records."

Marla pictured the young man seated at his desk. How could this be possible? She leaned against the storeroom counter where she'd gone to take the call. What had Ryan learned that he'd meant to tell her?

"This is going to hit that group hard," she said.

"Some of them, maybe not all. I sense a rat there."

"Do you think Ryan got killed for the same reasons as Ken? The insurance fraud agent's involvement suggests a broader operation. That could be why her department has been keeping mum. They don't want us locals to spook the big fish."

"I'll get in touch with them. There's one good thing to come out of this situation," Dalton said in a taut voice. "Ryan's murder falls under my jurisdiction."

"Will your captain let you get involved?"

"Langley could take charge, but this one's my baby. I've already been in touch with Mallory. Ryan's death affects his case as well. Now he'll have to cooperate."

Marla drew in a sharp breath. "What if the dead woman wasn't investigating Ken as a suspect? What if he was working with her?"

"It would help if her people would tell us who they were interested in among that group."

"Maybe they don't know, and that's why they enlisted Ken's help. Are you going to close the office?"

"Not until I talk to Louise Harrison's boss, or I might inadvertently screw up whatever her team has in the works. There's something going on here that is eluding us."

"What if I'm right, and Ken was cooperating with their agency? Why would he have gone out that night? And what made Tally jump in the car with him?"

"She could have been worried about his safety, if he'd clued her in on things."

"I can't see Tally risking her life and leaving Luke that way." Marla brushed a hand over her face. This case kept getting more complicated.

"Perhaps her concern for Ken outweighed her other interests in the heat of the moment. We don't know what message he received. Ken must have repeated it to Tally, and she became concerned for his welfare."

"Do you think Ken knew Louise was a captive in the

warehouse? Maybe the bad guys lured him out to rescue her," Marla suggested.

"Or they could have threatened him. If he didn't follow their instructions, they'd kill her. Which they did anyway," Dalton added in a glum tone. "That would only be effective if Ken and Louise were working together."

"He could have been a mole to gather evidence, and she was his handler. Do you have a photo of her?" Maybe Louise was the strange woman she'd seen in Ken's company at Wilton Manors.

"I'll get one. But these are merely theories. Ken could still have been involved in whatever fraud scheme was underway. I'm betting he had a partner who double-crossed him, and Tally was collateral damage. Ryan was getting close to the truth, and so the partner offed him, too. It has to be somebody in their office."

"Darryl is the most likely suspect, but we shouldn't overlook the ladies, either. They both have secrets they want to keep. Did you find the murder weapon? Maybe you can trace the killer through ballistics."

"Not yet. If it was left at the scene, we haven't found it."

"Then there's Shawna's idea, assuming she isn't blowing smoke because she's guilty. If Tally hadn't gone with Ken, she and Luke would have been home alone."

"So somebody wanted to put Tally in a vulnerable position. Why?"

"Who knows? She's been running around town lately, making new friends. It could be she stirred the wrong pot."

"That seems like a wild shot, forgive the pun."

Marla straightened her spine, aware her next customer would arrive any minute. "You're the one who told me to examine all the options. I think I should look into this angle while you focus on Ken."

"Sounds like a plan to me." His voice deepened. "Have I mentioned what a good team we make?"

"You have, but you can tell me again later ... in bed. Love you, hon."

Marla repeated her news to Nicole first chance they had together.

The other stylist's eyes rounded at Marla's tale. "I'm so sorry. How awful. If Ryan could have shared what was on his mind, he might not have been killed."

"Tell me about it."

"Did Dalton say if they recovered his cell phone?"

"No, why? Because of what information we might find on it?"

"That would be helpful, but I'm thinking along different lines. What if the bad guy looked through the call list and saw that Ryan had sent you a recent text message? He'd be wondering how much you know," Nicole explained.

"Dear Lord, surely he wouldn't come after me, not with Dalton on the case?"

"That wouldn't be a deterrent to this guy. And when Tally wakes up, she may be in danger, too, if the killer thinks Ken confided in her."

"Dalton mentioned putting a guard on watch, but that was back when Mallory was in charge. Ryan's death puts a new spin on things. I'll text him right now."

"So what will you do next?" Nicole asked once Marla had completed her task. She stood by her station preparing a stack of foils for her next highlights customer.

Marla hovered nearby. "I'm still not convinced Ken was the target, although it seems the most logical explanation with the dead agent in the warehouse. Dalton will investigate that angle. I'll get better acquainted with the tea circle ladies to see if Tally mentioned anything relevant to them."

Nicole jabbed a finger in the air, an excited gleam in her eyes. "What about her recent phone calls, contacts, and meet-ups? Did Dalton check her email messages?"

"No, he's been looking in the other direction. So has

Mallory, who's in possession of their home computer hard drive and Ken's work device. I've suggested Dalton check for backup data in the Cloud, but we need our friends' passwords. Mallory will have to give Dalton access to his findings now that there's a related murder victim on his turf."

"You both have lots of trails to follow."

"Want to go with me? I mean, to check out the places where those tea ladies have met."

"Sorry, but I promised Kevin I'd help him study for his paramedic exam. It's on Monday, and we have plans for the weekend."

"Hey, that's great. Wish Kevin good luck for me. I hope he passes."

The fire department EMT had rescued Marla's poodle from a hazardous hole in the ground next door. She'd thought he and Nicole might hit it off and had invited them both to a barbecue at her house. Nicole had been dating him ever since.

Not wishing to jinx their relationship, she changed the subject. "I should bring Luke into work so you guys can see him. He's the cutest thing. I felt so helpless when he was sick."

"I'd love to see the baby." Nicole gave her a penetrating glance. "Say, are you and Dalton thinking any further about—?"

"Not yet. You know how I feel on the subject."

"Yes, but I thought you were coming around."

Marla spied a woman headed their way. "Here comes your client, Nicole. We'll talk more later." Relieved to have dodged that conversational ball, Marla prepared to receive her next customer.

*****

Thursdays were Marla's late day at work, so she had the following morning free. After dropping Luke off at day care, she headed for the yoga studio listed on the tea circle group's itinerary. A class was already in full swing when she entered through a set of double front doors. The instructor's voice echoed down the hall.

A receptionist glanced up from her seat behind a granite-topped counter. She had curly auburn hair, tanned skin, and friendly blue eyes. Behind her on the wall was a bulletin board full of notices on one side and a collection of framed certificates on the other.

"May I help you?" the woman asked in a pleasant voice.

"I'm thinking of joining a yoga class. One of my friends came here a few weeks ago and recommended the place. Her name is Deanne Tinsley." Marla mentioned the skinniest of the tea circle ladies, assuming Deanne worked out to maintain her figure. "She came in with a bunch of other women. I believe they took a class and then hung around to chat."

"Do you mean the meet-up group organized by Rissa Kyle?"

"Yes, that's the one. Do you remember them?"

"I'll let you talk to their instructor. If you care to sit in our lounge, she'll be finished with her class in ten minutes."

"Can I take a peek?" At the receptionist's nod, Marla headed down the corridor. Polished wood flooring flowed between the areas, creating an expansive pattern. Her low-heeled sandals made a discreet tap-tap as she strode along.

She followed the instructor's voice to a large, well-lit room filled with students. Their trim bodies encased in athletic garb made Marla envious. She watched as they twisted into various positions on colored mats. Water bottles and towels lay by each person's spot. No one wore shoes. A rack of cubbyholes by the door provided storage for foot wear. Other containers held extra mats, Mexican blankets, and equipment that was foreign to Marla. Portraits adorning the walls displayed photos of famous yogi masters.

The instructor stood at the far end, between two windows shaded by blinds. Her blond hair tied in a ponytail, she demonstrated the poses for her disciples to imitate. Behind her sat a shelving unit holding a collection of rock crystals amid potted greenery. Speakers mounted on the walls played New Age music from a digital player.

Not wishing to break the women's concentration or disturb the vibe in the room, Marla retreated to wait in the designated lounge. Comfortable seating areas made for a quiet respite. Vending machines offered snacks and drinks, while another corner held gear for sale. Yoga mats in plum, teal, or royal blue; tee-shirts with the studio logo; and books on yoga, meditation, and massage were available for purchase. Marla sat on a couch and picked up a health magazine from the coffee table.

She was reading an article on yoga for pregnant women when the instructor found her. The young woman strode forward, a fountain of energy. Her skin was flushed from the aftermath of exercise. She wore a silver angel pendant on a chain around her neck.

Marla remembered someone she'd met recently had liked angels. Who was it?

Shawna's image floated into her mind. The account executive had worn a similar necklace. Did both women share the same interest in angels? That had to be a coincidence, right?

"Hi, I'm Shannon Courtley. I understand you have some questions?"

"Marla Vail." She jumped up to shake hands with the instructor and then resumed her seat.

The other woman sank into an armchair with a weary sigh. "It feels good to relax for a few minutes. How can I help you? Are you interested in classes?"

"I might be. A friend referred me to your place. Her name is Deanne. She meets with a group of women on a bi-weekly basis, and they explore new sites together. They like to eat and drink tea at these gatherings." Marla showed the piece of paper she'd brought along with the dates of the group's outings.

Shannon smiled, her teeth gleaming white. "Oh yes, those were the ladies from Boca. They did well in my class and seemed to enjoy themselves."

"They've probably taken sessions before. I'm wondering what your impressions were of these women. Was there a tall, leggy blonde among them? Her name would be Tally."

Shannon gave a vigorous nod. "She's the one who could have been a model. I loved the outfit she wore. The royal blue color looked stunning on her."

"She owns a dress boutique. I'm surprised she didn't give you her card."

"None of the girls said much about themselves. The lady in charge was more interested in sounding out our other students. You know the one I mean?"

"If she's a redhead, that would be Rissa."

"When the girls in my class were changing after the session, she went around and spoke to each one of them. They exchanged a few words, and Rissa gave out her card."

Rissa must have been trying to recruit more members for their group. "Did Tally seem engaged with her friends? Did she mingle with them?"

"I'd say so. She appeared quite enthusiastic about the class. She told me she'd recently had a baby and needed to get back in shape. We have prenatal classes as well as sessions for new mothers." The instructor's eyes narrowed as she glanced at Marla's figure. "Are you—?"

"Not me, either way. I'm married, but we don't have kids of our own yet. My husband's teenage daughter is enough for us to handle. Tell me more about your studio," Marla said, hoping to divert the instructor's attention.

Shannon crossed her legs, fitted with black athletic pants. She'd slipped on a pair of ruby ballet flats that matched her top. "We offer a variety of classes for different levels depending on your goals. Yoga has been around for thousands of years. It helps you gain flexibility, balance, and strength."

"So does dance. What's the difference?"

"Yoga is a full mind-body workout that combines strengthening and stretching exercises with deep breathing and meditation."

I'd meditate all right, but mostly about my to-do list, Marla thought. "Don't you have to contort yourself into different poses?"

"Most people find yoga to be relaxing. It can provide relief from stress and tension, and it helps to lower your blood pressure. Some forms are fast-paced and intense, like Power Yoga. That helps you burn calories and increase strength. Other types are more gentle and suitable for beginners."

"What if it hurts me more than it helps me?"

"As with any physical activity, the risk of injury is present. You should check with your doctor if you're not sure how this exercise may affect you. We require our students to sign a waiver of liability."

"I wouldn't know where to begin." Marla spread her hands in a helpless gesture.

The instructor rose and pulled a brochure from a rack by the vending machines. "Here, this explains the various options along with our pricing packages."

Marla stood and accepted the item. "Thanks so much for your time. Is there anything else you remember from my friend's visit?"

Shannon scrunched her face in thought. "The redhead was the last one to leave the parking lot. A guy who looked like a panhandler sauntered over. I'd have been scared, but she reached into her purse and gave him a handout. Very generous of her, I must say."

"Had you seen this fellow around here before?"

"No, he wasn't familiar. Usually, these people stake out the bigger intersections."

"Maybe he spotted her group coming in and figured they'd be a soft mark."

"Maybe." Shannon gave her an impish grin. "Anyway, it was great meeting you, Marla."

"I'm a hairstylist. If you're ever in the area, stop by my salon. I'll give you a discount on your first visit." They exchanged business cards before Marla departed.

Once back on the road, she considered what she'd learned. Rissa appeared to be the ringleader of the tca circle group. She was a schmoozer from the sound of it, introducing herself to strangers and handing over her business card.

Speaking of handouts, how did Shannon know what Rissa offered to the panhandler outside? Did she see cash exchange hands, or was that a guess? Did homeless people usually hang out by yoga studios? And why was Rissa still there when the other women had already left?

As she veered onto I-95 to head north toward the hospital, Marla shook away her unease. Likely, she was building mountains out of molehills. But it made her visits all the more imperative to the other places where the tea circle ladies had met.

Chapter Thirteen

Tally didn't seem any different to Marla when she arrived at the hospital a few minutes past eleven o'clock. Visiting hours had just started in the ICU. Marla couldn't stay long, so she consulted with the nurses, combed Tally's hair, and pulled up a chair at her bedside. Her friend's body seemed to be shrinking under the sheet. Tally's face was pale, her golden hair spread like a halo against the white bed linens. Today she had on a gown with a blue plaid pattern that might have matched her eyes had they been open.

Would her gaze be intelligent when her lids lifted of their own volition, or would they be void of memory and experience like a newborn? Was anybody home upstairs?

Regardless of her mental state, it would be a long road to recovery when she woke up. The doctors seemed to think it was a matter of time and healing, now that she was past the critical stage. Even when she left the hospital, Tally wouldn't have the stamina to care for Luke or to go back to work for a while. But they could cross that bridge in the future.

Marla reached for the book she'd brought in her handbag. During her last visit to Tally's house, she had grabbed a bunch of mystery novels she'd seen on the bookshelves, thinking she could read to her friend while sitting there. First she rambled on, sharing Luke's antics and hoping Tally could hear her somewhere deep inside her brain. Then she picked up the novel and began reading, her mouth forming the words while her mind raced ahead to her next plan of action.

Time passed rapidly. That afternoon ran into the next one. Despite her best intentions, Marla wasn't able to pursue the case until later on Friday. She was at work that day waiting for a customer to arrive when Dalton called.

"What's up?" she said into her cell phone. She headed outside for a breath of fresh air and a modicum of privacy. With a weary sigh, she sank onto the unoccupied bench in front of her salon facing the parking lot. The chilly temperature cooled her skin, but her sweater provided enough warmth.

"Mallory and I met to exchange information. Now that I'm officially on the case with Ryan's death, he's shared what he knows."

"So Ryan's murder and Ken's accident are related?"

"He's calling Ken's death a vehicular homicide. The search is still on for the other car, but it must be garaged somewhere. It hasn't surfaced."

Dozens of questions came to mind. "Does he know what Ken was doing on that road in the middle of New Year's Eve?"

"Mallory has been cooperating with the Department of Financial Services. Their regional LEO revealed that Ken was working with them as an informant."

Marla knew LEO stood for law enforcement officer. She sucked in a breath at this news. "So he was on the side of the good guys." A sense of vindication filled her. She should have had more faith in him.

"That's right. He came to them, when a client tipped him off to a possible fraud scheme. The field officer told him to sit tight, because Ken wasn't sure who in his office might be involved. Their investigation became more widespread than expected. They're not sure how far up this thing goes."

"Did they tell Mallory what type of fraud is involved?"

"No, they're keeping mum in that regard. The dead agent, Louise Harrison, was Ken's handler. I don't want to overlook other possibilities, so I'll be investigating everyone Ryan has been in contact with recently."

"I'm sure you'll be as thorough as always. How about the computer data from Ken's machines? Were the techs able to find anything significant?"

"Ken was doing research into claims histories, but that could have been part of his job. The insurance bureau will better understand that stuff."

"Why do they believe Ken was killed? Did the rat in his nest discover his role?"

"That's the presumption," Dalton stated in his wry tone.

"Then who made the phone call to him that night? And for what purpose?"

"We may never know. How did Louise end up in that warehouse? Had she been grabbed earlier and taken there? Or maybe she'd found something and called Ken to come meet her. The killer overheard their conversation, bound and shot her, and then ambushed Ken."

"Or the bad guy could have forced Louise to call Ken and plead for help," Marla suggested. "That would explain his rushed departure on New Year's Eve. The crook would have known that road was dark and bordered a canal. He planned a trap for Ken."

"And Tally was in the wrong place at the wrong time," Dalton concluded. "She wasn't meant to be there."

Marla fell silent, watching the cars come and go in the parking lot. A breeze rustled dead leaves on the ground, bringing an earthy scent to her nose.

"If this all falls on Ken, there's no purpose in my following Tally's trail." She hated to give up, but the evidence appeared solidly in Ken's court.

"On the other hand, what if it's a smoke screen?" Dalton replied, his voice terse in her ear.

"What do you mean?" She sat upright, pressing the phone tighter to her head as a supply truck rumbled past and belched fumes.

"Somebody knew Ken was home, lured him out, and targeted Tally in the house alone with Luke."

"You're saying Louise's abduction was part of a plan to get Ken out of the way? This person would need to have far-reaching strings to know about the fraud case. And why go after Tally? I haven't uncovered any secrets worth her death."

"Maybe you haven't dug deep enough. Keep at it. I have the insane feeling that everything is connected."

"All right. Are you coming home before we go to dinner tonight?" They were supposed to meet Anita and Reed. The older couple was leaving on a cruise the next day.

"Sure, I'll let Langley follow the paper trails. How about if I meet you at the restaurant?"

"Okay. See you there."

*****

Marla felt like she was part of a cavalcade with Brianna and Luke in tow. The three of them made it into the restaurant where the others waited. Anita enjoyed playing with the baby and feeding him his bottle as he sat in his portable seat. Dalton engaged her mother's boyfriend in conversation. That left Brianna texting friends on her cell phone and Marla ruminating over what she'd do for the rest of the weekend.

"Have you learned anything new about your friends? How is Tally progressing?" Anita asked once they'd received their entrees at the lively Italian place.

"The doctor says she's improving, but I don't see much difference," Marla replied. "She's stabilized for now, and that's a good thing. Plus, her bruises have faded."

"Did they give you a time frame for her waking up?"

"It could be any day now. She's moving around in bed, and her reflexes respond to stimulation. But her mental state remains to be seen. We won't know more until she's awake." Marla pushed the broccoli around on her plate. She couldn't wait for Tally to regain consciousness and yet dreaded the outcome.

"Have you learned any further details about the accident?" Reed asked in his deep baritone. He spoke with a cultured voice that suited a retired literature professor.

Marla's gaze flitted from his graying red hair to his green eyes the color of shamrock to his straight, narrow nose and trim beard. He cut a handsome figure in his camel jacket, pressed brown pants, and white dress shirt open at the collar. Anita looked petite in comparison, even with her layered white hair fluffed atop her head.

"We have a new case that relates to the vehicular homicide." Dalton stuffed a forkful of angel hair pasta into his mouth. In full detective mode, he gave them a rundown.

"So it appears someone in the insurance agency is a rotten egg," Reed stated, his eyes expressing keen interest.

"Yes, but whoever it is knows how to cover their tracks. I can't help feeling we're missing something important."

Anita wagged her finger at Dalton. "Give yourself a break from work. Insights come when we least expect them. Let's talk about Luke instead."

The conversation segued to baby care, Brianna's school projects, and other mundane topics.

"When are you visiting Tally again?" Dalton asked as they strolled to the parking lot after paying the tab. They'd treated the older couple for a change.

"I'll go on Sunday. I promised your folks that I'd bring Brianna for a visit. Kate said I could leave Luke there, too, so I could get some other things done. Will you come?"

He shook his head, the silver highlights in his hair gleaming under the street lamps. "I'm going to be busy working Ryan's case."

She swallowed her disappointment, being used to his irregular hours by now. So when Sunday rolled around, she dropped the kids off as promised at her in-laws and headed to the hospital on her own.

Inside the solemn institution, she took the elevator and

hurried past the ICU nursing station toward her friend's cubicle.

Except Tally wasn't there. The bed was empty, freshly made with clean white sheets.

Dear Lord. This can't be it.

Her limbs heavy, she reversed direction and accosted a nurse she recognized.

"Where's Tally? What's happened to her?" she asked in a raspy voice. Her heart pounded so hard that her temples throbbed.

"Oh, I'm sorry, luv. Didn't anyone notify you? Your friend has been moved to a neurovascular intermediate unit."

Marla's heart slowed from its rapid staccato. When she'd regained a sense of calm and her knees stopped shaking, she followed directions to Tally's new location. The room was semi-private, but its other bed remained unoccupied. Marla moved closer to the bedside. Tally lay with her eyelids at half-mast.

"That's what we call doll's eyes," the nurse said after Marla introduced herself to the staff. "Her eyes are the slightest bit open, but you'll see they are mostly fixed. She almost seems to widen them when we call her name. She's even yawned and moved her mouth. These show great progress."

Marla shared the news with Brianna on their way home. The teen sat in the back to keep Luke company.

"I nearly had a heart attack when I saw that empty bed." Marla still felt shaken over the incident.

"It's a good sign if they've moved her out of ICU. Maybe she'll just open her eyes one day and be her normal self," Brianna offered in a hopeful tone.

"I wish. Do you mind if we stop by her house? I'd like to make another sweep. We've been concentrating so hard on looking for clues to Ken's end of things that we've ignored Tally's role."

Brianna stayed with Luke while Marla dashed inside her friend's vacant home. First she collected the mail and piled it in the foyer. Then she searched through Tally's drawers looking for any items that might help reveal the killer's identity. Nothing turned up to interest her.

Was it foolish to suspect Tally of being involved in something more than stumbling into the wrong place at the wrong time? Ken's work site appeared to be case central, although Dalton agreed things didn't totally add up in that direction.

Marla sat on the family room sofa, debating what to do next. She seemed to be running into dead ends at every corner. Meanwhile, Brianna and Luke waited for her in the car. She pressed her hands against the cushion to push herself upright when her fingers encountered a hard ridge. What was that? Something rested beneath the padding.

She stood, yanked it out, and gave a yelp of delight. An iPad! Tally must have stuffed it in there for security before she left the house on New Year's Eve. She was always advising Marla to hide her valuables when expecting service people.

Feeling as though she'd struck gold, Marla put the iPad inside a plastic shopping bag from the laundry room along with the pile of mail she'd gathered. She couldn't wait to get home and turn on the device. Oh, wait. It might need charging. Where did Tally keep the wire?

As Marla searched for it, another thought struck. Did Tally bring her iPad to work with her, or did she own a laptop? If so, where was the notebook computer? She'd have to make another visit to Tally's boutique and ask the manager.

Brianna waited patiently in the car with the windows down. Occupied with her cell phone, she barely glanced up as Marla approached. Luke appeared to be fussy, his movements accompanied by whimpers. It had been a long day. Time to make him comfortable and lay him down for a nap in familiar surroundings.

"You found something," Brianna observed, her saucy

gaze meeting Marla's in the rearview mirror as they snapped on their seatbelts.

"Tally's iPad. It was hidden in the family room sofa."

"Let me see it." The teenager took the tablet from Marla's outstretched hand. "The battery is down. It needs to be charged."

"I found the wire in a kitchen drawer. It's in the bag along with their mail."

"You could have used my charger."

"It might be a different model. Listen, I should make another visit to Tally's shop. She might have a laptop there that she uses in the back office. I didn't even think to look at her computer when I visited the place."

"Why would that matter?"

Marla put the car in gear and backed out of the driveway. "It's possible Tally was meant to be the target that night. She would have been home alone with Luke once Ken went out."

"But what about the two dead people? They relate to Ken and the insurance fraud case."

"We're trying to figure out the connections. Your Dad is working on Ryan's case. I'm focusing my efforts on Tally, and I've been neglectful in that regard. Tally's manager told me about a couple of people I should interview." She steered down the street toward the development's exit.

"Who's that?" Brianna asked.

Marla waited until she hit the main road before replying. "The landlord and a former employee both have reasons to resent Tally."

"Hey, I have an idea. We should make one of those crime boards like Dad uses at work. We can do one of our own. Then you won't forget anyone."

"*We* won't be doing anything. You have to finish your homework, and Luke will need his bath and bottle." Nonetheless, it wasn't a bad idea. Maybe she'd find more connections by laying it all out in a diagram.

Now wasn't the time, though. Back home, Marla got occupied with baby care and meal preparation. In a spare moment, she plugged Tally's iPad into the kitchen wall socket. While the battery charged, she turned on the power button and swept her finger to activate the interface. A keypad popped up asking for a password. Damn. Marla tried every combination of dates that might be important to Tally, but none of them worked.

This might be a job for Dalton's cyber techs, but she hated to give the tablet to them. Maybe the dress shop manager had Tally's codes.

She let the thing charge while fixing a quick casserole with cut-up cooked chicken, broccoli florets, cooked orzo pasta, cannellini beans, and stewed tomatoes. By the time Dalton came home, the aroma of Italian spices filled the room.

After dinner, Marla broached his daughter's suggestion to set up an evidence board. Dalton's mouth curved in amusement at the idea.

"You do know we use a software program at work for this purpose now."

"Yes, but a visual isn't a bad idea. We're not sure how the victims connect to each other, if you include Tally in that category."

"I suppose we could do our own link chart. But we don't have a bulletin board that's large enough."

Brianna chimed in. "I have an extra poster left over from my science project. You could use sticky notes."

"That might work," Marla said with a proud grin. Brianna always came up with fresh ideas. "I have kitchen string that we can use to connect the dots. How about people photos? We have pictures of Tally and Ken, but no one else."

"Use a blank head with their name on it," Dalton suggested. "In real life, we don't get high-resolution photos of suspects like they do on television."

"All right, let's clear the dishes and get started."

When they had a basic chart assembled, Marla pointed out the loose ends from Tally's viewpoint. "Tomorrow, I'll visit the vegan restaurant and the chocolate factory where the tea ladies met, and then I can track down the landlord and former employee."

Dalton clamped a hand on her shoulder. "Good plan, but take care. We aren't clear about what type of nest we're disturbing."

Brianna pointed to the chart, her ponytail loosened and wisps of hair fanning her face. "Look, Ken is the one person who links to everyone else."

"True, but there's something we aren't seeing yet," her father replied.

Marla agreed. Maybe she'd learn what it was on Monday. She had the entire day free and could complete many of her tasks.

The next day, she pondered her to-do list after dropping Luke off at day care. Which item should she tackle first? She'd have to hit the vegan restaurant around lunchtime, since the place didn't open until eleven. It was too early for the chocolate factory as well.

That left Tally's landlord and her former staff member. Marla, sitting in her parked car, accessed her cell phone notes. She'd typed in their contact info from Tally's shop manager.

The landlord wasn't in when she called, so she left a voice mail stating her relationship to Tally and that she'd like to speak to him.

Fortunately, the former employee answered her ring. After identifying herself, Marla had to distance the phone from her ear at the loud voice that responded.

"I've got nothing to say about that bitch. She doesn't have a heart," Iris Caswell said. "I told her my situation, and she didn't believe me."

"Maybe you can tell me about it," Marla replied in a soothing tone. "Where do you live? I can meet you nearby."

"What's it to you?"

"As I mentioned, I'm Tally's best friend. She's in the hospital. I just need to ask you a few questions."

"Why, do you think I put her in there? What happened, did someone beat her up?"

"No, she was in a car accident. Her husband got killed."

Iris inhaled an audible breath. "Oh my God, I'm so sorry. I wouldn't wish that on anyone. How bad is Tally?"

"She's recovering from a head injury. I'm handling her affairs for now. Are you available to meet in person? I can explain more later."

"I have to go to work this morning. Tally might not have liked me, but my new boss appreciates my talents."

Marla realized she should offer an incentive. "I own a hair salon. If you'd like to come in at eight a.m. tomorrow, I'll give you a free wash and blow-out while we talk."

"That's nice of you, although I don't understand what you want from me."

They confirmed arrangements. After Marla disconnected, she sent a text to Robyn. Her receptionist would schedule Iris for an early appointment on Tuesday.

With those two leads on hold, Marla did other errands until lunchtime. Then she headed to the vegan restaurant that Tally's tea ladies had visited. Hopefully the menu would offer something appealing to her.

A long counter on one side had stools for seating while offering a view of the cook fixing meals. The dark-haired fellow looked like a guy off the street in rumpled clothes and a stained apron. Along the opposite wall were four lime green, high-top tables, so wide it would be difficult to hear the person across from you. The accompanying seats looked as bare and uncomfortable as the tabletop. Harsh florescent lighting shone down from overhead.

Figuring she had a better chance for conversation at the counter, Marla took a seat. Condiments vied for space with plastic-covered menus. As she scanned the ordinary meal choices, she wondered who would eat there. Maybe local business people came in for the sandwiches and salads.

A draft blew on her from an air-conditioning vent as she studied the menu. The waiter took her drink order for an iced green tea, which Marla noted cost three dollars. When it arrived, she took a sip of the pinkish fluid and wrinkled her nose.

"This is too sweet, and it's flavored. Don't you have regular brewed green tea that's unsweetened?"

"Nuh-uh. That's it," the waiter said. He was a scrawny fellow with tousled brown hair and a prominent Adam's apple. His youthful complexion, marred by various blemishes, reddened under her scrutiny.

"I'll have an iced coffee then, with cream on the side. And I would like to order the hummus sandwich with avocado and tomato." The meal was pricey at fourteen-fifty, especially for such a simple place with an unappealing ambiance.

She waited until the waiter delivered her food before getting to the point of her visit. "A friend told me about this place. Do you recognize her?" Marla showed the waiter and the cook a photo of Tally on her cell phone.

"Sorry, we get a lot of people in here," the waiter replied with a shake of his head.

"She would have come with a bunch of other ladies." Marla gave their descriptions. "Here, this might jog your memories." She handed each fellow a ten-dollar bill.

"Oh, I remember them," the cook declared, his face brightening. "They were a fussy bunch. You could tell this wasn't their regular kind of joint."

She gave him an appraising glance. Was he telling the truth, or making up a tale to please her? "Go on. Did you hear what they talked about?"

"The usual girlie stuff. Kids. Husbands. Movies and TV shows." He leered at her. "Undergarments that either suck it all in, or new styles that attract a man."

"How about my friend in particular? The woman in the picture?"

"She said her husband left her out of things to protect her, but she knew when something bothered him. A marriage should be a true partnership with no secrets. The other women laughed. They all kept secrets, one of the other blondes told her, and it should be that way. They argued over this point until the subject changed."

"Do you always listen to customers' conversations?"

The cook toed the floor and glanced away. "It's research. I like to write stories."

"You're a writer?" Marla gaped at him. From his street-wise accent, she wouldn't have guessed he had literary aspirations.

"I've been at it a while, but don't tell nobody."

Marla sipped her iced coffee. "One more question. Did you see the gang with anyone else? It was just the five of them?"

The waiter, loitering nearby, cut in. "I had to push two tables together. There were six gals altogether."

Marla knew other women must belong to the group besides the ones she'd met. "Did anything strike you as peculiar about their visit?"

The young man scratched his head. "I saw a dude outside hanging around the parking lot like he was waiting for someone. I thought he might come in here and ask for a meal, but he made a move on the redhead when she was leaving."

"Really? How so?"

"He approached her as she headed to her car. She said a few words to him then reached inside her bag and gave him a handout. I assume she felt sorry for the guy. He looked like yesterday's trash."

Oh, and you're an example of good grooming? "Were the other women still there, or had they already left?" This incident sounded eerily like the one Shannon had mentioned at the yoga studio. The redhead had to be Rissa.

"They'd gone. This chick took her time getting outta here."

"What did the man wear? Can you give me a better description?" Marla bit into her sandwich, licking her lips after swallowing. It was actually quite good. The hummus had a garlicky flavor.

"He wore a hoodie so I didn't see his face."

"Had you ever seen this person before, or has he been here since?"

"Nope. Maybe another shopkeeper chased him away. It's not good for business to have beggars hanging around."

"Do you have video surveillance outside? You know, cameras to monitor activity in the parking lot or the storefronts?"

"No, our landlord is too cheap."

Marla offered him a card. "If you see this guy again, can you give me a call? I'd appreciate it."

The kid shot her a suspicious glare. "Are you a cop?"

"No, I'm a hairdresser." She glanced at his stringy, unkempt hair. "Come into my salon, and I'll fix you up. I guarantee the girls will like you better."

Marla reviewed what she'd learned while driving to her next stop. Tally had mentioned Ken wanting to protect her. The women admitted they kept secrets from their husbands. And at each location where they'd met, Rissa gave a handout to a scruffy man in the parking lot.

Next on her list was the chocolate factory. This was the last place she meant to visit until the tea circle ladies met this Thursday. They planned to tour the Flagler Museum in West Palm Beach and partake of the high tea at the on-site café. Marla looked forward to the visit as she'd never been there.

It was easy to see how a day's outing would appeal to these women. Their adventures were different from mommy and me classes focused on babies. Not all the women were new mothers, but they were all looking for an escape. They visited interesting places. If she weren't employed full-time, she'd consider participating in the group on a regular basis. It didn't seem so strange to her anymore as to why Tally might have joined.

The jangle of her phone on the car's system jarred her. She pushed the answer button. "Hello?"

"This is Ollie Weaver. You called me?"

The name gelled in her brain. *That's Tally's landlord.* "Yes, I'm wondering if we can meet. I'm representing Tally Riggs, who's been in a serious auto accident."

"Are you her lawyer?"

"I'm her best friend. I've been using her power of attorney while she's disabled."

"Can you come to my office? I'll be available in a half-hour." He related his address.

"Sure, I'll be there shortly. See you then." Her heart racing with excitement, Marla pressed on the accelerator and sped down the road.

Chapter Fourteen

The landlord's office was located in a stand-alone building belonging to a large real estate firm. This wasn't any mom-and-pop owner who'd invested in a single shopping strip, Marla realized. That meant the landlord would be less sympathetic to Tally's plight. She might have to fight for her friend's right to stay in her current location.

Wishing she had armed herself with more knowledge about Ollie Weaver's company, she swung the door open and marched inside to a small reception area.

It didn't take long for the landlord to come out and greet her. He was a roly-poly individual with a balding hairline and a gruff but cheerful manner. His slate gray suit matched the color of his remaining hair.

"Mrs. Vail, it's good to meet you." He gave her a firm handshake. "Please come this way."

She followed him down a corridor lined with offices, impressed by the upscale furnishings. His space occupied the far corner with a view of landscaped greenery out a wide window.

"Tell me what's happening with Mrs. Riggs," he said, claiming a leather chair behind his polished wood desk.

She settled into an armchair facing him and laid her purse in her lap. Glad she'd worn comfortable black pants, she crossed her legs. "How much have you heard about Tally's condition?"

"She was injured in a car crash. Her husband didn't make it. What a horrible tragedy."

"The doctors expect her to recover. Meanwhile, I'm handling her business affairs. I understand you've asked her to move before the lease is up."

"We have an offer on the shopping center, but the buyer has plans that do not include our present tenants. Everyone else has agreed to our proposal except for your friend."

"Maybe it doesn't matter as much to the others there, but Tally's customers know her place and live in the area. Moving would be disruptive to her business."

"It'll be more disruptive if she doesn't go. I'm offering to cancel her remaining balance on the lease and to provide a relocation bonus. This buyer requires a response by the end of the month. Can you make a decision for Mrs. Riggs?"

"I won't go against her wishes. Is there an alternative that would work for both of you?" Maybe *he'd* caused the accident, anticipating that Tally's heirs would want to sell the business.

"I'm afraid not. She'll have to move anyway, when I follow the terms in the lease and initiate eviction proceedings. Then all the other tenants will be mad at her for making them lose this opportunity."

"The home goods store doesn't have to move."

"They're a free-standing building and an anchor for the shopping center."

Marla noted the stubborn tilt to his chin. He wasn't going to budge on the issue. "What does the buyer intend to do?"

"Seamus Cross plans to make it into a multi-use site with rental apartments, retail, and dining. Here's his proposed site plan." He grabbed a blueprint and showed Marla the improvements.

"Why can't Tally rent one of those spaces? Won't the buyer need tenants?"

"He has a different clientele in mind and has already

begun offering leases. The demolition and construction is expected to take two years after the sale and all approvals."

Marla had to admit the plan would modernize the location and potentially bring in new customers. Even if Tally wanted to rent a space in the remodeled property, she'd have to wait too long to reopen. Plus, the new owner might not even want her business.

It was a tough call and one Marla wasn't prepared to make.

"What happens if she doesn't comply? I'm not ready to make a decision for her, and Tally might be unable to give a response by your deadline."

Mr. Weaver folded his hands on his desk. "Then I suggest you read the early termination clause in the lease. If she doesn't accept my offer by January thirty-first, I'll send her an official notice under the contract terms. She won't be liable for the remainder of the money, but she'll lose my bonus offer."

"When do people have to vacate the premises?"

"March fifteenth is the deadline. After that, we'll file for eviction." His lips curved in a sly smile. "If you're willing to cooperate, I can offer a finder's fee. Believe me, it'll save your friend a ton of hassle. She doesn't need to deal with these issues while she's recovering. Make it easy for her."

Marla's spine stiffened. "Are you offering me a bribe?"

He waved a hand in an imperious gesture. "Certainly not. I'm merely suggesting you deserve compensation for your time. It would be a wise decision. Think of the trouble you'd be saving your friend when she's dealing with the recovery process along with a personal loss."

"What are we supposed to do with her stock if we close the shop but don't have anywhere to go?" Marla could envision all the problems ahead.

"Sell it to another store owner? Put it in storage? Although if it's seasonal items, that wouldn't be smart. You'll figure it out. Do we have a deal?" He grinned, his eyes gleaming with avarice.

"I'll think about it. You've made your point. I'd like time to examine the options."

He rose and moved toward the door. "Don't take too long. I'll need a positive decision by the end of the month."

Marla left, unhappy that nothing was resolved. She really needed Tally to wake up. But even if her friend had a miraculous recovery, would she be capable of moving her place of business that quickly? Had she already researched other locations?

Marla had meant to revisit the boutique anyway to search their computer. Now it became imperative that she speak to the manager again. She couldn't solve Tally's dilemma, but maybe she'd get fresh insight into the alternatives.

Fortunately, Stacy was present when Marla walked in the door to the dress shop. Spying the auburn-haired manager sorting silk scarves on a display counter, Marla felt an odd jolt of recognition. She'd been assuming Rissa was the redhead in the tea circle who'd met the vagrant outside, but what if it was another woman? She should obtain a photo of Rissa to show around.

No, this line of thought was absurd. Stacy wasn't free to leave work on a weekday. And Rissa did appear to be the ringleader of the group.

"Hey, Marla, what's up?" Stacy's eyes crinkled in an expression of concern. "Oh, dear. Is Tally okay? You're not here with bad news, are you?" She let go of the scarves and wrung her hands together. A tape measure hung around her neck. She wore a short sweater dress with leggings, silver bangle bracelets, and matching hoop earrings.

"Tally is doing better. She's in an intermediate unit now. Her reflexes are good, and she appears to be more responsive. We're hoping she'll open her eyes soon."

Stacy gave a visible sigh of relief. "Thank goodness. And Luke is all right?"

"Yes, thanks for asking. By the way, I spoke to the landlord. Mr. Weaver says Tally has until the end of this month to make a decision on relocating, or he'll initiate early termination proceedings. Does she keep a computer in the back office? I'd like to look over the contract terms. Or did Tally bring in a laptop from home each day?"

"We have a computer in the back. Come this way."

Marla followed her to the rear office. Soft jazz music played in the background, while a pleasing citrus scent permeated the air. She paused at the inner sanctum, observing the order forms scattered across a broad workspace. A printer sat on a separate table, while an older model desktop unit rested under the desk.

"I haven't bothered to turn it on." The manager indicated the blank monitor screen. "But now that you're here, perhaps you can help me pay for some of our outstanding accounts. I should have thought to ask during your last visit."

"Do you have Tally's passwords?"

Stacy pointed to the file cabinet. "She keeps a copy in there. It's always locked."

That's the second place a thief would look, after the cash register. "Where's the key?" Marla asked in a dry tone.

"In the desk." Stacy's face flushed. "Not very secure, is it? But we have an alarm system. Tally probably figured things were safe. A robber would go after the cash, not the computer codes."

While Stacy hunted for the list, Marla turned on the unit and flexed her fingers. A few minutes later, she had the codes in her hand and had gained access to the desktop screen.

Financial spreadsheets, invoices, and copies of bank statements indicated things were balanced, so the shop wasn't short any money. An employee who'd been embezzling had been at the back of Marla's mind, but now she discarded that possibility.

She found records of Tally's business bank accounts and

Nancy J. Cohen

noted the numbers on a spare sheet of paper. These hadn't shown up at the bank when she'd used her power of attorney. Tally must keep them separate from her personal accounts.

My bad. I should have thought of this earlier. Now she'd have to make a stop there to speak to a bank officer again before she could pay bills for the shop.

Her glance roamed to a framed photo of Luke and Ken on the desk, a miniature clock made in England, and a Brighton pen set. A separate cherry wood box held another collection of pens, including a couple Marla had given Tally as gifts. Moisture seeped into her eyes. Her friend should be here. It wasn't right for Tally to be absent.

She blinked, chasing away her swell of emotion and focusing on the computer. A search through the files revealed a pdf copy of the lease. An early termination clause existed as Mr. Weaver had said. All either party had to do was give thirty days written notice.

Marla didn't see any way around it. Tally wouldn't have a choice. Even if the buyer agreed to rent her a space, the rates were likely to be higher and construction would take years. Resistance was futile.

She should copy these files before telling Dalton about the computer. He might want to confiscate it as evidence. While Stacy waited on a customer up front, Marla retrieved the thumb drive she kept in her purse with her own backup files. Would there be room for these?

She initiated a copy sequence, minimized the window, and opened the Internet browser. The code for Tally's email was on the printed list from the locked file drawer. Marla would take the paper with her, as it wasn't safe to leave here. Didn't Tally realize Stacy knew where she kept the codes? Or did she trust her manager more than her husband?

Unfortunately, the list didn't include the password for the iPad. She'd have to let Dalton's team work on that device.

Huh, what was in this folder labeled *Iris* among the saved

emails? Wasn't that the name of the employee Tally had fired? Marla opened it and found a series of complaints from Iris alleging Tally's unfair treatment of her. Iris claimed she hadn't been lying to customers about having a sick relative, and they'd been generous to offer support. Tally had no right to dismiss her because she spoke honestly to clients.

My sister Edie told me how you contacted her, Iris wrote in one recent missive. *You should have seen I was telling the truth. Edie needs help to pay her medical bills and to care for our ailing mother. Now things will be worse for her, thanks to you.*

And later: *I can't believe you and Edie are friends now. I used to work with you. How can you stab me in the back like this? I was simply trying to help my sister. Don't think that you can take my place as her friend. I'll see that you pay for your betrayal.*

Oh, my. The former employee had threatened Tally. Had she carried out her intentions?

Wait, Tally was now friends with the sister? Edie Herman was a member of the tea ladies circle. Maybe that was how Tally had gotten involved. She'd contacted Edie to verify Iris's story, and Edie recruited her for the group.

Was this their mode of operation? Did Edie truly have an illness and an elderly mother, or did they sucker lonely women into joining them and donating money?

Tally wouldn't fall for such a scheme, would she? Or maybe she'd found Edie's tale of woe to be true and had joined her group out of guilt.

Further research on the tea ladies climbed a notch on Marla's priority list. So did interviewing Iris to see if she'd carried out her threats.

Marla returned her attention to Tally's inbox. Going through all that email would take hours. Nothing else popped out at her, so she went to the browser history.

Halfway through the dropdown list, she stopped. Tally had done a search on someone named Liam Kelton. She followed the links. The man was director of the insurance fraud division in the state's Department of Financial Services.

Hadn't Dalton mentioned his name earlier?

Perhaps Kelton filled the role of higher-up in the ongoing fraud investigation. Why else would Tally be researching him? Was this when she'd learned Ken worked for their department as an informant? Marla scanned a couple of articles profiling the guy. He appeared to be aiming for the Chief Financial Officer seat when the current occupant won the governorship.

After the files finished copying, she removed her thumb drive and shut everything down. Now that she had Tally's codes, she could access her email from home.

A pile of unopened envelopes sat on a counter where the manager must have placed them. Marla hadn't noticed any payments due among Tally's emails, but some of the invoices might arrive via regular mail. She scooped up the batch and reentered the shop proper.

"I'll take this stack home with me," she told Stacy, who'd just finished ringing up a sale at the cash register. "I haven't found any unpaid bills yet, but I might have missed something."

"That would be great, thanks. I don't know what I'd do without your help." Stacy pursed her lips. "Did you find a copy of the lease in Tally's files?"

"Yes, and there is an early termination clause as the landlord said. Would Tally want to stay here if she's the last holdout? The other tenants would be resentful, and the sale is likely to take place regardless. So where could she move that isn't too far from your customer base?"

"Maybe it's better if we close down," Stacy said in a disconsolate voice. "Tally has her child to raise when she recovers. She might decide to stay home with Luke."

"She'll have various options to consider when the time comes. Meanwhile, perhaps you can come up with a plan to dispose of this stock if necessary."

On the way out, Marla realized she was prepared to take charge as though this place were her own. If Tally didn't wake up soon, the landlord's ultimatum would have to be met. Possibly, Tally had already begun searching for a new site. But Marla hadn't found anything in this regard on the computer or in Tally's notes. Nor had Tally mentioned this business matter to Marla. How many more secrets had she kept?

Marla glanced at her watch. It wasn't time to get Luke yet. She could still make it to the chocolate factory, the final site on her list where the tea circle ladies had met.

Twenty minutes later, she arrived at the place. It was located on a road lined with plant nurseries and a fruit farm offering u-pick strawberries. Marla parked in front of an A-frame building. With its fanciful trim, it reminded her of a cross between a gingerbread house and a Swiss chalet. Monday afternoons must be a slow period, judging from the few vehicles in the lot. Good, she'd have the shopkeeper's attention.

Inside, the smell of chocolate wafted into her nose. Display cases offered an array of artistic candies that tempted her taste buds. She wandered over to the counter, her mouth watering at the aroma in the air. Each individual piece of chocolate was like a miniature work of art. Labels described the fillings. On a back wall, wrappers from chocolate bars around the world attested to the sweet's popularity.

"Can I help you?" said the sales clerk with a warm smile. She wore her dark hair in a ponytail and a white lab coat over her street clothes.

"I see you have a café." Marla pointed to a collection of round tables and chairs at the opposite end. "A friend of mine visited here a few weeks ago along with some other ladies. I have questions to ask about them."

"Teri is our tour leader. She'd be the person you want. She's about to take the next group out, however. Would you care to buy a ticket?"

"Sure, why not?" *Like, do I have a choice?*

Ten dollars later, Marla stood in an anteroom with several other guests. Plaques on the walls described how chocolate was discovered. Early South American natives would harvest cacao beans and grind them with water and spices to create a beverage. Spanish conquerors brought the plants home to Spain, where the drink became a treat enjoyed by royalty. From there, it made its way to France. At some point, somebody added sugar to the mix. Cacao eventually entered the United States, where Hershey noticed it. The rest, as they say, is history.

"You don't want to eat mass-produced chocolate," said a perky blonde wearing a white lab coat and a name tag identifying her as Teri the chocolatier. "We'll show you how American craft chocolate is made. Small batch chocolate-making gives us control over the flavor, quality, and ingredients. You'll find our chocolate isn't tainted by unhealthy additives or products like corn syrup. We start by using the best ingredients. The cocoa beans must be perfect. Not only do the origins and genetics matter, but also how the beans are fermented and dried. We get our beans from fair-trade growers in Ecuador."

Teri explained the refinement process while pointing out various pieces of equipment in her artisan factory. "Here's where we temper the chocolate before pouring it into molds. Then we tap the molds like this to get the bubbles out. We also do custom designs by hand. Come, let's give you some samples."

In another room, guests helped themselves to chocolate bits in various dishes. The tastes ranged from bitter to sweet. Finally, they exited through a door to the café.

"I'll be happy to answer questions while you sip a cup of hot chocolate or try some of our specialty desserts," Teri said, her tone energetic even though she must have given this same speech hundreds of times. "We do parties here if you want to reserve the café. We'll even teach a chocolate-making class for an additional fee."

At the café, the scent of chocolate mixed with hints of vanilla and cinnamon. Marla peered at the selections inside a glass case, wavering between the chocolate lava cake and the chocolate bombe filled with mousse. It had been a while since lunch, but she resisted temptation for the sake of her waistline and settled for an iced mocha drink instead.

"Teri, I'm wondering if you remember my friend who came in here a while back." Marla drew their tour guide off to one side and accessed Tally's photo on her cell phone. "Tally would have come in with several other ladies."

Teri examined the picture. "Sure, I remember her. She was a striking woman, tall with a lively presence. Her group made a reservation for seven people but only six showed up."

"Did Tally seem happy among them?"

"They all had a good time. Why do you ask?"

"She's been in an accident, and I'm trying to fill in the blanks of her movements in the past few weeks. Did you overhear anything that might seem unusual?"

"Huh. I didn't like how the thin lady with straight black hair kept saying chocolate was bad for you."

The chocolatier must mean Deanne, the health advocate among the group. "I thought dark chocolate was supposed to have health benefits," Marla replied.

Teri gave a fervent nod. "Cocoa contains flavonoids that are powerful antioxidants. These prevent cellular damage due to free radicals and help to lower your risk for heart disease. Flavonoids also improve blood flow to your brain and cause your body to release endorphins. Dark chocolate has a higher content than milk chocolate. You'll want to avoid cocoa powder that has undergone Dutch processing. It's been treated with alkali agents that reduce the flavonoid value."

"How about caffeine? Like, if I eat too much chocolate, won't it make my heart race?"

"Cocoa contains some caffeine, but it also has theobromine. Both of these compounds can increase your heart rate. Again, dark chocolate has a higher concentration than milk chocolate. And these chemicals are usually not present in white chocolate."

Marla thought of her pets back home. She'd heard cautionary tales about canines and sweets. "Why is chocolate so dangerous to dogs?"

"They metabolize theobromine more slowly. Dogs can get theobromine poisoning from even a small amount of milk chocolate. Dark chocolate is even more toxic to them. It can lead to seizures and death. The same risk is reported for cats, but they're less likely to eat anything sweet."

"When my friends were here, did they try your desserts?" Marla pointed to the other tour guests sitting at various tables and indulging in treats.

Teri chuckled. "Yes, they made an afternoon of it and seemed to enjoy their visit. Well, two of them did appear to be arguing."

"Which two? Can you describe them?"

"One had a round face and was on the chubby side. The other one was taller with highlighted brown hair and a tattoo on her shoulder. She wore a tube top and a short skirt. Her necklaces must have weighted down her neck."

The second woman didn't sound familiar, but the chubby lady could be Edie. "What else did you notice?"

"Your tall blonde and I got into a discussion on recipes. She's a chocolate fan, did you know? One of her favorite recipes was handed down by her mother. It's for a chocolate zucchini cake."

"I'll bet that's good, and at least it's a trifle healthy."

"Tally has a recipe for an English trifle, too. She's lucky to have inherited her mother's collection. They both shared a sweet tooth."

"Tally and I have often exchanged recipes, but I'm not into desserts so much. She likes vintage cookbooks, but I prefer regional ones from places I visit. They make good souvenirs."

"Sometimes you can discover hidden treasures in those old recipe books. Dollar bills, pressed flowers, handwritten notes. Tally admitted she'd found a love letter inside one of her mother's cookbooks. It was addressed to her mom and predated her marriage."

"Oh?" This was news. Tally hadn't mentioned anything to Marla about it, but that seemed to be the norm for their relationship lately. "Did she say any more on the subject?"

"Yes, it led her to an unexpected, and unnerving, discovery."

"Like what?"

"Sorry, you'll have to ask your friend for more details. Now, please excuse me. I need to tend to another guest who's been waiting."

"Hold on; I have one more question. After everyone left, did Rissa hang out in the parking lot? She's the redhead in the group."

Teri's eyebrows lifted. "Well, now that you mention it, I did see something odd. A homeless guy wandered over to her, and she was kind enough to give him some money."

"Did you actually see cash exchange hands?"

"No, I just assumed—"

"Can you describe this fellow? Had you seen him around here before?"

"I'd have called the cops if I had. We don't allow panhandlers on the premises. This person wore a hoodie, so I didn't get a good look at him. After their encounter, the lady got into her car and the man went away. I've never seen him again."

Teri scurried off before Marla could ask more. She lingered by the sales counter until the shopkeeper came over. Tempted by the glistening sweets in the display case, she bought a selection of dark chocolate-covered marzipan, pistachio ginger bark that Dalton might like, and chocolate-covered orange peels. Maybe she'd get some health benefits from her purchase. On the way out, she stuffed a catalog into her shopping bag. Custom-made pieces could be cute for holiday business gifts.

So what had she learned? Marla reviewed their conversation as she walked outside to her car. Rissa had encountered a vagrant in the parking lot. Their meet-up sounded similar to the other occasions.

Edie had argued with another tea circle lady whom Marla hadn't met yet.

Tally had discovered an old letter belonging to her mother in one of her cookbooks. Why would this particular find have rattled her friend? So her mom had an admirer. The woman had probably dated lots of guys before she'd met Tally's father.

Curious to learn more, Marla determined to make another visit to her friend's house to look for this letter.

She crossed the pavement toward her Camry, so deep in thought that she didn't pay attention to her surroundings. A sudden roar made her lift her head.

She gasped as a car barreled straight toward her.

Chapter Fifteen

Marla leapt to the side, crashed against a parked sedan, and slid to the asphalt. With a squeal of tires, the car sped away. She glimpsed a flash of silver and the back end of an SUV.

Shaking from head to foot, she rolled to her knees and managed to stand. It wouldn't be smart to wait around in case the driver returned to make another pass at her. She had no doubt this had been a deliberate attempt to injure her, or worse.

She brushed off her pants, grabbed her purse from the ground, and hobbled to her car.

Safely locked inside, she examined herself for damage. Her wrists throbbed, having taken the brunt of impact. They didn't appear to be broken, thank goodness. And her hip felt bruised but nothing more. She'd been lucky.

She sat immobile, her heart racing like a squirrel on steroids. *Get a grip, Marla. You're okay. This proves you're on the right track if you've riled someone enough to take a potshot at you.*

She was lucky it hadn't been a shot for real. Both Louise and Ryan had been killed by a bullet. She'd lost her sense of caution. This brought it back home to her.

Her fingers trembling, she called Dalton on her cell phone. "Someone tried to run me down in a parking lot," she told him, her voice weak. "They drove a silver SUV."

"Where are you?"

"I'm outside the chocolate factory where Tally's group of

friends had met. I must have been tailed from one of my earlier stops."

"Are you okay?" he asked in his detective's tone.

"Yes, I'm all right. I'll pick Luke up early and go home. I've finished most of what I had to do today." She'd meant to make another visit to Tally's house to search through her cookbooks, but it would have to wait for another time.

"Do you need me to come and get you?"

"No, I can drive. And before you ask, I didn't get a plate number."

"Your well-being is more important. I want you off the case. It's getting too dangerous."

"Are you serious? We need to talk about who I might have spooked."

"We'll compare notes later. Send me a text when you get home. And watch your back."

She hung up, tucked the cell inside her handbag, and turned on the ignition. Dalton was right. They could discuss things that evening. For now, safety took precedence.

Her mind calmed after she'd retrieved Luke. His baby smell permeated the car, and he made cooing noises from the back seat as they drove into her neighborhood. Nobody appeared to be following her, but she'd taken a circuitous route anyway. At the day care center, she'd reiterated her instructions that absolutely no one was to get Luke except her and Dalton, not even their mothers.

A fierce protective instinct swarmed her as she changed his diaper inside the house. His cute little face gazed up at her, melting her heart and bringing reassurance she hadn't known she'd needed. She bent to kiss his forehead, savoring his soft flesh and powdery scent. As she straightened, he fixed his innocent blue eyes on her with a smile that made her blink away a swell of moisture.

"Hey, little guy, we'll do everything in our power to keep you safe and loved."

She and Dalton exchanged news at dinner that night. Brianna sat across from them, an apt expression on her young face. It pained Marla to think the teen would be off to college in a few years. How fast children grew up.

"I'll have to make another visit to Tally's house to look through her cookbooks," she concluded. "I can't imagine what the letter might say that upset her."

"The lady in the shop told you it was a love letter addressed to Tally's mother?" Dalton's forehead creased in thought.

"Yes, but why should this matter now?"

"Good question. Guess you'll have to read the message to see what's so important."

"I can run over there on my way to work tomorrow." She told him about her other discoveries. "Iris, the fired employee, turns out to be Edie's sister. I gather this is how Tally learned about the tea circle. Edie must have mentioned it to her."

"Who is the Liam fellow that Tally was researching on her work computer?" Brianna cut in, sticking a forkful of shrimp brown rice into her mouth.

Marla redirected her attention to the teen. "Liam Kelton is head of the state's Insurance Fraud Division. He could be involved in the investigation affecting Ken, although you'd think the local bureau would be in charge. Liam has political aspirations, from what I've read online. He's vying for the CFO's seat when there's a vacancy."

"I learned something new today, too." Dalton took a swallow of water from his glass. "Sergeant Mallory got a report on that oily residue found at both crime scenes. It contains red dye and may have come from the killer's shoes. He's asked for further analysis."

"That's weird." Marla frowned as she remembered something else. "Listen to this. The people at all three stops from the tea circle mentioned some guy Rissa encountered in the parking lot. His description is the same at each place. He

Nancy J. Cohen

looks like a homeless person in a hoodie. Each time, Rissa appears to give him a handout."

Dalton's gaze sharpened. "Did your witnesses see what exchanged hands?"

"No, but the folks who told me about it assumed Rissa had offered cash."

"And she did this willingly?"

"Nobody said anything about a holdup or a scuffle."

"Maybe she's being blackmailed, and these were payoffs. Have you any idea what prompted someone to come after *you* in the parking lot?"

Marla shrugged. "It could be related to anything—the tea ladies, Ken's investigation, Tally's research. Oh, I checked the terms of her lease. The landlord does have the right to early termination. What should I do? He wants her decision by the end of this month."

"Does she have a choice?" Brianna asked, her ponytail swinging when she tilted her head.

"Not really. If it were me, I'd relocate and take the bonus money."

"You might have to make that decision for her," Dalton said in a somber tone.

"Tally has to wake up soon. I'd hate to pre-empt a move that goes against her wishes."

"Yes, but right now, you have POA. And that means you may have to decide the outcome before the landlord evicts her."

"Maybe a miracle will happen before then." Marla could only pray that would be the case.

*****

Tuesday morning, Marla stopped by Tally's house on her way to the day care center. She didn't believe in miracles, but rather in arming yourself with knowledge. That way, you could influence change. She hoped to find the letter written to Tally's mother by a former boyfriend. Perhaps it would hold some clues to current events.

"Luke, are you sensing you're home?" she asked the little guy, bending over his stroller where she'd parked it in Tally's kitchen. She tickled his tiny fingers. He squealed in response, giving her a smile that softened her heart. A strong yearning to cuddle him all day gripped her.

She stood back, fearful of losing focus. Luke had the ability to drag her attention away from everything else. Caring for a baby could do that to you.

Would Tally really be broken up if she had to relocate her shop? Now that Marla had found a reliable day care center, maybe she'd want to move her store closer to that end of town.

But never mind that now. Aside from the few cookbooks Tally kept in the pantry, she'd shelved the rest of her collection in the family room. Marla walked over and scanned the volumes with a groan. Tally had dozens of them arranged haphazardly.

If a letter was stuck between the pages somewhere, it might fall out when Marla shook the book. So she took them out one-by-one, turned the books upside-down, and flitted through the pages.

She hit pay dirt when she shook a worn Betty Crocker cookbook. A folded paper with browned edges fluttered to the floor. Marla replaced the recipe book in its place after searching for an inscription and finding none. She grabbed the note with eager fingers and smoothed it out on the kitchen table. The message contained a handwritten scrawl.

To my dearest Lilly,

Knowing how much you like to cook, I thought this would please you as a parting gift. I'm glad you understand that while I have deep feelings for you, relationships have no place in my life at present. You'll always have a fond spot in my heart regardless of where the future takes us.

Love and kisses, Liam

Marla's heart skipped a beat. Liam? As in, Liam Kelton? Was it possible Tally had a connection to this man beyond Ken's insurance fraud case?

Teri had said the letter led Tally to believe something unnerving. Marla checked the date. It was the year before her friend had been born. When had Tally's parents married? And wasn't her father named Rubin?

Marla didn't think a continued search would be fruitful. This had to be the letter that upset Tally. Liam worked for the state. That meant he lived in Tallahassee, didn't it? Or was that merely his governmental residence? Could he own a home elsewhere, like Sunny Grove? Perhaps the discovery of this letter had compelled Tally to visit that town.

First chance she got, she'd dig further into Liam's background. Meanwhile, other items took priority.

She dropped Luke off at day care before heading to the salon. There she prepared for her early morning appointment with Iris Caswell. Tally's former employee was due to arrive for the free services Marla had promised. Marla itched to question her about Tally's affairs.

Iris sauntered in on a pair of heels that must have added three inches to her height. She had highlighted brown hair that needed a trim and a tattoo on her upper arm. A set of beads hung around her neck. They drew attention to her ample bosom under a tube top that she wore along with a pair of distressed jeans.

Hmm, hadn't Teri at the chocolate factory mentioned a woman with Iris's description as joining the tea circle that day? And this woman had been seen arguing with Edie?

Marla introduced herself and made suggestions for Iris's

unruly hair, including a trim for her split ends. Then she shampooed the woman herself. They were alone in the salon since the place hadn't officially opened yet. The receptionist would be in at nine.

She sat Iris at her station and towel-dried her hair. "So tell me about your relationship with Tally," she began in a noncommittal tone.

Iris scowled at her. "That witch fired me. What else do you want to know?"

"How about starting with the truth?" Marla sniffed in the strawberry scent from the shampoo she'd used as she dropped the damp towel on a counter and picked up a comb.

"Tally didn't pay enough for me to make ends meet. When I told customers about my problems at home, they felt sorry for me and offered a gratuity for my service. Tally got mad and said I was telling lies to solicit money."

"If you weren't earning enough there, why didn't you quit and find another job?"

"Like what, cleaning rich folks' houses? I don't have any skills."

"Why not acquire a wealthy husband like your sister, Edie? How can she have problems paying for medical care?"

Iris gave her a startled glance. "Edie has more troubles than you can imagine. She's in a worse place than I am. I've tried to help her."

"I've met her at the tea circle. Is Edie the one who recruited Tally into the group?"

"Tally was getting restless staying home with the baby, so Edie told her about this social network she'd joined."

"What does Edie get out of the meet-ups?"

"It gives her an excuse to escape from the house. With her husband in the slammer, she has to take care of our ninety-year old mother and her teenage son. She can't work, not with her health issues. And I don't have room for mom in my tiny apartment."

Nancy J. Cohen

"Did you tell customers at the dress boutique about these problems and how you wished you could help your sister?"

"So what if I did?"

"I could understand your resentment if you felt your compensation was inadequate, but it's bad for business to hit on customers. Tally was right to object."

"She should have given me a raise. I worked hard and took over some of the slack when she got pregnant."

"Were you resentful enough to want to get even?" Marla selected a pair of shears. She lifted a section of Iris's hair with the comb and cut it at an angle, aware that once the blow-dryer started, conversation would be difficult.

Iris glared at her in the mirror. "Hey, I don't like Tally, but I wouldn't hurt her."

"Do you know anyone who would?"

"Where are you going with this, Marla?"

"Their car crash wasn't an accident. The police found evidence that another car was involved. Somebody caused Ken to lose control of his vehicle."

"Heck, don't look at me."

The bell over the front door jangled as Robyn arrived fifteen minutes early. Marla gave their receptionist a brief wave and got back to work. The air-conditioning kicked in, sending a cool blast her way. Somebody had put it down too low, making her shiver in the draft. Or maybe it was the gloomy clouds outside bringing another cold front that made her feel chilled.

Marla asked what kind of car Iris drove. It wasn't a match for the vehicle at the accident scene, nor was it a silver SUV like the one that had nearly run her down.

"Did Tally mention anything about insurance fraud to you?" she asked the other woman, while snipping her hair with skilled movements.

"Not while I worked in the dress shop. She worried about Ken, though. He'd been keeping long hours at work."

206

"Tally suspected he might be having an affair, but that didn't turn out to be the case. How about someone named Liam? Did you ever hear his name?"

That question produced a frown on Iris's face. "I did overhear her ranting on the phone in the back room one day. It was right before she made a sudden trip to Sunny Grove. I remember what she said because it was odd: *He'll either help us, or he'll wish he had done the right thing all those years ago.*"

Marla cut too much off one strand. Oops. Now she'd have to even things out on the other side. She hastened to complete her task, eager to research Liam Kelton again on the computer. He had to be the reason why Tally had gone to Sunny Grove. Had her primary purpose been to seek help with Ken's insurance fraud problem, or had the visit been related to Lilly's letter? If Marla had to guess, she'd choose the latter.

One thing was certain. Marla had to clear her schedule for a trip to Central Florida.

She didn't garner any fresh information from Iris. Pleased with how the woman's hair turned out, she wished her good fortune at her new job. At least Iris would look more professional when she went to work, although her abrasive manner wouldn't help her cause.

Marla checked in with their receptionist before dashing over to Bagel Busters to collect their daily order. Arnie Hartman beamed when he saw her walk through the door. The proprietor wore his customary apron over jeans and a tee-shirt. He stepped out from behind the cash register to give her a quick embrace. Business was already booming with the deli's regulars, mostly senior citizens who awoke early.

"Hey, Marla. How come you're picking up the order today?"

"I wanted to see you, why else? Oy vey, Arnie, you wouldn't believe my life these days."

"Oh yes, I would. I imagine it's as hectic as ever. How is Tally doing?"

"Her responses are improving. That's a good sign."

"Glad to hear it. Can you sit a minute?" He signaled to Ruth, a waitress, to man the cashier station.

Marla checked her watch. "My nine-fifteen will be in soon. I need to get back, but I wanted to fill you in on what's been happening."

"So you'd like for me to keep an eye on the parking lot in case that hooded vagrant shows up in our area," Arnie said once she'd finished her tale. His dark eyes took her in, as though assessing the toll recent events had taken on her. He'd been a dear friend for years.

"That's right. Let me know if you see the guy, or if you spot a silver SUV like the one that nearly hit me."

"Did you get the make or model?"

"No, sorry. It all happened too fast."

"Good luck, then. This parking lot is filled with silver SUVs. Do you think the hooded person and the driver who nearly hit you are one and the same?"

Startled, she stared at him. "I suppose it's possible. The person Rissa met each time was obviously familiar with the stops made by her group."

"What about the other car from the accident? Was that an SUV?"

"No, it's a sedan. Besides, that vehicle has probably been repainted by now and any damage repaired."

"I'd be more concerned about the guy who nearly hit you. How did he know where to go? Were you followed from somewhere else? Or was he watching that particular place, waiting for you to show up there?"

"If I knew those answers, I could put the pieces of the puzzle together. Please keep an eye out for trouble, that's all I'm asking."

"Consider it done, doll."

Ruth brought over her platter of bagels and cream cheese for the day. Marla thanked her, paid the bill, and left. Back at the salon, she got busy with clients and forgot about her concerns until later, when she had a spare moment. Then she took over Robyn's post at the front desk computer.

A search for Liam Kelton brought up a number of news interviews and articles relating to his position but offered nothing about his personal life. Next, she put his name plus Sunny Grove into the search window. He'd attended some charity functions there, but again, she didn't find much on him personally.

How could she dig deeper into his background? Surely there had to be a connection, but time ran out when her next customer walked in.

"Robyn, I'm trying to look up someone who lives in Sunny Grove, but I'm not having any success."

The receptionist regarded her from behind a pair of black-framed eyeglasses. "Would you like me to have a go at it?"

"That would be great, thanks. Try querying the Chamber of Commerce. You'd think they would be proud if a state politician had a home there. His name is Liam Kelton."

"I'll get on it right away."

Marla left the matter in the woman's capable hands, sent her client to get shampooed, and headed back to her station. On the way, her cell phone buzzed from inside her pants pocket. She pulled it out and squinted at the caller ID. What did Rissa Kyle want?

"Hey, Rissa, how's it going?" she asked the leader of the tea ladies circle.

"Not well, I'm afraid. Too many of our members can't make the meeting this week, so we have to cancel. However, I wanted to invite you to a party at my house seven o'clock on Friday night. It's women only, so come alone unless you want to bring a female friend."

"Thanks, it sounds like fun." Marla was curious to see where the socialite lived.

Excited by the chance to learn more about the group's ringleader, she had a hard time returning her focus to work.

But once she started on her client, the rest of the day passed in a blur. So did Wednesday. Marla didn't have time to think about anything else except her daily routine.

Late on Thursday morning, she arrived at the salon with news trembling on her tongue. She'd been to see the gynecologist and had decided to go off the pill. Now that she was married, she wasn't comfortable with continued hormones surging through her body. She still grappled with how this decision might impact her future. Her self-doubts about being a mother had been allayed by caring for Luke, but being responsible for her own children was another issue. Was she truly ready for that step?

She had to tell somebody, so she confided in Nicole when they both had a spare moment between customers. The other stylist's eyes widened at Marla's revelation.

"No way, girlfriend. You're going *au-naturel*? There are other means, you know."

"Yes, but this is something I want to do. I think." She leaned against the counter at her station, where Nicole stood by. They spoke in soft tones so no one could overhear.

"It's baby Luke, isn't it? He did this to you."

"He's had an influence, I'll admit. I've seen that I can manage a family and a career."

"And you've discovered you can be a wonderful mother," Nicole surmised with a wise nod. She picked a comb off the counter and flicked its tines with a polished fingernail.

"That, too."

"When will you tell Dalton?"

"Soon enough. I need to let my body adjust. I wouldn't want to get his hopes up about starting a family, and then nothing happens."

"You're right, it could take a while."

"How did Kevin do on his paramedic exam?" Marla asked, to change the subject.

Nicole put the comb down and grinned at her. "He

passed the test. I'm so happy for him. We're going out to celebrate this weekend."

"That's great. Say hello to him for me." Marla hoped their relationship would continue to progress.

Robyn gestured to her from the front desk. Marla strode over, realizing she had a long day ahead. She'd dropped Brianna off at the school bus stop and Luke at day care before her early doctor's appointment. Thursdays were her late day at work. She'd come in at eleven and wouldn't leave until eight. Dalton would pick up the kids later, but then he had to go back to the office. Brianna would babysit Luke until Dalton came home for dinner.

Marla was appreciative of her family's support. How would Tally manage to raise Luke alone? It seemed an insurmountable task, and yet single mothers did it all the time. They had to rely on their inner strength.

Shoving aside those pervasive thoughts, Marla approached her receptionist. "Have you discovered anything significant about our Sunny Grove politician?"

"I found someone who has the resources to help," Robyn said with an earnest expression. "There's a business in Sunny Grove called A Friend in Need Agency. It's run by Keri Armstrong and offers virtual assistant services. They have access to private databases."

"So did you hire her to find this guy?"

"Yes, and she came up with a home address. It's Liam's personal residence. Apparently, he's due in town this weekend for a charity event."

"This weekend? I need to talk to him." She mentally rearranged her plans. Liam might know something about the fraud case and the dead agent in the warehouse, not to mention the letter addressed to Tally's mother.

Robyn rolled her eyes and groaned. "Don't tell me to reschedule your clients again."

"I'd leave tomorrow if I could, but I have too many

obligations. I could run up there on Saturday morning. When is the charity function?"

"Saturday night. You'd have enough time to see him."

"If not, maybe I can get tickets to the event. Give me the contact info for that agency. I'll call for an appointment. It'll take me four hours to drive up there. I could meet them around one-thirty, assuming their office is open on weekends."

"You're not going alone?" Robyn said in an admonishing tone.

"I might have to bring Luke if Dalton has to work this weekend. Or maybe I can drop him off at Kate's condo. Delray Beach is on the way."

"Why not bring Brianna for company?"

"She has plans for Saturday." Normally, Marla would call Tally to accompany her. A pang of longing hit her, stabbing like an open wound.

"Hey, I'd love to come." Robyn poked Marla in the side. "Call somebody over from the day spa to man our front desk."

Marla gave her a bemused glance. It might be fun to have Robyn's company. "Okay, you're on. Meanwhile, you'll need to notify my customers and reschedule their appointments."

The day spa's receptionist assured Marla that she would cover for Robyn. Marla spent a few minutes touching base with the staff over there. Then she hurried back to the salon for her next client. Her pulse raced. Surely she was onto something important. She texted Dalton her plans to give him advance notice.

"Can't you just talk to the man on your cell phone?" Dalton said, upon calling her back.

She heard the irritation in his voice. Doubtless he wasn't pleased by her scheme. "I want to see his face when I mention Tally's mother and show him the note."

"That could be dangerous if he's involved in Ken's accident."

"Oh, come on. He's too far removed up the ladder, although I'm hoping he's heard about the fraud investigation. I think Tally went to see him for personal reasons. She wanted to learn about his relationship to her mother."

"Then a trip there is pointless. It wouldn't help solve any of the homicides."

"You've always told me to examine all the angles. You never know what might be hiding under a rock, especially one this big."

"You may be right, but I don't like it. Wait until I can go with you."

"You're tied up with Ryan's case. I'll be fine. Robyn will be good company." She hung up, wondering if she was doing the right thing. Would a trip to Sunny Grove be a waste of time? Did it matter if Liam had a relationship with Tally's mother in the past?

She shook her head on the way back to her station. Curiosity compelled her to pay this man a visit regardless of the consequences.

Chapter Sixteen

Marla went to work on Friday, eager to get through the day and start on her weekend plans. She had her bag packed for an overnighter to Sunny Grove, not wishing to drive four hours and return the same day. Dalton had made her and Robyn a hotel reservation for Saturday night. That way, he'd know where they would be staying. Now it was just a matter of getting past her Friday clients and Rissa's party that evening.

At two o'clock, her cell phone rang while she waited for her next client to get shampooed. A glimpse at the screen told her the call came from Ken's insurance agency. Her stomach clenched. Now what? She remembered with a sense of unreality that it wasn't Ken's business anymore. Tally owned the place. And since Marla acted as Tally's representative, the responsibility fell upon her shoulders.

"Hi, it's Darryl. I was hoping to follow up on your interest in a long term care policy. Did you have any further questions for us? I'm sure you and your husband would be easily approved once you turn in your applications."

Relief swept over her that nothing disastrous had occurred. "Now that you mention it, I do have a few more questions. We've been too busy to give it much thought. I don't get out of work until five, though. How about if I swing by your office then? Will you still be there?" She had to pick up Luke later, fix dinner, and get ready for Rissa's shindig.

"Yes, we don't close until six."

"All right. I won't take up much of your time." Marla disconnected, wondering at his call. Was there something else on his mind that he meant to discuss?

The clock read five-thirty by the time she pulled into the parking lot by the insurance agency. She'd left her jacket at home and shivered outside in the late afternoon air. Goosebumps rose on her flesh until she entered the office.

Jeri got up to give Marla a quick embrace. The scent of roses accompanied the older woman. "Hello, sugar. It's good to see you again. Are you here to give us a report on Tally's condition? Is she awake yet?"

"Actually, Darryl called me about long term care policies. But Tally is doing much better. Thanks for asking." From the corner of her eye, Marla noted the other front desk stood empty, cleared of Ryan's personal effects. She couldn't understand how the staff could carry on under the circumstances, but like her, they must have clients who depended upon them.

"And Luke, is he okay?"

"Luke is a doll. I love taking care of him."

"Bless your heart. I can tell you'll have trouble giving him up when the time comes."

"It'll be difficult, but I'll be happy when Tally can take him home."

Jeri shot a furtive glance toward the inner door. "Any more details on what caused the car accident, or who shot Ryan? I still can't believe he's gone, poor guy. I miss his cheerful manner."

"Sorry, I'm not allowed to discuss either case."

"I'm wondering if Ken was onto something, and then Ryan found out about it. You don't think—" Loud voices sounded from within. "Good gracious, Shawna and Ronnie are at it again. Those two are like fuel together. They're combustible if you leave them alone."

"Why is that?" Marla wondered what Jeri had been about

to say before the interruption but decided to follow this train of thought instead.

"I'd bet Ronnie wants to break things off, but Shawna won't let him."

"Is that so?" Whatever the reason, the account executive and financial planner must have been having quite a row, because Shawna slammed the door to her office and lowered her voice.

Darryl appeared in the doorway, a broad grin on his face. "Marla, I'm glad you're here. Sorry about the ruckus. Shawna and Ronnie are having a minor tiff about a client referral. Jeri, I'll take it from here."

Jeri's demeanor altered immediately. She bent her head, muttered a platitude, and sank into her desk chair without another word. When had the dynamic between those two changed?

Darryl led her back to Ken's domain, which it appeared he'd taken over now that the cops were finished scouring the place. He must have packed Ken's possessions because they were no longer in evidence. He'd barely waited until the dust had settled over his employer's demise, Marla thought with a disdainful curl of her lip.

After she took a seat opposite him, Darryl favored her with a Cheshire cat smile. "I appreciate your stopping by. So what questions do you have about the long term care plan?"

Marla folded her hands in her lap. "I forgot to ask how payment is made. Is it an annual premium or monthly installments?"

"It's your choice. You can have automated payments withdrawn from your checking account each month, or you can choose to pay in full once a year." He lifted a folder and handed it to her. "Here, I've taken the liberty of filling in these applications based on the information you gave us at your prior visit. Let's set a deadline for your decision. The sooner you act, the lower the premiums you'll lock in. Don't make the mistake of thinking you don't need this now. Once you have health issues, it becomes more difficult to get approved, and your payments will be considerably higher."

"Thanks, I'll try to get back to you soon. It's tough with so much else going on." Marla placed the folder by her purse.

Darryl tilted his head to regard her with a gleam of curiosity. "Have you thought about what you'll do when Ken's life insurance claim is accepted? Can you deposit a check on Tally's behalf, or would you prefer a wire transfer?"

"Actually, I believe Dalton said the money goes into an irrevocable trust. How about if you let me know when the approval goes through? I'll have to contact Tally's lawyer to see what we should do at that point."

"Okay. How is Tally doing?"

"Her reflexes are more responsive. I'm hoping she'll snap her eyes open one day and ask us what's been going on."

"Let's hope you're right. What are the chances of her memory returning? Do the doctors have any idea of her mental state?"

"Not yet. She could have residual damage or none at all. And what isn't physical could be psychological. She's lost her husband in a horrific accident. The emotional trauma might add to her impairment."

Marla didn't envy the doctor who had to tell Tally the outcome of the crash. Her friend would be heartbroken she'd missed the funeral, but that part was over. It was time to move on for all of them, including Ryan's colleagues. They had to be feeling his loss.

"Keep us updated on her progress, would you? We're all concerned." Darryl leaned back, his chair creaking with the movement. The aroma of wood polish entered her nose. The place was spotless, as though he'd taken extra care to clean the room. Did Darryl already consider it his space?

Disturbed by his presumption, she gathered her bag and rose. "Thanks for the follow-up call. To be honest, I'd completely forgotten about the LTC policy. But you're right in that it isn't something we should put off." Hopefully, they wouldn't need it until far into the future. And if she and Dalton applied while still young, their payments would be reasonable.

Darryl smoothed his receding hairline as he walked her to the door. "How is your husband's case coming along? Ryan's loss was a terrible blow to us. Is Detective Vail close to finding the young man's killer?"

"He has some leads to follow. I'm not at liberty to discuss them."

"We're hoping to see the perpetrator of this senseless crime put behind bars." Darryl spoke stiffly, as though it was the proper thing to say, but his tone lacked sincerity.

"So are we, Darryl." She strode into the front section, startling Jeri who'd been hovering by a shredder near the door. Marla didn't recall hearing the machine turn on. Had Jeri been listening to their conversation?

Marla noticed that the office had become unusually quiet. Shawna was busy at work behind her desk, and Ronnie had vanished. A reflection from a framed picture on the wall showed Shawna's computer monitor swirling with colorful bubbles from a screen saver. Had she been eavesdropping as well?

Wishing she were miles from here, she waved at them all and left. Ryan's spirit haunted the place, as did Ken's lost soul. Marla would bet something unethical was going on at their agency, and it had cost two good men their lives.

Hopefully, the politician in Sunny Grove would have some useful information relevant to the case. The sooner she made her visit there, the better.

Meanwhile, she had Rissa's party to attend that night. She whisked over to the day care center to collect Luke. Baby care being her first priority, she fed, bathed, and changed him at home in record time. While Brianna and Dalton ate dinner, she showered and donned a black sheath dress. The set of Swarovski jewelry that Dalton had given her for the holidays would complement it perfectly.

"Text me when you get there, and don't drive home too late," he called after her as she exited to the garage.

The moon had risen by the time Marla reached Rissa's address in Boca Raton. The gated community had luxurious lawns, tropical shrubbery, and sprawling houses with screened pools in back. For a wealthy neighborhood, the residences were crammed close together with little space in between. She liked the one on Rissa's corner that had a stone-faced turret and bay windows.

Rissa's place had an impressive entrance lush with green foliage and flowering plants. A brightly lit crystal chandelier shone from inside the foyer through glass panels in the polished cherry wood front doors. Marla adjusted the cross-body strap of her purse while waiting for someone to answer the doorbell.

When nobody responded, she twisted the knob. It opened easily. She entered to face a living room directly ahead and a dining room to her right. Voices assailed her from farther in the house. People must be gathered in the kitchen and family room.

Thinking it wasn't safe to leave the front door unlocked so burglars could enter, she shut the door and headed toward the sounds in back. Her heels clicked on the tile floor. As she rounded a corner to enter a spacious kitchen, she spotted Rissa. The redhead stood among a cluster of guests.

Rissa hurried over to exchange air-kisses. "Marla, I'm so glad you came."

Marla noted men in the crowd. "I thought you said this was a girls-only party."

Rissa pouted her cosmetically-enhanced lips. "These guys are special. You'll see what I mean. Look, Bridget is here." She pointed to the blonde dressed in a low-cut dress that clung to her curves. A bevy of men surrounded her while she simpered under their attention, most of which fixated on her chest.

A note of unease crept up Marla's spine. The proportion of women to men seemed off, favoring the former gender. Why couldn't she have brought Dalton? And who were these ladies? Did they belong to the tea party circle, or were they neighbors?

She observed a commonality among them. They boasted taut faces, wide-open eyes that didn't show the ravages of age, perfectly-styled hair, and stiff mouth muscles when they smiled. They wore a lot of makeup with a predominance of bold lip colors. Their outfits showed a generous view, enhanced by body language easily interpreted as a come-on.

"Who are these people?" she asked Rissa in a sharper tone than intended.

"They're friends of mine. What would you like to drink? You need to loosen up."

"A glass of Chardonnay would be great."

"Who's your little friend, Rissa?" a man said from behind, tapping Marla on the shoulder.

She whirled around, bristling at his form of address. "I'm Marla Vail. Who are you?"

A sheen of sweat covered the man's forehead. Clearly, he'd imbibed a few drinks too many. He was a heavyset guy with slick black hair and a condescending smirk on his jowly face.

"Nice to meet you, darlin'. I haven't seen you here before, or I'd have made a beeline in your direction. I like your style." His overt once-over made her feel grimy.

"Thanks. My *husband* likes it, too," she said, emphasizing the word.

"That's not a problem here." Coming closer, he draped an arm around her.

Marla shook him off. "I think you're getting the wrong impression."

He chuckled. "So that's how it is? The pretty newcomer plays hard to get. I like it." His breathing deepened, and a lustful gleam entered his eyes.

"Marla, here's your drink." Rissa slipped it into her hand before Marla even realized the woman had left her side.

Her fingers gripping the glass, Marla tucked her arm into Rissa's and walked away from the guy leering at her. "What's going on here?"

"It's just a party, dear. Come, let me introduce you to those fellows standing alone."

Marla withdrew her arm. "I didn't come here to meet men."

"Of course you did. You just need to relax." Rissa's gaze hardened as she tipped the drink in Marla's hand. "Here, you need this. It's okay. Everyone's always nervous the first time."

"The first time for what?"

Rissa didn't answer. She dragged Marla over to a pair of men standing by the fireplace. "Boys, this is Marla. As you can tell, she's new here. Maybe you can put her at ease."

"Sure thing, sweetheart." The man wearing a cowboy hat grinned at her. "So where did Rissa find you? Are you another bored housewife from the neighborhood?" He and the other guy shared a loud guffaw.

I'm not a housewife, loser. I own a business, and I'm married to a police detective, Marla wanted to say but didn't. Instead, she wondered if Tally had ever been invited to a party like this and what had transpired.

"You might say so," she said with a ditzy smile. Playing along might garner her more information than appearing the outsider. "How did you guys come to be here? Are you friends of Rissa's?"

"I'd say we're more fans than friends, wouldn't you, buddy?" he asked his pal.

"You got it." The other guy waggled his brows at Marla. "We'd like to be your fan, too."

Rissa interceded before Marla could formulate a retort

that wouldn't get her in trouble. "Okay, you've met these two. Let me introduce you around." Rissa hauled her over to a different group. Her grip was unusually strong as she clamped onto Marla's upper arm.

"Guys, meet my new friend, Marla." Rissa released her. "Take a drink, luv. You'll feel a lot better after you wet your throat."

Will I? Or is this drink designed to make me woozy and more suggestive?

She remembered Dalton's oft-repeated advice to his teenage daughter: "Get your own drink. Otherwise, you don't know what someone else might put in it."

Marla glanced at a guy seated in the family room. He wasn't wearing yuppie clothes like the rest of the bunch. Jeans and a sport shirt revealed a paunch and a hairy chest. His unshaven jaw and scraggly hair gave him an unkempt appearance. Yet the pair of men approaching him seemed deferential in their manner. As they engaged him in conversation, he morphed into a more authoritative figure with straightened shoulders and a stern glare.

After listening a few moments and nodding his head, the scruffy man gestured to one of the women. A heated discussion ensued between him and the other guys. A jolt of familiarity hit Marla. Could they have met before?

She felt her face blanch. Could this be the man who'd met Rissa in the parking lot on each stop of the tea ladies' circuit? Was he the same person who'd tried to run her down?

Stepping aside, she withdrew her cell phone and frowned at it as though reading a message. She turned on the camera and aimed it at the man on the couch. One of the other fellows passed him a wad of bills. Then he headed for the woman indicated earlier, whispered in her ear, and led her from the room. His companion looked disappointed. The couch potato consoled him with a few words. With a cheery grin, the second man set off to hunt new prey.

Because that's what purpose these women served, Marla realized, switching off her video and pocketing the phone. She dare not let the pimp on the couch notice her observing him.

Moving on, Marla followed a couple of women toward the dining room where a buffet offered snacks. The girls giggled and chatted together as they grabbed plates and helped themselves to the food.

A man who'd been stuffing olives into his mouth caught sight of her and sauntered over. "Well, aren't you a sight for sore eyes. When does your number come up, honeybuns?"

Marla raised her glass to him and smiled. "I'm new at this game. How do I find out?"

"Ask your boss. A sweet thing like you will be popular tonight."

"I certainly hope so. Rissa didn't say anything about a number, though." Did the men bid on the women? Was that how it worked?

"Oh, she ain't the boss, hon. I mean the guy in the other room. He sits on the couch like it's his throne, but this is his kingdom, after all."

"I thought the house belonged to Rissa and her husband. Where is he, by the way?"

"Poor sop is out of town. Rissa stages these parties during his absences. The idiot has no idea what's going on."

"So the man in charge … sorry, what was his name?"

The potential john stared at her. "Don't you know? Yuri would have screened you first before inviting you here."

"Rissa invited me."

"Oh, right. She does a great job as recruiter. No matter. I'll cast my net for you anyway."

His slap on her bottom gave her the impetus to move away. "Thanks, I'll look forward to it."

She found a bathroom, where she shut the door intending to dump the contents of her drink down the drain. Wait, would there be enough residue for Dalton to have the liquid tested if she brought the glass home? Then again, an item that big wouldn't fit inside her purse. Maybe she could soak a cloth in the wine.

A tray filled with paper guest towels gave her the solution. She stuffed one into the glass, swirled it around, and retrieved it before discarding the remaining contents in the sink. After wringing out the soggy paper, she wrapped it in a dry napkin and fitted it into a corner of her purse. Hopefully it wouldn't get her other items wet.

Now how could she make a graceful exit? Putting a loopy smile on her face, she opened the door and sashayed toward the dining room. She placed her empty glass on a side table and was approaching the front door when a hand on her arm stopped her.

"Where do you think you're going?" Yuri demanded. The pimp spoke with a strong accent she couldn't place.

"I, uh, need something from my car." She pointed to the front door, so close and yet frustratingly far under the circumstances.

"You're not leaving, are you? Because I'd hate to believe you were a tease." The menacing light in his cold blue eyes told her she'd better comply.

She yanked her arm free and gave a flirty laugh. "Of course not, darling. I brought along a few toys in case tonight got exciting. I need to get them, that's all. I'll just be a minute."

He signaled to a muscular fellow who hovered near the door. Marla hadn't noticed him there before. "Ivan, this lady wants to retrieve some items from her car. Go with her, *da?* See that she returns and doesn't try any tricks. The only tricks being turned tonight will be ours."

"Don't worry; I won't disappoint you," she said in a sultry tone. "Come on, big fella. My car is parked at the curb."

Accompanied by the bruiser, Marla exited into the cool night air. She had to get rid of this guy somehow. Leaving the bright lights and loud chatter behind as she strode down the darkened driveway, she debated what to do. It would be handy to have a weapon in her purse like Dalton had advised her to carry, but she'd been resistant. Maybe she'd reconsider the idea in the future, if she had one.

"Which car is yours?" Mr. Muscles demanded, his powerful form casting a shadow in the streetlight.

"I parked down the road. There weren't any spaces nearby." Her heels clicked on the pavement. Wait, that was it. She *did* have a useful weapon on her.

The white Camry was up ahead. Key in hand, she beeped the remote so the driver's door would open upon contact.

A few feet away, she stumbled and cursed. "Damn shoes. I'm not used to wearing high heels, but they make my legs look good." She lifted her foot, took off the shoe, and whirled around to bash the bruiser's nose with the point of her heel.

As he howled in fury and pain, she sprinted to her car, threw open the door, and dove inside. A moment later, she'd shut the door and pushed on the ignition. As she put the car into reverse, she gained enough space to shift gears. She zoomed ahead onto the road.

Marla didn't dare to look back until she'd exited the gate at the development's entrance. She made it to the turnpike in record time with frequent glances at the rearview mirror. Plenty of headlights came into view, but none of them seemed to stick on her tail. If Yuri figured out who she was, though, he wouldn't need to have her followed. He'd know where to find her.

That thought chilled her blood as she attempted to calm her racing heart. Her icy fingers gripped the steering wheel. At least she'd discovered Rissa's secret. Had Tally found out as well? Did Yuri send someone to silence her? Or had he been personally present the night of the accident?

Marla couldn't wait to tell Dalton what she'd learned. When she got home, she flung her purse on the kitchen counter and accosted him on the family room sofa where he sat watching the history channel. The rest of the house was quiet, the baby and Brianna presumably asleep. Her dear husband had waited up for her safe return.

She snuggled against his warm form and kissed him. "I've never been gladder to be home."

He turned off the TV via remote. "How was the party?" When she told him, his eyebrows drew together like gathering thunderclouds. "Good God, you barely escaped."

"Tell me something I don't know. Look, I took pictures." She got up, retrieved her cell phone, and resumed her spot to show him.

"I'll contact the vice department up there tomorrow. They might already have a lead on this guy. It makes you wonder how Rissa got involved in the first place."

"Maybe she was bored with her husband being out of town so often. Bridget was there, too. She belongs to the tea circle."

"And the other women? Did they look like hookers?"

"Not necessarily. They looked like typical wealthy Boca Babes." She gave a snort of derision. That lifestyle would never suit her.

"Hmm, I recall hearing something along these lines before." Dalton got up, paused to put on the house alarm, and headed into their home office to use the computer.

Marla went to get changed, eager to wash away the remnants of the evening. Once comfortable in her cold-weather jammies, she padded in slippers into the room where he sat frowning at the monitor screen.

"Listen to this," he said, pointing to the display. "A Boca Raton police officer's wife was accused of running an illegal escort business as a front for prostitution. The investigation was initiated when a woman from Peru claimed she had been forced to sell her body for money. She was told that if she didn't perform, she'd face deportation."

"Rissa doesn't run an escort service, and the women present tonight were not foreigners." Marla tapped her chin in thought. "It's possible she started her tea ladies' group to recruit affluent housewives. Like her, those members are looking for some extra spice in their lives."

Dalton clicked another link. "Here's a case from Central Florida. An upscale prostitution ring there brought in half a million dollars per year for a woman and her partner. They hid the cash in storage units."

"It's a lucrative business, that's for sure. Do you suppose Rissa works for Yuri, or are they in it together as partners? How do they launder the proceeds?"

"Yuri might have the connections." Dalton squinted as he scanned the data on the screen.

"You mean, as in organized crime?"

"You said his name is Yuri, and he speaks with an accent. His henchman is Ivan. I'm wondering if the Russians have moved into the territory. If so, it's possible their operation is already under investigation. I'll find out and let you know."

"It's too bad I didn't do a complete search of the house. I'll bet Rissa has hidden cameras in the bedrooms. Then she could blackmail the women into continuing to work for her. They might think it's a lark the first time, and then they're trapped."

"I shouldn't have let you go there on your own."

"Nonsense, it was my decision. I got away, so things turned out all right." Her shoulders slumped with fatigue, but tension kept her too alert for sleep. She couldn't help ruminating about the near miss she'd had. "I could use a glass of wine. It'll help me relax so I can stop replaying tonight's scenario in my mind."

"I'll come with you into the kitchen."

"Wait, that reminds me. I soaked a napkin in the drink Rissa handed over. Would you be able to have the lab analyze it? I'm betting she added something to make me cooperative."

Dalton shut down the system for the night and rose from his chair. "Sure, I'll drop it off tomorrow. How deeply do you think Tally was involved?"

"I doubt she'd be unfaithful to Ken, not even if she believed he was having an affair. Maybe she got wise to Rissa and threatened to warn the other women in their group."

"Are they all potential candidates for recruitment?"

"Edie doesn't have the figure for it. As for Deanne, she's very body-conscious. I don't think she would do anything harmful to her health."

"It's likely Rissa uses the group as a front to choose which individuals to approach for her lucrative side business."

"Then she rounds them up at a house party to snag them into her net." Marla had to admit the tea circle leader had the talent to guide women down the wrong path. She would never have guessed Rissa's secret on her own.

"I hope you were cautious enough in getting away so this Yuri fellow doesn't come after you." Dalton accompanied her toward the kitchen.

"Rissa thinks I'm married to a security expert. If she tells Yuri, it might warn him off. You'd think he would steer clear of me then."

"Oh, yeah? She invited you to the party for a reason. They could have hoped to entrap you, thinking the resultant blackmail would ensure your silence."

"If so, they failed. Assuming you're right, I must have spooked them somehow. I'd wondered if Yuri might have been driving the car that tried to run me down, but he didn't seem to recognize me. I suppose he could have sent Ivan to do the job." She halted as another thought surfaced. "Maybe Yuri targeted Tally in a similar manner. He thought she knew too much about his operation and sent Ivan to deal with her."

Dalton caught her inference. "You mean, he caused the car crash?"

"That's exactly what I mean."

Chapter Seventeen

"If you believe this Yuri person might be guilty of running your friends off the road, why are we driving to Orlando?" Robyn said from the passenger seat of the Camry.

"I need answers, and Liam Kelton might have them." Marla focused her attention on the turnpike. Hugging the right lane, she didn't mind the Saturday morning traffic zooming by on their left. They'd passed Mount Trashmore but still had about three more hours to go.

"Can you review everything again for me? I still don't understand how Liam fits into the picture besides working for the state's insurance industry." The salon's receptionist tugged at her long-sleeved embellished top that she wore with jeans and short boots.

Grateful for the company, Marla figured it would help to review things in her mind, too. "Okay. Ken gets a phone call on New Year's Eve. He heads to Davie along a darkened road by a canal. Another car bumps him, causing him to swerve to the right. His car rolls over down a ditch and ends up partially submerged in a canal."

"You said he told the babysitter it was a work-related call, but nobody from his office claimed responsibility."

"That's correct."

"And Tally decided to go with him last-minute. So it would appear Ken was the target, and not his wife."

"True, unless the person making the call knew he would

leave. When Tally accompanied him unexpectedly, they followed her and caused the accident."

"I see several holes in that theory. At the end of the road was a warehouse. Inside was a dead woman. This lady had been working with Ken on an insurance fraud case." Robyn adjusted her sunglasses. Despite the cooler temperature, Florida's bright sun still produced a glare.

"Maybe Louise, the agent, is the one who called him. She could have been forced to make that call to lure Ken out of the house," Marla said. "What if he'd raced outside that night because he feared for her safety?"

"It still means another person was involved who knew about her connection to Ken." Robyn punctured the air with her finger to emphasize each point. "And Ryan's death makes it even more likely that Ken was the target and not Tally."

"We know somebody from his office has to be part of this, especially if the fraud division enlisted Ken as an informant. Ryan must have found out this person's identity, and that's why the murderer went after him."

"Is it possible the Russian mob is connected to the insurance fraud operation?"

Marla shot Robyn a quick glance. "They could be separate issues. I'm hoping Liam can tell us more on that subject."

"You said a fellow tried to run you down. For what reason? Because you're a threat to whoever murdered Ryan and the investigative agent?"

"Yes, I must have made someone nervous with my questions."

"Didn't you say Rissa met with Yuri at each of their tea circle stops?"

"True, I think he's the vagrant from the parking lots. Rissa wasn't giving him a handout as people thought. More likely, she was transferring cash from her illegal side business."

"Why would Yuri risk exposing himself at a party?"

"I don't know. Not everything makes sense." Marla

shuddered over her memory of the evening at Rissa's house. She hoped Tally hadn't been snagged in their net.

"Let's look at this from another angle," Robyn suggested. "Have you eliminated any suspects?"

Marla chuckled. "Now you sound like Nicole. Do you read mystery novels, too?"

"Who has time to read, darling? I'm too busy. Just because I gave up my corporate job doesn't mean I don't keep up with marketing news. And I work out at the gym in my spare time. You should join me."

"I walk the dogs. That's enough exercise as far as I'm concerned."

"I'll bet Luke keeps you on your toes. Imagine when he's a toddler."

"I hope Tally will be taking care of him by then. Every time I visit, she seems to be getting closer to the surface."

"Maybe the emotional trauma is keeping her from regaining awareness. Too bad you can't bring Luke to the hospital. That might make a difference."

"What a great idea! I'll take a video to play on my next visit." Marla should have thought of this before. Playing a video of the baby at Tally's bedside might help to rouse her friend. Hearing Luke's coos and gurgles might motivate her to rejoin the land of the living.

"Despite your doubts, you make a good mother, Marla. I can hear in your voice how much you love Luke."

She gave a resigned sigh. "I do. I'm anxious for Tally to be normal again, and yet that will mean she'll take Luke from us."

"You have Brianna, although she'll be going to college in a couple of more years."

"Yes, that's why I—" She cut herself short, almost confessing about her change in birth control methods ... or lack thereof.

"What? Don't tell me you've had a change of heart regarding kids."

"You should talk. I don't see you settling down."

"I haven't met the right guy." Robyn stared out the side window at various housing projects. Most of them offered box-like structures with little variety.

"Come on, Robyn. You've been a corporate exec. You must have met lots of men."

"Yeah, and most of them wanted me to become someone else. They don't like the brains as much as the beauty. I'd like to meet a guy who appreciates me for who I am, but it's not a priority. Better to be alone than in a bad marriage, like my mother for all those years."

A tanker truck sped by on their left. Marla eased up on the accelerator until it gained a safe distance. Hazardous payloads on the highway made her nervous.

"Are your parents still around?" she asked her friend.

"No, they're both gone. I grew up in Connecticut. My folks divorced when I entered high school, but it should have been sooner. My father's response to stress was to drink. He rarely showed up for school events and always disappointed my sister and me. When he lost his job, it was the last straw for my mother."

"You have a sister? I didn't know that about you."

"Diana is married with a family in New Orleans. Her husband is a chef, and they have two kids. She's younger than me. When our mom died, I moved to Florida since we have cousins in the area. They invite me over for the holidays, so I'm not alone here." Robyn unscrewed the water bottle she'd put in the cup holder and took a sip.

"Tally's parents were divorced, too," Marla mused aloud. "She never told me the reason why Lilly and Rubin decided to separate. It happened when she was in college. Now that I think about it, this probably accounts for her odd behavior the second summer. She seemed unusually distant that year. I was wrapped up in my own problems and didn't pay her much attention."

"Do you think Tally's father found out about his wife's

earlier affair? That might have caused him to initiate their divorce."

"Why should it?" Marla countered. "People have flings all the time before they get married, although it wasn't as common back then. If Rubin loved Lilly, it wouldn't have mattered."

"How do you know the affair ended when Lilly got married?"

"Tally found a love letter Liam had written to her. He's the one who broke off their relationship. Lilly married Rubin, and then Tally was born the following year. You see, I'm not only visiting Liam because of what he can tell me about the insurance fraud case. I really want to know about his connection to Tally."

*****

"Get off at Fairbanks," Robyn instructed her several hours later. They'd stopped for lunch at a turnpike plaza and reached I-4 in Orlando by one o'clock. "Then keep going until you hit Lake Avenue. I'm glad you booked us a hotel room," she said, fiddling with her cell phone. "Look at all the things to do in Sunny Grove—museums, boat rides, botanical gardens, shops, and restaurants."

"There's no way I could have driven back the same day. It's too tiring," Marla replied, amazed by the traffic on I-4 at this time of day. She was relieved to get off at Fairbanks, past the skyscrapers of downtown Orlando.

"You're lucky we didn't have to take the baby along."

"That's for sure. Kate and John were delighted to watch Luke for us. I just wish Dalton's mom would stop dropping hints about us having kids, though."

"She wants more grandchildren. You can't blame her."

Marla bit her lip to avoid telling Robyn about her recent decision. Instead, she focused on the scenery. Heading east, they passed a seafood market and a popular barbecue place, judging from the number of cars cramming the parking lot.

At the intersection for Lake Avenue, she turned left as instructed. This brought them to an upscale neighborhood where shops and cafés spilled onto the sidewalk to their right, and a green expanse called Lakeview Park stretched to their left. People walked babies in strollers and dogs on leashes.

"Look," Robyn said, pointing. "The farmer's market is over there past the train tracks. They even have an Amtrak station. You could take the train up from Fort Lauderdale."

"I suppose. Where do we go from here?" Marla didn't care about sightseeing at the moment. She'd come on a mission.

"We're meeting Keri Armstrong at her agency. She doesn't always work on Saturdays but was nice enough to see us today. Her office is on a side street."

They found the address on a lane shaded by live oaks with gray moss hanging down like men's beards. Marla parked in a free public lot farther along the road.

Outside, the cool January air brought the smell of wood smoke into her nose. It had to be in the fifties. For a Floridian, that was downright cold. By early next week, the temperature was expected to rise into the seventies again, so the blast of northern air wouldn't last long. She huddled in her leather jacket as they strolled along the sidewalk.

Robyn's eyes lit with excitement. "I love this town already. It's near a big city and yet has a distinct sense of community. The history dates back to the 1800s. Look at the brick on those buildings."

"Yes, it's charming." Marla located A Friend in Need Agency and pushed open the door.

Inside, a young woman sat behind one of four desks facing forward like at a travel agency. She rose upon their entrance and came over to greet them.

"Hi, I'm Keri," she said with her hand outstretched. She had dark brown hair with layered ends that curled inward, electric green eyes, and a model-perfect face. The business owner looked to be in her late twenties.

Marla shook her hand and introduced herself. "This is my friend, Robyn Piper. Thanks for meeting us today. I appreciate you coming in on your day off."

Keri smiled at her remark. "I often work on Saturdays. Please, have a seat." She indicated two chairs opposite her desk in the rear row.

Marla settled herself comfortably. "What kind of agency is this exactly?"

Keri's eyes gleamed. "We're available to act as your personal assistant for anything you need done. No job is too big or too small. We have three staff members. Sharon does most of our virtual assistant jobs and party planning. She handles the big corporate events, too. Purdy manages our scheduling and vets our vendor list. I prefer field work. It's gratifying to work directly with customers."

"How did you get started?" Robyn asked, a rapt expression on her face.

Keri fingered a strand of hair. "I got laid off from my position as marketing director for a large firm. It was like Fate handing me a second chance. My mother had gotten sick, and I'd been too focused on work to listen to her. When she died of a sudden stroke, I felt guilty. Then when I started getting palpitations, I decided it wasn't worth the stress to stay on the corporate track."

"I know what you mean." Robyn wagged her forefinger. "I lost my job in marketing, too. Now I'm the receptionist at Marla's hair salon and loving it. I like the daily interaction with people and the lack of deadlines."

"This job can have its frenetic moments," Keri admitted. "Things get really busy around the holidays."

"What kind of things do you do?" Marla's curiosity compelled her to ask.

"We run errands for busy professionals, such as gift shopping or taking their clothes to the cleaners or mailing packages at the post office. Planning social events and business meetings are a large part of our job. In addition, we'll staff booths at trade shows, write company newsletters, or help plan advertising campaigns. I'm especially pleased when elderly people hire us. We pay their bills, drive them to doctor's appointments, and do their grocery shopping."

"I could use someone like you closer to where I live," Marla remarked with a chuckle.

"It's gratifying to know you're freeing people's time for the more important things in life. I felt if we could help folks take care of their mundane chores, it might allow them to pay more attention to their families."

Like you failed to do with your mother, Marla surmised. Guilt was a great motivator. She'd learned that lesson the hard way.

"It's awesome," Robyn said. "I gather you're the sole proprietor?"

Keri gave a proud grin. "Yep, I started the business. The demographics work well for us in Sunny Grove. And our online clientele list keeps growing." She handed them each a brochure with more details.

Marla offered a business card in exchange. "You're an entrepreneur, like me. I own the Cut 'N Dye Salon and Day Spa. Please keep us in mind if you have any clients coming to the area who need these services."

"I'll do that, thanks. So I found out what you wanted to know about Liam Kelton." Keri shuffled through a pile of papers on her desk and withdrew a sheet. "He has a condo in Tallahassee, where he works for the state government. But he maintains a residence in Sunny Grove and comes home for the occasional weekend. Currently, he's in town for a charity event. Here is his address."

Marla took the printout, folded it, and stuck it in her purse. "So do we show up at his door and ring his bell?" She'd prefer to confront him in private.

"That move would be up to you, Marla. I was just hired to locate him."

"Is his record clean? I mean, can you do full background checks on people?"

Keri's eyes narrowed. "I didn't realize you wanted an extensive search."

"I'm wondering what else you might know about him."

"He has a sterling reputation and is well-respected as a hard-working official. It's known he has political ambitions. He'd like to be appointed as the state's next chief financial officer. The current CFO hopes to move up to governor."

Marla exchanged a glance with Robyn. What they suspected about him could lead to scandal if it leaked out. Then again, all she had was supposition and no proof, other than the letter found in Lilly's cookbook. Or had Tally found further evidence that linked them together?

They'd better head over to Liam's house while the day was still young. Later, he'd be busy getting ready for his charity event. She fumbled inside her purse and took out her checkbook.

"I appreciate your research on our behalf," she told Keri. "How much do I owe you?"

Keri gave her a warm smile. "My discounted rate for new clients is twenty dollars an hour. This didn't take me much time at all, so let's consider it a complimentary first visit. Any future referrals you can send my way would be welcome."

"Are you sure? You gave up your free time to meet with us today."

"No problem. I had a few things to catch up on this afternoon anyway."

"That's generous of you. If you're ever in Palm Haven, stop by my salon and I'll return the favor." Marla put away her checkbook and rose.

A short time later, she and Robyn rang the doorbell at an imposing two-story house with a lake view. This neighborhood must range upwards from half a million, Marla thought. Many of the homes had docks for small boats in the back. Meticulously landscaped lawns were the norm along with flowering shrubbery and graceful palms. Liam's house, like the rest, had a circular driveway in front and a garage attached to the side.

A uniformed housekeeper opened the door. She had black hair tied in a bun and a careworn face. "May I help you?" she said in a slight accent.

Marla handed over a business card. "We're here to see Mr. Kelton. Tell him it's about Lilly and her daughter."

The woman's expression eased upon learning they weren't members of the press or constituents soliciting money for a cause.

"Wait here, please." A few minutes later, the maid returned and gestured for them to enter. "Mr. Kelton will see you in the parlor." She took them into a sunny room facing a screened pool and a boat landing over the lake. "Can I get you something to drink?"

"Not for me, thanks." Marla stood admiring the view while Robyn echoed her reply.

"Ladies, what can I do for you?" boomed a deep male voice a few minutes later.

Marla spun to face a gray-haired gentleman wearing a dress shirt and navy pants. He had broad shoulders, a lean build, and piercing blue eyes that reminded her of Tally.

"I'm here to talk about Lilly." *Awkward.* She didn't know Lilly's maiden name. "Lilly was married to Rubin, and they had a daughter. But you knew Lilly before she wed Rubin."

Liam's brows folded together. "And who are you, exactly?"

"Oh, sorry. I gave your housekeeper my card. I own a hair salon in Palm Haven. Anyway, I'm a close friend of Tally Riggs. She's the only child of Lilly and Rubin. Or at least, that's what she'd been led to believe until she found your letter." Marla rummaged in her purse for the copy she'd made.

Liam snatched it from her. His face darkened as he read the scrawled handwriting. "Where did you find this?"

"Tally discovered it hidden inside one of Lilly's cookbooks. I stashed the original elsewhere for safekeeping. Oh, this is Robyn, my friend and neighbor. She came along for the ride." Marla gave her comrade a sheepish grin.

"Don't mind me," Robyn said. "I need to stretch my legs after the long drive." She meandered off to examine the items on a set of bookshelves. Framed photographs and travel books vied for space with a collection of knickknacks.

"What is it you're hoping to prove, Mrs. Vail?" Liam's voice was calm, but his tense stance radiated hostility.

"Tally came to see you, didn't she? She wrote the date down in her appointment book."

"She did come here," he admitted, turning away to pace the tile floor. "She wanted information on her mother. I didn't have much to offer. Lilly and I had dated in our younger days, and then we'd lost touch."

"Really? And Tally means nothing else to you?"

"Absolutely not."

"Are you aware of her car accident?"

His response was a fraction too slow. "I'm sorry. I don't follow."

"She was in a rollover accident not that long after she came to see you. She survived but is in a coma at the hospital."

"That's terrible. I had no idea." He put on an appropriately sad face.

"Her husband was killed in the crash. On the good side, their baby was home safe. I've been taking care of Luke since she's been disabled." Marla showed him a photo of the baby on her cell phone. Was it her imagination, or did a flicker of softness enter his eyes?

"Cute kid. I don't see what this has to do with me, though."

"Well, here's the thing. When Tally and I were in college, we used to enjoy spending time together during the summers. Her parents got a divorce after our sophomore year. Tally never told me why her folks had separated, but I think she discovered the reason in this letter."

Liam jabbed a finger at her. "Give it to me straight, Mrs. Vail. What are you saying?"

"I believe you and Tally share a closer relationship than you'd want anyone to know."

"Is that what this is about? Next, you're going to ask for money in exchange for your silence? As a man in the public eye, I've been down this road before."

"Have you? Did you deny the truth to Tally? Because her very existence could prove difficult for you. Are you a married man, Mr. Kelton? Do you have children?" She walked over to the photographs on the shelves. "Lovely family you have here. And who is this?" She pointed to a picture of Liam as a younger man beside a girl who looked oddly familiar. Was that Lilly?

"That's Daphne, my sister. We were much younger then." His voice turned wistful. "Time flies when you're not looking, as my mother used to say."

"Regardless, our earlier indiscretions have a way of returning to haunt us."

His gaze hardened. "I'm afraid I'll have to show you to the door. I have an engagement this evening that requires preparation."

"Do you mind if I use the bathroom?" Robyn asked, wandering their way. She looked weary, as though a rest in the hotel room would do her good. She'd revive soon enough if Marla mentioned shopping, however.

"The guest bath is to the right down the hall," Liam said with a curt gesture.

"Me, too," Marla added with an ingratiating smile. "It was such a long drive from Fort Lauderdale. Do you have another bathroom I can use? Then we'll be out of your hair."

"Go upstairs. It's the first door to your left."

Marla scampered up the carpeted steps. Hearing the housekeeper humming somewhere nearby, she bypassed the second lavatory to head for the master suite. If caught, she'd say she got lost. Liam's wife wasn't home, but her expensive shoes and clothes were evident from a peek at their closet.

Marla shut the bathroom door and used their private facility. Washing her hands, she spotted a hairbrush near a man's shaving set. A few swipes with a tissue later, and she'd snagged a few gray hairs. She stuffed the bundle into her purse. Then she exited before anyone came looking for her.

Downstairs, she met Robyn in the front hallway. She wondered how to bring up the other matter on her mind.

"Thanks for seeing us," she told Liam, who stood ready to let them out. "I realize you're very busy in your political role. You're director of the state's insurance fraud division, correct?"

"I'm sure you researched me before coming here. And what was the point? You didn't ask for anything. Most people want favors from me."

"I thought you might care about what happens to Tally. She's going to need help when she leaves the hospital. She'll have to raise Luke on her own."

"That's not my problem, ladies. Just because I knew her mother in the past doesn't mean I owe any obligation to Lilly's daughter. Now if you don't mind—"

"Of course, Tally wouldn't be laid up in a hospital bed if it weren't for her husband's involvement in a case of insurance fraud. Doesn't that fall under the auspices of your department? Surely you must know his agency is being investigated. I'm hoping you can tell me what kind of fraud is being perpetrated and who else in his office has come under suspicion?"

Liam's mouth flattened, and his gaze chilled. "I've listened to you long enough. This conversation is over. Please don't bother me again, or I'll see that you regret it."

Chapter Eighteen

"Liam is very sensitive on the topic of Luke and Tally," Marla told Dalton and Brianna at Sunday dinner. "He wouldn't admit to a connection between them, but his face changed when I showed him the baby's picture."

Luke squirmed in his stroller parked beside them at the table. In another month or two, he'd be sitting up much steadier. She couldn't believe how fast he was growing. Her fingers stretched out, and she let his tiny hand clamp onto hers as she gave a happy sigh.

"So he admitted Tally visited him, but you still can't prove anything," Dalton said.

She swept her gaze back in his direction, strengthened by his presence. "Oh, my. I forgot to give you this." She disengaged herself from the infant and rose to get her purse from the kitchen counter. Inside was the hair sample she'd obtained. Marla handed it over with an explanation. "See if you can get it analyzed and compared to Tally's DNA," she requested.

"We can get a swab from Luke for comparison. That might be easier." Dalton got up to bag the evidence.

"Wouldn't this guy have known you're married to a detective?" Brianna asked, before sticking a forkful of baked chicken tenderloin into her mouth.

"Why should he?" Marla resumed her seat. "Even if he's involved in the fraud case, he's too far up the ladder to be concerned with details."

"I disagree. As head of his division, he should know about major investigations. That's part of his job." Dalton's brow creased in thought. "Which do you think upset him more—the potential for scandal from his relationship to Tally, or his role in the fraud inquiry? I'm not clear on how you think he's implicated there."

"Me, neither. I don't have any theories. Call it a hunch." Marla took a bite of roasted red potatoes with garlic and rosemary. She could barely smell it over the scent from a lit pumpkin candle.

"We still know somebody from Ken's office is involved. I wish the guys from the local fraud agency would be more open about their investigation."

Dalton's morose expression prompted Marla to lighten the mood. "I'd say it was a worthwhile trip. Robyn had a great time checking out the shops on Lake Avenue. She bought a cute outfit in one of the dress stores, and I liked the spice place. We'll have to go to Sunny Grove for a long weekend. You'd both enjoy the farmer's market and botanical garden, and the Morse Museum has a collection of stained glass art."

Dalton's gaze steeled. "I'm not going anywhere until we solve Ryan's murder."

He was waiting for more test results on that oily residue found at both murder scenes. Marla wouldn't hold her breath about it. Yet what other hope did they have? They weren't any closer to pinpointing a culprit.

The person in Ken's office could have been working alone. Liam's connection could be purely personal. Or, the Russians could be the ones who'd ordered Tally to be silenced, meaning insurance fraud had nothing to do with the accident except for getting Ken out of the house. But then, wouldn't Yuri have made another attempt on Tally's life while she lay helpless in the hospital?

Maybe they know she's unconscious and doesn't pose a threat that way. Did this mean if she woke up, she'd need protection? Dalton had determined a police guard wasn't necessary. Should Marla suggest he revisit that decision?

"Did you learn anything about the Russian mob and their possible involvement in Rissa's affairs?" she said instead.

"I've contacted the Boca unit. They haven't gotten back to me yet. You're thinking Tally might have been the target of the accident, and not Ken?" He shook his head. "It has to be related to the fraud case. Why else would he have been heading to the warehouse that night?"

"We've discussed this scenario. It could have been a smoke screen to lure him out of the house."

"You two are missing the big picture," Brianna cut in with an annoyed frown. "Who stands to gain the most from their accident?"

"Lots of people," Marla answered with a wry twist of her lips. "We need to narrow the list of suspects. Like, who can we eliminate?"

Dalton pointed his finger at her. "May I remind you that this is *my* case? You need to back off for safety's sake. You've already painted a big red target on your back. Your visit to Liam may have added another one."

"Then let's hope *we* get a break soon." She wasn't about to let him shunt her to the sidelines, not when she'd dug up a fair share of the data.

Marla rose shortly thereafter to clear their empty dishes. "I plan to visit Tally tomorrow. Robyn gave me a great idea. I'll record Luke on my cell phone and play the video at Tally's bedside. Hearing him might penetrate her brain and give her a reason to wake up."

*****

At the hospital on Monday, Marla combed Tally's hair while chatting about inane daily topics. Her friend remained silent, eyelids closed and limbs still. Then she played the video of

Luke. Her friend's eyes seemed to jump to life under her closed lids, and her legs shifted restlessly.

"Come on, Tally, wake up! Your son needs you. *I* need you." She wrapped Tally's hand around her fingers. "Listen, squeeze once for yes and two for no. Can you hear me?" A faint pressure on her hand resulted. "Are you in any pain?" She felt two barely perceptible movements. Her heart leapt in joy. But beyond that progress, Tally's status remained unchanged.

Out in the corridor, Marla confronted the nurse. "Has she been responding like this recently?"

The brunette beamed at her. "She's been answering questions with hand squeezes. She kicks her legs, moves her mouth like she's trying to talk, and has better eye tracking. The physical therapist is helping her get back in shape with mobility exercises."

"She seemed to tilt her head toward the sound of her son's voice."

"That's a good sign. She'll regain awareness one of these days, you'll see."

Marla left the hospital and strode to her car with a sigh of relief. It always felt good to leave that place. Relishing her freedom, she drove toward Las Olas Boulevard to meet her mother for lunch. Ma had returned from her cruise over the weekend, and Marla was eager for a report.

"The trip was wonderful," Anita said after they'd ordered their meals. She described the ship, the ports of call, and the food. Then she thrust back her short, white hair and showed off a pair of diamond hoop earrings. "Look what Reed bought me."

"Wow, that's a nice gift. I guess things are serious between you two?" She didn't know the former literature professor too well, but he seemed to be rushing things.

"He cares about me, and I like being with him. We're going with the flow for now."

"O-kay." Marla wasn't sure how she'd feel if the guy

proposed and Ma accepted. At least Reed was a vast improvement over her mother's previous boyfriend.

She spoke about Tally and Luke and showed the video she'd taken of the baby.

"You're a natural with him," Anita commented with a delighted grin. She jabbed a painted red fingernail at Marla. "Doesn't this make you yearn for your own child? You'd make a terrific mother. You're already great with Luke."

Marla gripped her water glass, a confession that she'd gone off the pill nearly spilling from her tongue. However, she held her silence and changed the subject to discuss the murder cases instead.

"Good heavens, Marla. Let your husband do his job. Stay out of it."

Marla, busy later with household chores at home, didn't have a chance to think about tracking down clues until Dalton phoned.

"The lab analysis I'd ordered came in earlier than expected. The oily residue from the crime scene derives from boat fuel. It's dyed red in Florida to denote commercial use and to qualify the buyer for reduced tax rates."

"Commercial use? What does that mean?" Marla put the unit on speaker phone so she could continue filing receipts at the desk in their study. "Port Everglades has freighters and container ships as well as major cruise lines. Is it possible this person works there?"

"I'm thinking smaller, like fishing boats or charter yachts." His tone denoted a certain smugness, as though his field of suspects had just narrowed.

"So your bad guy presumably got this stuff on his shoes." She recalled the yacht photos at Ken's insurance agency on the walls by Darryl's desk. "Darryl likes boats, remember? He rents them in his spare time from that dock near Bahia Mar. Would this be the same kind of fuel he has to use?"

"I gather red diesel is readily available at commercial

marinas," Dalton acknowledged. "That site where we interviewed Darryl has charter boats and tourist cruises. It's possible he refuels his rental of the day. Residue from the fueling station might have stuck to his shoes. It's worth checking out."

"How, by making another trip down there? That won't prove anything. You need access to Darryl's closet at home to check his footwear. Is this enough reasonable cause for you to get a warrant?"

"Unless you know someone else who owns a boat, he's our best guess. I'll contact the judge."

"Darryl will be at work today. How will you get into his house?" She considered the set of lock picks that a friend had given her. Lack of practice made her skills rusty, but she could manage the basics.

"I'll show up at his workplace once I have a warrant and demand his house key."

"Oh, that's smooth. And if he's guilty, you think he'll just hand it over?"

"He'll pretend nothing is wrong and will comply. A refusal is too close to a confession."

"I hope you're right."

She hung up, a puzzled frown on her face. If Dalton did find a shoe in the man's closet with the residue, then what? Wouldn't he have to get it tested to confirm it was a match for the substance at the murder scene? That seemed too circumstantial as a cause for arrest, unless they could also match his DNA to trace evidence from the victims. Even better would be locating the murder weapon.

Dalton's plan seemed too much of a long shot. Marla glanced at the wall clock in their study. It read two-thirty. She had plenty of time before picking up Luke at day care. What if she ran down to Bahia Mar to verify that the commercial boats there used red fuel? Otherwise, Dalton could be heading down the wrong path.

She tidied the desk, refreshed her makeup, and headed out the door.

*****

The marina across from Fort Lauderdale Beach bustled with tourists and boat owners as the sun burned brightly overhead. Creaks and groans from sailing vessels competed with the splash of water as Marla strode the pavement in a pair of white-bottomed sneakers. She'd worn jeans with a long-sleeved top and felt comfortable with the temperature around seventy. The tang of an ocean breeze freshened her nose and cleared her sinuses.

She approached the boat rental booth, her cross-body purse strap slung diagonally across one shoulder. "Excuse me," she said to the bearded fellow inside. "I'm interested in reserving a boat for a friend of mine, Darryl Trent. He usually likes a particular vessel, but I can't remember the name. He comes here on weekends."

The man flipped through a log book. "Do you remember when he visited last?"

Marla gave the date when she and Dalton had met him there.

"Oh, yeah. He took out the Sea Lion."

"Tell me something. Do these commercial boats use fuel that's been dyed red? I've read about how this distinction allows for a tax-free sale."

"Many boat owners will choose that option. It's available at the fueling station."

"Is that a separate facility from here?"

"Yep, you got it." He grimaced at his log book. "You know, I think we just rented the Sea Lion for a trip to the Bahamas. We have reciprocity at a harbor there." He ran his finger down the entries. "See, I'm right. Your guy was here less than an hour ago. He'd requested the Sea Lion yesterday, but it was in use. The renters brought it back in this morning. He should be there now getting ready to cast off if you want to catch him."

Marla's heartbeat accelerated. If Dalton went to the insurance office to look for the account executive, he wouldn't be there. Did Darryl intend to flee to the islands? If so, she had to stop him.

Or not. Dalton would want her to call for backup. But what if Darryl had his boat shoes with him? Footprint impressions hadn't been taken at the crime scenes to her knowledge, but the fuel residue might still be present on his soles. However, she couldn't retrieve his footwear without compromising the evidence. Obtaining it properly was Dalton's department.

Before moving on, she sent her husband a text regarding the situation. Then she found the boat slip and halted beside a sleek motor vessel. She glanced at the flying bridge deck and noted a couple of lounge chairs facing aft for guests to catch the sun. Darryl sat at a command console forward toward the port side. Should she call out to him?

No, alerting him to her presence wouldn't be smart. She should at least take a peek to see if he'd brought any luggage on board. That would give a strong indication he didn't plan to return home. She'd do a quick search and get off the boat before Darryl noticed her.

Her heart thumping, she hopped onto the swim platform and entered the salon through an unlocked sliding glass door. To her left, she spied an L-shaped beige sofa cleverly designed with an extra berth beneath. Another seating arrangement sat opposite, facing glossy wood cabinetry that framed a large flat-screen TV with a high-tech sound system.

Marla stared in blatant admiration. She couldn't imagine a life of leisure where you cruised the waterways, enjoying the view along with these luxurious amenities.

Ahead toward the left was a galley with a full range of

gleaming appliances and granite countertops. Just beyond was a spiral staircase leading downward that beckoned to her. Her scalp prickled as she padded over and crept down the carpeted steps. She'd just need a minute to glance at Darryl's belongings, and then she could vamoose out of there.

A quick exploration showed her a master suite plus two guest cabins all decorated in the same brown-and-beige color scheme. Inside the master stateroom, bulging suitcases occupied a double-sized berth edged by two built-in nightstands. A chest of drawers with a TV on top, built-in cabinets, and a desk below a window completed the furnishings.

Overhead, the low ceiling had a hatch like a skylight in the middle. A person could easily reach it by standing on the bed.

A rumbling vibration underfoot jarred her just as she noticed a partially open metal case. Curious to see what this one held, she went over and opened it. Stacks of one-hundred-dollar bills were lined up inside. Whoa, what was this? She had enough presence of mind to take photos with her cell phone. Then she did the same for the other suitcases filled with clothing. Darryl must have packed hastily. None of them were locked.

At any rate, this confirmed her notion that Darryl planned to run for the islands and not come back. She sent the pictures to Dalton and stuck her phone in a pocket before backing out toward the door.

"Where did you come from?" Darryl snapped.

Marla whipped around. His form filled the doorway, his eyes gleaming with menace. He held a gun in his hand.

Her stomach lurched. Was that the same weapon that had shot Louise to death and later done in poor Ryan?

"Actually, I'm waiting for my husband," she said in a smooth tone that belied the panic squeezing her chest. "Dalton knows I'm here, and he's on his way along with backup. You'd be smart to cooperate."

"I could say the same to you. We're about to get underway. I didn't count on a stowaway, but I can deal with you once we're out to sea."

"Like you dealt with Louise and Ryan?" she said to force a confession. "You're the one who killed them, aren't you? Did they get wise to your fraud scheme?"

Damn, she should have left her phone turned on. Could she reach it in her pocket? Not yet; Darryl's gaze was pinned too closely on her.

His lips curled in a snarl. "I had a good thing going. Florida is rife with boats that become prey to storms or modern-day pirates. It's unfortunate when owners lose their vessels, but they're insured."

"Through your company, I assume. How much kickback do you get on these claims? I'm guessing you help those boats along to their watery graves. Do you have a special place where you scuttle them?"

"You don't need to know the details." He gestured with the gun for her to move farther inside the cabin. His gaze moved to her bag. Would he take her purse or ask for her cell phone?

"Did you run Ken off the road that night?" she asked quickly to distract him. "You must have figured out his role as informant for the fraud division. Am I correct?"

He shrugged. "It doesn't matter now. Sit tight, Marla. I hope you don't get seasick." With a sinister chuckle, he slammed the door shut. Clunking noises sounded from outside in the corridor, and then his footsteps stomped away.

She tried the door, but he must have jammed it from the other side. Shortly thereafter, the vibration increased as they moved away from the dock.

She'd better text Dalton again before she lost service. She sent him the name of the vessel, their destination, and how she'd gotten trapped. She'd face his wrath later, if there was a later.

The message went through, or at least she hoped it did. She tucked the phone inside her purse without waiting for a response.

At the window, she noted their progress with a growing sense of alarm. Her attempt to open the window failed. Probably the glass was too strong to break.

She had to escape before they hit the open sea lanes. Her gaze rose to the hatch overhead. Could she open it by herself?

She crawled onto the bed and stood on top of a stuffed suitcase. Her fingers touched the latch. Rust must have stiffened it as the thing barely moved. After several tries, she managed to shove it into the unlocked position.

With a grunt, she pushed on the heavy circle of glass. It banged open with a crash.

She winced, hoping Darryl was in another part of the boat and hadn't heard. Or maybe he'd think she was pounding on the stateroom door in an attempt to free herself.

Balancing precariously, she carefully straightened her spine. It wasn't easy with the boat rocking. They were going slow, probably to clear the buoys before reaching open water. This would be her last chance for freedom.

She grasped the rim and hefted herself up, straining her arm muscles. Adrenaline gave her an added boost. She hauled herself out the hatch and collapsed onto a wooden deck.

Uh-oh. The channel ahead led out to sea. She didn't have much time.

It took an effort to stand as the boat's movements increased. She steadied herself over by the railing. Now what? Should she jump overboard?

She peered at the seething depths. Another boat might come along if this was a trafficked lane, but could she tread water for any amount of time? Her arms might be strong from her work as a hairdresser, but did she really have the stamina to stay afloat while getting slapped in the face by waves and buffeted by the current?

Then again, did it matter? This being January, the water was bound to be cold. She might die of hypothermia before anyone reached her.

Hopefully that meant the sharks had gone elsewhere. Usually, they swam close to shore in Fort Lauderdale. If she had a choice, jumping into the water wouldn't be her first option. That meant she'd have to choose the alternative of disabling her captor.

She glanced at the flying bridge, and her heart skipped a beat. Darryl wasn't there.

Had he noticed her escape? Her throat tight, she scanned the deck for a handy weapon. An axe mounted on the wall for fire control caught her eye. That would have to do.

She'd just detached the tool from its mounting when a growl sounded from behind.

"How did you get free? Never mind, we'll do this now. You're shark meat."

Marla gripped the axe handle, lifted it, and swung the blunt end into Darryl's skull.

His eyes rolled up in his head, and he slumped to the deck.

Feeling relieved but not yet secure, Marla realized she needed to tie him up before she could call for help. With the boat speeding toward the open channel, she widened her stance to steady her feet. Presumably, Darryl had put the vessel on autopilot, if there was such a thing for boats.

There, that coil of rope would do. She used the axe to hack off a couple of sections and then trussed Darryl at his wrists and ankles before lashing him to a pole. Her limbs trembled from exertion. Ignoring her discomfort, she headed to the command deck.

With the boat swaying even more, she had to grip the hand rail to climb the ladder. Her stomach responded to each pitch and roll as she got higher. The wind blew hair into her face, making it difficult to see ahead. She squinted, nearly blinded by the sun's glare.

Nancy J. Cohen

Once under the covered area, she donned the sunglasses she kept in her purse, still strapped across her shoulder. She tried to make a cell phone call, but got the no service signal.

A wave of dizziness hit her unexpectedly. She sank into the chair behind a big steering wheel and put a hand to her mouth. *Come on, Marla, don't get sick. You have to think.*

She examined the array of instruments. There must be a radio among all this tech. But even if she recognized a microphone or communications unit, she wouldn't understand how to operate it. Living in Florida, why hadn't she ever taken a boating course?

Her ears picked up the sound of a siren. She peered over the side to see a Coast Guard vessel bearing down on her. Dalton must have notified them.

Oh, thank God. She waved her arms in joyful relief. She'd never been happier to see the authorities chasing after her.

Chapter Nineteen

"That was a brilliant move to call the Coast Guard," Marla told Dalton for the umpteenth time on Tuesday as they reviewed the case. She sat with her husband in a Cuban restaurant near Hollywood Boulevard. They'd dropped Brianna off at acting class and were enjoying a leisurely dinner together. Luke was home with Ma babysitting. Her mother had said she'd "missed the little tyke" and wanted to see him, so this gave her the opportunity.

"The outcome would have been a lot different if I hadn't," Dalton replied with a scowl. "You should never have gone aboard that vessel alone."

"I was only going to peek inside to see how much luggage Darryl had brought. I didn't mean to get trapped there."

Dalton grasped her hand from across the table, a fake candle flickering between them. "You gave me a fright. I almost lost you."

"I'm sorry. I didn't expect to get caught. But if Darryl had gotten away—"

"He didn't." Her husband's expression mellowed. "And you're okay, so we're good. However, a basic boating course might be a smart idea for both of us."

Relieved he didn't dwell on her mistakes, Marla withdrew her hand and lifted her wine glass. "Here's to solving your case," she said to distract him. They clinked glasses. "Darryl wrapped everything up nicely when he confessed to killing Louise and Ryan."

Dalton's gaze clouded. "Yeah, a little too nicely. A couple of things still don't add up."

"How so? He was running the insurance fraud scheme. Ken got suspicious when a client complained. He wasn't sure which agent from his office was involved, so when Louise suggested he should spy on his colleagues and play informant, Ken agreed. Darryl found out, grabbed Louise and took her to the warehouse. He called Ken using a burner phone and had Louise plead for help. Then he killed her."

"That would explain why Ken tore out of his house on New Year's Eve. He thought he could save Louise. It was a work-related call in a way, so that much was true. Darryl laid in wait for Ken, recognizing his car on the road and forcing him into the ditch. He hadn't counted on Tally coming along." Dalton took a sip of Cabernet, swirling it in his mouth before swallowing.

"Tally probably knew about Ken's involvement by that time and worried for his safety," Marla added. "Then poor Ryan got wind of the operation. Darryl took care of him in the same heartless manner. The man is a monster. I hope he gets put away for a long time."

Dalton's gaze narrowed. "His troubles began when his wife left him. I've met guys like him before. He hides a lot of anger behind a curtain of charm. His resentment stems from his own inadequacies that he projects onto everyone else."

"Lots of people have issues. They don't go around murdering their friends."

"Ken's work evaluation said Darryl wasn't worthy of promotion because he's not a team player. He acts competitive and petty, hiding it under a smooth veneer."

"I'd tend to agree. Did you interview his ex-wife to learn more about him?"

"The wife said he viewed porn sites on the computer and liked to visit strip lounges. These perversions are why she left him. She said he's especially spiteful to anyone who is more successful."

"So that's why he started the scam? To thumb his nose at everybody else?"

"It's one reason. Plus, he meant to save enough money to buy his dream yacht."

"So what bothers you?" Marla bit into her shrimp sautéed with onions and bell peppers, her appetite gone but eating for strength and energy.

"I don't know. Something seems off. I'm not able to put my finger on it."

"Let it go for now, hon. Darryl has confessed to the murders, and you can confirm it once you link him to the scenes via DNA evidence and residue from his shoes."

"And his weapon, now that we have the firearm," Dalton added.

She pondered their conversation on the way home after they'd picked up Brianna. But Marla didn't care to revisit the topic or disturb the peace she felt with Darryl behind bars. His arrest wouldn't bring Ken back to life, but it took away the threat to Tally whenever she awakened.

Marla glanced at Dalton's stern profile. She wanted nothing more than to put this tragedy behind them and move on. Now that the bad guy was behind bars, she'd put all her efforts into caring for Luke and advocating for Tally.

*****

On Wednesday morning, Luke woke with a fever. Aware of her crowded work schedule, Marla called Mrs. Phelps to babysit. Neither her mother nor Dalton's mom would get there in time, and she didn't want to bother them.

"Thanks so much for coming at short notice," Marla said, greeting the older woman at the door and ushering her inside. "I've alerted the day care center that Luke would be absent today. I'll show you his meds. Call me if his temperature doesn't come down in an hour or two. I've already given him a dose this morning."

"What time do you expect to be home?" The sitter's blue eyes regarded Marla with a kindly expression.

A jolt of familiarity slid along her spine. Short on time, she shook the feeling aside. "I'd like to get through my morning clients. I'll check with you later, but let me know if Luke gets worse."

"Don't worry about a thing. I'll take good care of him."

Marla gave a heavy sigh. "I wish I could stay home, but I've too many customers."

"Go on to work. We'll be fine, and you'll be back before you know it." Mrs. Phelps chuckled. "Time flies when you're not looking, dearie."

Marla frowned, the hairs on her nape prickling with unease. What was throwing her comfort level off-kilter today?

She collected her purse and left the house, her cares fleeing as work consumed her. She finished her early appointments, wishing time would move faster.

It was past lunch when her cell phone rang. Dalton's name showed on the caller ID. At least it wasn't the sitter saying Luke's temperature had spiked.

"I received a preliminary report on the hair sample you took from Liam Kelton," Dalton said. "There's a ninety-eight percent chance that he and Luke are related."

"What? How?"

His deep voice responded. "Wasn't it your theory that he and Lilly had a child?"

"Yes, and this could be the reason why Tally's parents ended up getting a divorce. Rubin learned another man had sired his daughter. I'll bet Tally went to Sunny Grove to confront Liam. He'd have urged her to keep quiet, since a scandal could ruin his reputation. He wouldn't want to lose his chance of becoming the state's next CFO."

"I'll have to do more research on this." Dalton rang off, leaving Marla standing with the cell phone to her ear.

She tucked the device back into her pants pocket, envisioning her visit to Liam's lakeside mansion. Wait a minute. Hadn't he used the same phrase as Mrs. Phelps? *Time flies when you're not looking.* He'd said it while gazing at the photo of his younger sister. The woman had looked familiar to Marla. Her blood chilled as she realized why. Surely there couldn't be a connection between the politician and her babysitter?

She rushed to the computer at the front desk. "Robyn, move aside. I have to check something."

Accessing a popular real estate site, she looked up Mrs. Phelps's house number that she'd programmed into her address book. The babysitter claimed she'd moved into Tally's neighborhood four years ago. She had started babysitting after her husband died. So how come the lady was always available when Marla called?

Her throat constricted. Oh, no. The address where Mrs. Phelps lived had sold within the past year. This sale would have been shortly after Tally's trip to Sunny Grove. And Mrs. Phelps hadn't bought the house with her husband. The buyer was listed as Liam Kelton.

With a dawning sense of horror, Marla stared at Robyn. "I think I know who's behind everything. I have to go home. Reschedule my clients for me, will you?"

She rushed back to her station, grabbed her purse, and dashed out the door without any further explanations. Her heart racing, she drove home like a wild woman, passing through yellow lights and barely pausing at stop signs. Her brakes squealed as she stopped the car in her driveway.

Mrs. Phelps's vehicle was gone.

Her stomach lurching, she entered through the front door and called the babysitter's name. No response. A horrible pit of despair opened inside her.

Nancy J. Cohen

She sprinted down the hall to Luke's nursery. His crib lay empty, the sheet rumpled.

A quick search through the rest of the house revealed a haunting emptiness. With trembling fingers, she lifted a mobile phone unit and dialed the babysitter's given numbers. Nobody answered. She sent a text from her cell, praying she was mistaken, and there would be a logical reason for the woman's absence.

Could Mrs. Phelps have taken Luke to the doctor? A call to the pediatrician's office confirmed her fears that they weren't there.

She called Dalton next and practically screamed at him when he greeted her.

"Dalton, you have to come home. Luke is missing. I think Mrs. Phelps kidnapped him. She's Liam Kelton's sister. They've been behind everything from the start."

"Whoa, calm down. Luke isn't in the house? Did she take him to the doctor?"

"No, I already checked with their office. I have an awful feeling about this." Her voice caught on a sob. If anything bad happened to Luke, she'd never forgive herself.

"Maybe she brought him over to her house. Did you check there?"

"I can do that. It'll take me twenty minutes to reach her place, though."

"I'll meet you," Dalton told her. "Park a few doors down, and don't do anything until I arrive."

Marla made it to Tally's neighborhood in record time and searched for the address. She found it easily enough and parked farther down the road as Dalton had suggested. Noticing that he'd arrived ahead of her, she walked toward him along the sidewalk.

The sitter inhabited a ranch-style house with a gray shingle roof. Sparse landscaping decorated the lawn that needed weed control. The driveway was empty, which didn't bode well.

260

"Why would Mrs. Phelps take Luke?" Marla asked her husband, where they stood out of view from the windows. "To blackmail us into keeping quiet about Tally's relationship to Liam? They must have been working together ever since Tally visited him in Sunny Grove. He wanted to make sure Tally wouldn't spoil his plans, and so he planted his sister here as a spy. No wonder Mrs. Phelps was always ready to come over at a moment's notice."

"Let's not speculate. We'll find Luke and worry about their reasoning later."

"There's no other car here. Did you peek inside the garage window?"

"The garage is empty. I'll ring the doorbell. Keep an eye out in case she escapes through another exit." Dalton loped over and rang the bell. No response. Same with rapping his knuckles on the door.

"I'll have to get a warrant," he said, his voice doubtful.

"You have reasonable cause for a kidnapping. And you're with me." Marla withdrew her lock picks. "I'm not very good at this, but I don't need court authorization."

"Don't tell anybody I helped you break in."

Together they got the door open and charged inside. Dalton headed to the right. Marla took the left-hand direction. She looked in one empty bedroom after another.

They met up back in the foyer.

"You won't believe it, but the kitchen has few dishes and even less food in the refrigerator," Dalton said in a somber tone.

"She doesn't even live here." Marla's shoulders sagged at the full implications of their mistaken trust.

"Hold on, I'll make a few calls." His face grim, Dalton took out his cell phone and turned away. When he got off the line a few minutes later, his voice sounded triumphant. "Okay, I got another address. It's where she'd lived previously, according to her driving record. And I put out an alert for her car. It's a good thing you took a photo of her license tag."

"Where is this other place?"

"Off Griffin Road to the west. Hopefully, she'll be there and not on her way to Orlando. I've notified the Sunny Grove PD to keep a watch on Kelton's place."

"Why would she bring Luke there?" Marla slid into the passenger seat of his car, preferring for him to drive. She could pick up her vehicle back here later.

"Kelton could want the kid as a hostage. I just spoke to Louise Harrison's superior. The politician is involved in a multi-state insurance fraud scheme. They've been keeping a tight lid on things because they wanted to track the leaders."

"Adding kidnapping to the charges won't help his case. Could he have ordered Darryl to cause the accident that killed Ken?"

Dalton, eyes on the road, gave a curt nod. "I'd say it's likely."

"We have to save Luke. He's sick, and there's no telling what that man will do to him." She wrung her hands in her lap, wanting to scream and cry at the same time. Once again, she'd failed a child under her care. She was wrong about being a good mother. It wasn't a role she deserved.

"It's not your fault, Marla. Mrs. Phelps fooled both of us. Don't blame yourself."

Dalton slowed as they approached the cottage-style house on a large tract of land bordered by a canal in back. Live oaks and cabbage palms decorated a huge expanse of lawn.

Marla sat up straight, a flurry of hope surging through her. The babysitter's car sat in the driveway. As Dalton pulled up to the curb a short distance away, Mrs. Phelps came out of the house rolling a couple of suitcases. She popped her trunk to load them inside.

"She's leaving. Where's Luke?" Marla said in a choked voice. Her hand on the door handle, she tensed, ready to confront the woman.

"Easy, Marla. We don't want to spook her into doing anything stupid."

"I should talk to her. You'll scare her off."

"I'm best equipped to handle this. She might have a weapon."

Marla's stomach flip-flopped. "Call for backup. Meanwhile, I can distract her while you go inside to look for Luke. If she has a gun, you can circle around us from behind."

"You should stay in the car."

"I can't wait here, not with Luke's life at stake." Once Dalton had made his call, she shoved open the door. She hopped out and hurried toward Mrs. Phelps.

"Her name is Daphne," Dalton called after her, before he disappeared around the side of the house.

"Hello, Mrs. Phelps," Marla said upon sauntering into view. "Going somewhere?"

The older woman slammed down the car trunk and spun to face her with a reddened complexion. "Marla! How did you find me?"

"I have my sources. Where's Luke?"

"He's safe inside. I'm taking him with me. He deserves to have a caretaker who's related to him."

Marla scanned the open garage. Various gardening implements lay about amid other clutter like a usual South Florida home. Without basements, houses needed storage space, and the garage often served that purpose. She edged closer to the wall, spying a rake mounted there.

"You're his great-aunt, aren't you? We've discovered your relation to Liam Kelton. He and Tally's mother Lilly had a fling many years back. Tally was the result, but Lilly never told Liam she was pregnant. That makes Luke his grandson."

Mrs. Phelps sneered at her. "The past doesn't matter now. Luke is mine. I'll raise him as my own. Liam promised me I'd have the baby after he removed Tally from the equation."

"What?" Marla felt her eyes bulge.

"You don't get it, do you? We captured Louise Harrison as a ploy to lure Ken out of the house. With him gone, Darryl was supposed to go inside, disable Tally, and steal Luke for me. But Tally called me over to babysit while she accompanied Ken. Darryl had to change his plans. He followed their car and bumped Ken off the road."

"So Tally *was* the target? Darryl's orders weren't merely to disable her, were they? Your brother wanted my friend out of the way so she couldn't ruin his marriage and cause a scandal."

The babysitter gave a smug grin. "We got rid of Louise who'd figured out our game. Liam wouldn't let anything stand in his path."

"What about Ken? Louise was his handler for the insurance fraud division."

"Liam wasn't worried on that score. He'd set Darryl up as the fall guy. He didn't think anyone could trace things back to him. Ken's death was an accident."

Marla kept talking to give Dalton time to get inside and find Luke. "You had ample chances to take Luke earlier. Why now?"

"My brother is helping us leave the country. Otherwise, you and your nuisance husband would track us down. I'd be constantly looking over my shoulder. But Liam wasn't ready until now. Your visit pushed him into taking action."

"Wait, Liam is here?" Good God, they hadn't expected two adversaries. Where was Dalton? Had he made it inside the house? Did he know Liam would be present?

"What have you done with Luke?" Marla's pitch rose as fear engulfed her.

"Come and see for yourself. I'm his auntie. I've taken good care of the little guy."

Marla followed her into the kitchen. Mrs. Phelps halted and gave a choked gasp as she glanced out the window.

Liam stood outside next to a canal at the rear of the property. He held Luke in his grasp. Dalton faced him from several feet away, weapon in hand.

Mrs. Phelps gave a shriek and dashed outside via the family room sliding glass doors. "What are you doing?" she cried to her brother.

Marla hot-footed it after her. "Daphne, wait."

The politician poised Luke over the water. "I'll drop him if you fire at me, Detective. Lower your weapon, and let us go."

Dalton cast Marla a grim look. "He flew into town earlier. We should have anticipated his involvement."

"You two have ruined everything," Liam said, his face mottled. "I've got enough money stowed away in the Caymans so we can have a nice life there. But I would have liked to achieve CFO for the state. Now I'll never realize that dream."

"You won't realize anything except a prison sentence if you don't hand Luke over to us." Dalton placed his gun carefully on the grass, while keeping both hands in view. Marla was aware he had a spare weapon holstered at his ankle. "Do you really want to abandon your current family? How will they feel when this comes to light? Surrender now and face lesser charges."

Marla could barely breathe. If he dropped the baby ... Oh, God.

"Daphne, don't let him do this," Marla pleaded. "You want to raise Luke as your own child, don't you? He'll take that chance away from you if he hurts Luke. Saving his skin is more important to him than the baby."

"Give him to me." Mrs. Phelps approached her brother with her arms outstretched. "They'll leave us alone as long as we have him."

Liam eyed Dalton. "Will they? We won't get far before we'll be stopped."

"Then let's tie them up. We don't have to go to the airport. We can hire a boat to get to the islands."

"Sorry, but the kid will drag us down. It'll be easier without him." He raised his arms, holding Luke threateningly over the rippling water.

Luke wailed, his cries stabbing Marla's heart. In the near distance, sirens added to the noise.

"No-o-o!" Mrs. Phelps rushed her brother, tackling him away from the canal.

Dalton raced forward, catching Luke as the pair tumbled to the ground. "Marla, come get the baby."

She raced over and snatched Luke from his hands. "Oh, my sweet child." She cuddled him close, while Dalton retrieved his weapon and aimed it at the hapless duo.

Luke's howls ceased, and a smile lit his face. Focused on the child, Marla didn't even blink an eye when backup arrived and uniformed officers rushed to their aid.

Chapter Twenty

"I'm glad Luke is okay," Nicole said at work on Thursday afternoon. She'd accosted Marla for details on the case during a lull in their schedules.

"Thank goodness, he didn't suffer any ill effects from his adventures." Marla had dropped Luke off at day care that morning, grateful his fever had abated as suddenly as it had come. That didn't matter now. She never wanted to have a fright again like they'd had yesterday when the sitter stole him.

She rubbed her belly, wondering what anxieties she'd face if she ever had a child of her own. She'd saved Luke, and that had allayed any lingering doubts she might have had about her worthiness to be a mother. A warm glow filled her. At any moment, new life might be taking form inside her. Now that she'd made the choice, she wanted it sooner rather than later.

"Was Liam Kelton the so-called friend who called the hospital to inquire about Tally's condition?" Nicole asked from the adjacent station.

"Yes, Liam had been afraid Tally might wake up and tell the cops what she knew. Besides their personal connection, he wasn't sure how much Ken had told her about the insurance fraud scheme." Marla stood nearby, not wishing their voices to carry.

"What type of fraud was it?" Nicole loved a good mystery and had hounded Robyn for details of their trip to Sunny Grove.

"People would sink their own boats and cars, and then

report them stolen," Marla answered. "Fifty-four cars were found at the bottom of a lake in Boca Raton. The Lord only knows how many boats were scuttled over time. Darryl had a hand in that part, but he was simply a player in Liam's game. The tentacles reach into other states through the politician's network."

"What tipped Ken off that something wasn't right?"

"A customer complained that his boat had vanished from its mooring. Ken ran a background check on the guy, and there weren't any financial judgements against him, bankruptcies pending, or things like that. But boats just don't vanish for no reason. Ken suspected a false claim, although this particular client was innocent."

"So some of the boat owners colluded with Darryl and his gang, but not all of them?" Nicole asked for clarification.

"That's correct. Dalton visited Ken's agency this morning to have a long talk with the three remaining employees. Shawna will run operations for now. I'm not sure what Tally will want to do when she's able to take over. She'd be better off if she sold the business."

"But none of the rest of them had taken part in this scam?"

Marla shook her head. "Shawna had been having an affair with the financial planner. They'd argued because he wanted to break things off, but neither one was involved in the fraud scheme. They're good at their jobs."

"And the other staff member?"

Marla glanced at another stylist working on a customer as the smell of holding spray entered her nose. "Jeri lied on her application. Dalton discovered she'd never gone to college. Ken had found this out and meant to fire her. She'll be leaving the agency. I feel bad for her, because her daughter is ill, and they need the health insurance. But that doesn't change the fact that she'd falsified her credentials."

Nicole glanced toward the front desk as the bell over the

door chimed. Her next client had arrived. The sleek stylist went over to greet the woman and tell her to get shampooed.

"What about those friends of Tally from Boca Raton?" Nicole asked upon her return.

"The leader of the tea ladies was running a prostitution ring. Dalton said the vice squad up there is handling things. It's true the Russian mob was involved, but they had no interest in Tally. She wasn't ever suspected of being a mole and didn't know enough to cause a stir."

"Will the tea circle continue to meet? I thought that was a cool idea."

"No, they've disbanded. The other women don't want to be tainted by their association to Rissa."

"Darryl was the one who tried to run you down in the parking lot? Not the Russians?"

"Yes, Darryl didn't like how I was poking around. And he wasn't sure how much Tally had told me."

"So all's well that ends well, huh? It's sad that Tally and Ken had to pay the price."

Marla hung her head. "Don't forget Ryan and Louise. At least we've learned the truth. I wish Tally had told me about her father, though." She still felt hurt that Tally hadn't confided in her. Where would their friendship stand when Tally woke up?

Perhaps she'd been embarrassed by it all, afraid Marla's respect for her would diminish upon learning she had a different parent. Why would that matter? Tally should have known Marla wouldn't care. But until her friend regained consciousness, certain questions had to remain unanswered.

"Did Dalton's tech experts ever crack Tally's iPad?" Nicole asked.

"Oh, yes. She'd done several searches on Liam Kelton and some on Rissa, believe it or not. Maybe she suspected something was wrong with that group. Her emails didn't show anything significant."

"So what now?" Nicole gave Marla a questioning glance.

She brushed down her long skirt. "I'm going to notify Tally's landlord that she'll be relocating her shop. It's unreasonable for her to stay there when she's the only holdout. The other shopkeepers would resent her, and the landlord *will* file for eviction. This way, she'll qualify for his relocation bonus. Maybe she'll find a place closer to Luke's day care center."

"What about the stock in her store?"

Marla arched her eyebrows. "I've had a great idea in that regard. We have space available in our spa lounge. We can sell her clothing and accessories there until she reopens her store elsewhere."

Nicole gave an approving smile. "That's very generous of you, Marla."

"It's the least I can do. Besides, it might be fun for our customers."

"You're already doing more than enough by taking care of Luke."

"True, but this will solve one of Tally's problems. She'll have plenty on her plate in terms of Ken's loss."

Nicole got busy with her client. As Marla rose and wandered toward Robyn to see when her next client was due, her cell phone rang.

Oh, no. It was the hospital. Her heart fluttering, she answered the call.

"Hi, this is the nurse caring for your friend, Tally Riggs."

"What's wrong? Has something happened?" Marla choked out the words. Tally couldn't have taken a turn for the worse, not when everything else had been resolved.

"A miracle has happened, ma'am. Tally is awake, and she's asking for you."

Author's Note

Hopefully, happier times are in store for Tally as she recovers from the accident and resumes an active life. She and Marla have to mend their friendship, but this is bound to happen as Marla is a forgiving soul. Tally will need her friend's strength to move forward. In return, Marla will ask for Tally's advice as she embarks on a new adventure she didn't anticipate.

If you enjoyed this story, please help spread the word. Customer reviews and recommendations are the best ways for new readers to find my work. Here are some suggestions:

Write an online customer review at Amazon, BN, and Goodreads.
Post about this book on your social media sites and online forums.
Recommend my work to reader groups, mystery fans, and book clubs.
Gift a Bad Hair Day mystery to your hairstylist or nail technician.

For updates on my new releases, giveaways, and author events, sign up for my newsletter at http://nancyjcohen.com/newsletter. Free Book Sampler for new subscribers.

Acknowledgments

A book is rarely written in a vacuum. We need the help of critique partners and research sources plus the family members who encourage us to pursue our dreams. I'd like to express my particular gratitude to the following:

Jay Esterson, President of Esterson Insurance Group, for answering my questions regarding the insurance industry. Your responses helped me formulate my story.

Heather B., who won a character naming contest and suggested the name Stacy Maria Scranton.

Beta readers Sally Schmidt, Linda Kuzminczuk, and Janice Sklar whose insightful comments helped me strengthen the story. Your input was invaluable in making this a better book.

About the Author

As a former registered nurse, Nancy J. Cohen helped people with their physical aches and pains, but she longed to soothe their troubles in a different way. The siren call of storytelling lured her from nursing into the exciting world of fiction. Wishing she could wield a curling iron with the same skill as crafting a story, she created hairdresser Marla Vail as a stylist with a nose for crime and a knack for exposing people's secrets.

Titles in the Bad Hair Day Mysteries have made the IMBA bestseller list, been selected by *Suspense Magazine* as best cozy mystery, and won third place in the Arizona Literary Awards. Nancy has also written the instructional guide, *Writing the Cozy Mystery*. Her imaginative romances, including the Drift Lords series, have proven popular with fans as well. Her first book in this genre won the HOLT Medallion Award.

A featured speaker at libraries, conferences, and community events, Nancy is listed in *Contemporary Authors, Poets & Writers*, and *Who's Who in U.S. Writers, Editors, & Poets*. When not busy writing, she enjoys fine dining, cruising, visiting Disney World, and shopping. Contact her at nancy@nancyjcohen.com

Follow the Author Online

Website - http://nancyjcohen.com
Blog - http://nancyjcohen.wordpress.com
Twitter - http://www.twitter.com/nancyjcohen
Facebook - https://www.facebook.com/NancyJCohenAuthor
Goodreads -
http://www.goodreads.com/author/show/91508.Nancy_J_Coh
en
Pinterest - http://pinterest.com/njcohen/
Linked In - http://www.linkedin.com/in/nancyjcohen
Google Plus - https://google.com/+NancyJCohen
Instagram - http://instagram.com/nancyjcohen
Booklover's Bench - http://bookloversbench.com
BookBub - https://www.bookbub.com/authors/nancy-j-cohen
Audible - http://adbl.co/2gMlVw1

Books by Nancy J. Cohen

Bad Hair Day Mysteries
Permed to Death
Hair Raiser
Murder by Manicure
Body Wave
Highlights to Heaven
Died Blonde
Dead Roots
Perish by Pedicure
Killer Knots
Shear Murder
Hanging by a Hair
Peril by Ponytail
Haunted Hair Nights (Novella)
Facials Can Be Fatal
Hair Brained

Anthologies
"Three Men and a Body" in Wicked Women Whodunit

The Drift Lords Series
Warrior Prince
Warrior Rogue
Warrior Lord

Science Fiction Romances
Keeper of the Rings
Silver Serenade

The Light-Years Series
Circle of Light
Moonlight Rhapsody
Starlight Child

Nonfiction
Writing the Cozy Mystery

For More Details, Visit http://NancyJCohen.com/books/

CPSIA information can be obtained
at www.ICGtesting.com
Printed in the USA
LVHW05s2320160818
587184LV00009B/608/P